PRAISE FOR JOANNE

QUIETE

D1040696

"A truly stunning academic mystery . . . You'll be all the richer for this nineteenth-century view of a very modern murder. A literary and intricate mystery with connotative power. Watch this one."
—*Mystery Lovers Bookshop News*

"Amanda Cross, move over. There's a new literary mystery novelist in town. Dobson is brilliant."
—*Great Neck Record*

"Emily Dickinson scholar Dobson's first novel has an appealing heroine, a nifty payoff, and a beguiling way with the extracurricular entanglements of her teaching stiffs."
—*Kirkus Reviews*

"Anyone who thinks the word 'academic' is synonymous with 'detached' needs to read Professor Dobson's tale of seething passions and deadly animosities within the English department of Enfield College. It's a cutthroat world, academia, polished and elegant though the blades may be, and the author captures all the nuances of jealousy and fear that lie beneath the foundations of the ivory tower. Emily Dickinson, shall we say, with a stiletto in her hand."
—Edgar Award winner Laurie R. King, author of *A Grave Talent* and *The Beekeeper's Apprentice*

"A witty and fast-paced academic mystery. Joanne Dobson has a light touch."
—Joan Hedrick, Pulitzer Prize–winning author of *Harriet Beecher Stowe: A Life*

"An intriguing plot with a motive for murder that's as old as human nature. Good characterization and fast-paced action make QUIETER THAN SLEEP an entertaining novel."
—*The Chattanooga Times*

"An engaging story . . . a tense confrontation . . . will have readers rapidly skimming pages to see how it ends. An entertaining read."
—*Gazette-Telegraph,* Colorado Springs

"Joanne Dobson skewers the world of academe with her murderously funny sleuth, Dr. Karen Pelletier. They both deserve a long tenure on any mystery lover's bookshelf."
—Francine Mathews, author of *Death in a Cold Hard Light*

ALSO BY JOANNE DOBSON

Dickinson and the Strategies of Reticence:
The Woman Writer in Nineteenth-Century America

Joanne Dobson

Quieter Than Sleep

BANTAM BOOKS
New York
Toronto
London
Sydney
Auckland

All of the characters in this book are fictitious, and any
resemblance to actual persons, living or dead,
is purely coincidental.

This edition contains the complete text
of the original hardcover edition.
NOT ONE WORD HAS BEEN OMITTED.

QUIETER THAN SLEEP

PUBLISHING HISTORY
Published in association with Doubleday
Doubleday hardcover edition published November 1997
Bantam paperback edition /August 1998

All rights reserved.
Copyright © 1997 by Joanne Dobson
Cover art copyright © 1998 by Millie Falcaro
Library of Congress Catalog Card Number: 96-53970.
No part of this book may be reproduced or transmitted in
any form or by any means, electronic or mechanical,
including photocopying, recording, or by any information
storage and retrieval system, without permission
in writing from the publisher.
For information address: Doubleday.

If you purchased this book without a cover you
should be aware that this book is stolen property. It
was reported as "unsold and destroyed" to the
publisher and neither the author nor the publisher has
received any payment for this "stripped book."

ISBN 0-553-57660-7

Published simultaneously in the United States and Canada

Bantam Books are published by Bantam Books, a division of
Bantam Doubleday Dell Publishing Group, Inc. Its trademark,
consisting of the words "Bantam Books" and the portrayal of
a rooster, is Registered in U.S. Patent and Trademark Office
and in other countries. Marca Registrada. Bantam Books,
1540 Broadway, New York, New York 10036.

PRINTED IN THE UNITED STATES OF AMERICA

OPM 10 9 8 7 6 5 4 3 2 1

In memory of my mother,
Mildred McKinley Abele, R.N.

Acknowledgments

Betty Couvares and Frank Couvares have been in on this book from the very beginning, and I am grateful for their generosity, hospitality, and good advice. Patricia O'Gorman's enthusiastic message on my answering machine at a crucial moment saved me from abandoning the project, as did my daughter Rebecca's query "How hard could it be?" Clare Lees and Sandy Zagarell supported this endeavor with friendship, enthusiasm, and academic savvy; Joan Hedrick provided an expert Beecher eye; and I am indebted to Karen Dandurand and Martha Ackmann for many hours of Emily Dickinson conversation. Lt. Richard W. Downey, Ret., Town of Greenburgh, White Plains, N.Y., Police Department, gave me the benefit of his professional expertise, as did Jeanne Christman, R.N. Walter Kendrick shared with me his crackerjack agent, Deborah Schneider, for which generosity I am forever grateful. My gifted editor, Kate Miciak, has taught me much from which I will continue to benefit. Among other friends whose support has enormously enhanced the writing of this novel are Phyllis Spiegel, Joan Bloomberg, Miriam Duhan, Becky McBride, Barbara Nagler, and Liz Wilen-Berg. But my greatest debt, as always, is to my family: My husband, Dave Dobson, whose love and faith encourage me to keep pushing back the boundaries, and whose agile imagination has contributed more to this tale than I even wish to acknowledge; Lisa Dobson Kohomban and Rebecca Dobson, who cheerfully read the manuscript more times than they probably wanted to; and David McKinley Dobson, who provided a writer's perspective and companionship.

Author's Note

There is no off-ramp on the interstate for Enfield, Massachusetts, no listing for Enfield College occurs in any of the guides to U.S. colleges and universities, and none of Enfield's academic characters has ever paid dues to the MLA. In short, *Quieter Than Sleep* is a work of the imagination, and any resemblance to contemporary academe and its denizens is generic rather than specific.

One

I MIGHT as well admit it: I was sick of desire. Of love, sex, and desire, and all their cumbersome baggage. First of all, I was lugging around the residue of a recently pulverized heart. I should have been used to it by now. It had been six months since I'd left Tony, my longtime lover, to take a teaching job at Enfield College. Well, I couldn't pass up an offer from one of New England's most elite private schools, could I? Well, could I? And Tony didn't want a commuting relationship. He said that was no way to love someone, long distance. So I left. And I was right. Wasn't I? But I couldn't forget him, and I was beginning to wonder if I hadn't, just possibly, made a terrible mistake.

Almost worse than my aching heart, however, was the all-too-close physical presence of Randy Astin-Berger. No, I wasn't in love with Randy. Far from it. Rather, I was in dire peril of being bored to death by his erudite discourse on literature and sexuality. And he kept hitting on me. Standing a good six inches closer to me than I could ever imagine ever wanting him to, Randy was treating me to an extended scholarly analysis of the erotic implications of *The Scarlet Letter*. No doubt he thought of this as an irresistibly seductive line.

"And, thus," Randy said, as he pushed a lock of lank black hair back from his forehead and then touched me lightly on the shoulder, "inevitably results the narrative disallowal of desire." Light glinted off the gold stud in his left earlobe. "As Foucault would say, the erotic . . ." I was paying very little attention but I did hear him say something about seduction, transgression, obsession, the tyranny of the body. It was enough to put me off sex forever.

With his broad shoulders and MTV-rugged face, Randy was not an unattractive man. It was just that he was so boring. I may have a Ph.D. in English but I've always preferred to hold my social conversations in words of three syllables or fewer. And I'd much rather talk to a warm-blooded, witty human being than to a pompous wind-up genius doll like Randy Astin-Berger.

I sighed, imperceptibly I hoped. Randy had evidently finished with *The Scarlet Letter* and had begun obscurely on some other letter and the transgressive nature of desire. He'd been indulging in something more exotic than the liquid offerings at the bar. His eyes glittered. His manner had become confiding and insistent. He began to loosen his tie.

Untenured assistant professors must be vigilantly attentive, and I was doing my damnedest to look fascinated. In spite of his relative youth, Randy had just been named to Enfield College's prestigious Palaver Chair of English. And rumor had it that he was next in line to be department chair. I had to be nice to Randy; he was the Man. But I was tired, hot, and seriously stressed out; I didn't know how long I could keep up the facade.

I concentrated on the iridescent chrysanthemum design of Randy's shiny black retro tie; at least *that* would keep me awake. He wore the tie with a soft white narrow-collared cotton shirt, unironed, of course, under a wide-shouldered linen jacket the color of very ripe honeydew melon. His wide-pleated black cotton twill slacks hung loose over Reebok running shoes. He looked just exactly like what he was: a hotshot academic superstar on the make.

"Epistolary conventions of eros demand . . ." Randy said.

I stifled a yawn. It *was* stuffy in the room.

"And, then, given the tenuous preservation of literary ephemera, leading to failed transmission of even the most fundamental biographical data . . ."

Good God. Would he never shut up? I stretched my neck, trying to ease the tension in my shoulders. It had been a hectic month: classes, papers, exams, frantic students with eleventh-hour crises—suicidal friends, dying grandmothers, obscurely terrifying medical diagnoses. I took the opportunity to look around.

The Enfield College faculty was making merry. The president's annual Christmas reception for faculty and staff was being held in the public chambers of the president's mansion. Excuse me: the president's *house*. At Enfield the word *mansion* would be considered vulgar. To me it looked like a mansion, but I've always been smart enough to take on protective coloration. If anyone asked, tonight I was at the president's *house*.

Three high-ceilinged rooms of late nineteenth-century design opened into a massive three-story-high central hall. From a dramatic balcony with delicately turned mahogany railings, a curved staircase swept down each side of the hall. Swags of Christmas greens decorated the banisters; electric candles twinkled in the hundred sconces of the hall's central crystal chandelier. Understated opulence.

I am not used to opulence, understated or otherwise, having grown up in a row house in Lowell, Massachusetts. In Lowell, we thought faded red paper fold-out bells were festive, and sagging loops of green and red construction paper. Lowell wasn't very far from Enfield, but in every way that mattered it was immeasurably distant. Not that my success as an academic had turned me into a snob. It was just that I'd learned early—very early—that poverty can breed ignorance, abuse, and fear. Learned it, so to speak, in my very bones. A little opulence, now and then, looks pretty damn good to me.

Suddenly, I'd had enough of Randy. Tenure was five years in my future; I'd tough it out. I gave him a fraudulent smile, touched my empty glass with a finger whose significance I assumed required no deconstruction, and began to back down the steps as smoothly as I could. I was heading for the bar.

"But, Karen—" Randy sputtered, as I moved away, "the letter . . ." And something about a desk—or a disk; I still wasn't listening.

In an alcove by the right staircase a string quartet played excerpts from the *Messiah*. Randy had buttonholed me on the lower steps of this staircase. It wasn't the first time he'd cornered me. And I was afraid it wouldn't be the last.

I began to cruise, looking for my friend Greg Samoorian, who'd just that day been tenured in the Anthropology Department. I did careful surveillance as I made my way through the crush of faculty members, administrators, and spouses. The last thing I wanted was to fall into Randy's clutches again.

The crowd was abuzz with news of the just-announced tenure decisions. Student waiters proffered trays of champagne in stem glasses, fueling already flaming academic passions. More than once I heard: "Executive Committee," "denial," "scandalous," "appeal." The tenure issue had been fiercely debated during the fall months, and my good buddy Greg had ended up being the sole Enfield tenure of the year. All the other candidates had been denied.

I looked around but didn't see Greg. Surely he must have come, if only to celebrate his triumph.

"Professor Pelletier?" Behind me, the voice was hushed, almost furtive. I spun around. "Would you like a glass of champagne?" Sophia Warzek. Pale. Blond. Much too thin. A townie on scholarship, working her way through Enfield. The black uniform dress hung loosely on her, as if it had been made for someone from a much more robust species—like, maybe, for a human being.

"Sophia?" I took a glass from the tray. Waterford. Nice. I sipped. The champagne was nice, too. "Sophia, are you losing weight or something? You don't look at all well."

"No. I'm okay." She gave me a bright smile. I wasn't convinced. "I'm just tired. It's been a rough semester." Sophia looked so frail holding the heavy silver tray, I had to resist an impulse to take it from her.

"Yeah," I said. "I imagine. You work too hard. And you're really much too thin. And all of a sudden, too." I narrowed my eyes, thinking of anorexia, not an uncommon problem with Enfield's women students. "What's going on with you?"

I would never have asked such a personal question of any other student. But, like me, Sophia was an outsider at prestigious Enfield. And there's no denying it: Like calls to like. With my factory-town upbringing and her immigrant parents, Sophia and I knew the American class system from the bottom up. The view was not a pretty one.

In the crowded, noisy room, Sophia contemplated my question as if she might actually answer it. Then and there. Tray full of champagne and all. Then someone jostled her arm, she staggered, and that time I did grab for the tray. A pair of large, muscular hands reached it first, righted it. Oh, God, no! Not Randy Astin-Berger again.

"Uhh." Sophia blanched as Randy's hand closed over hers on the tray. Then she turned back to me, and her voice became furtive again. "Maybe I'll call you. About that late paper, I mean."

Late paper? Sophia was a fastidiously punctual student. Her final research paper had been sitting, unread, on my office desk for over a week, while the others filtered in days late. She faltered, obviously thinking she'd been too presumptuous. "What I mean is, if that's all right?"

"Sure," I replied. "Anytime." But she had scampered away with her heavy tray, looking as if she should be at home, confined to strict bed rest, rather than serving fine wine to professors already too tipsy to appreciate it.

"Karen," Randy said, but he was staring after Sophia. When she disappeared in the crowd, he turned back to me, fixing me with his torrid eye. "I've made up my mind." His smile was munificent, Zeus showering a mere mortal maiden with his divine largess. "I've decided to share some delightful news with you."

Share? The thought of sharing *anything* with Randy Astin-Berger left me more than a little nauseous.

"You'll be thrilled. I guarantee it. But first I've got to see—someone." He waggled his fingers in the air. The someone was a mere annoyance. Would be disposed of with dispatch. "But after that, what say we blow this scene?" He gave me a suggestive little leer. Surely his eyes were just a bit too bright? His pupils slightly contracted?

This was a problem. I wasn't about to go anywhere with this smirking, self-important blowhard. Even if he *was* a sure bet to be future chair of my department.

"Jeez, Randy, I'm sorry. I've got a date later." A date with my own narrow bed, thank you very much.

"Yeah?" Eyes narrowed. Thinking about asking me with whom. Still sober enough, thank heaven, to rethink such a crude impulse. "Well, okay, listen, I'll catch you before you go. Look for me. Right?" An intimate squeeze of the upper arm, a follow-up leer, and he was weaving away through the crowd.

Not if I can help it, dude. All I wanted now was to find Greg, congratulate him, and get the hell out of here. I'd worry about Randy's unwanted attentions later.

But I couldn't get his words out of my mind. Thrilled? I'd be thrilled? What could Randy Astin-Berger possibly have to tell me that would *thrill* me?

The last real thrill I'd had was the job offer from Enfield the year before. A fairy tale come true. Who would have believed it? Karen Pelletier (that's *PELL-uh-teer,* the New England pronunciation, not the more elegant French) from Lowell, Massachusetts. Pregnant and married at eighteen. A mother at nineteen. Divorced and destitute at twenty-one. And now—a professor at Enfield College.

It hadn't been easy. Night school, waitressing, scholarships, loans, teaching fellowships: I'd patched together piecemeal the education that seems to fall, ripe and succulent, into my students' laps. And I'd raised Amanda, too—and hadn't done a bad job of it. She was a major pain in the neck, of course, but then, who wasn't at eighteen?

After two years as an assistant professor at a New York City education factory, I'd been recruited by Enfield last year on the basis of my forthcoming book on class and classical American writers. I was—as I said—thrilled to accept their offer. Even left the man I loved to do so.

Was it worth it? Well . . . I was beginning to wonder.

I cruised by a cluster of colleagues engaged in spirited debate over the most recent rap group censorship case. All the faces were white; most were middle-aged. Jill Greenberg, by far the youngest in this contentious group, reached out and fingered the sleeve of my white silk dress. Raising her eyebrows in approval, she smiled at me, kept hold of the silk, and smoothly peeled away from the others.

"Do you think any one of that bunch has ever actually *listened* to rap?" she muttered as she guided me in the direction of the hors d'oeuvre table. In the fervor of argument, Jill's unruly red hair, gathered with a purple ribbon in an asymmetrical bunch on the top of her head, had begun to sag over her forehead. Anyone else would have looked slovenly. Jill looked adorable.

"Neat dress," she said, relinquishing my sleeve and stacking a small plate high with crabmeat puffs. "Emily's?"

I was startled into laughter. "How'd you guess?"

I'd bought the dress as a kind of private joke, a wry allusion to Emily Dickinson, who for many years had dressed only in white. I happen to know a great deal about Dickinson. That's one of the reasons I'm here at Enfield.

"Oh, I read." She looked at me slit-eyed. "You're

too tall to be Emily, you know. And not quite virginal enough for the Nun of Amherst."

"What makes you think she was virginal?" I retorted. "There's all sorts of speculation—"

"Yeah, yeah, I know. But I'm talking about you. Why don't you wear your hair down like that all the time? And the makeup . . . I never thought you could look quite so—well—*hot.*"

"Jill!"

"Oh, I know, I'm embarrassing you. Sometimes I'm really indiscreet. But I'm just really interested in, you know, *style.* And I always thought that professorial look of yours was some sort of camouflage." The wild red topknot flopped over her left eye. She tugged off the purple ribbon and shook her head. Curls fell about her face like a miniature firestorm.

"Now, me," she went on, "I like to be outrageous." She flapped the purple ribbon in the air. "But you—restraint is super on you. Keeps 'em guessing. Those innocent sleeves. That demure neckline. That clinging white silk revealing just—well, you know." She nodded vigorously and popped a crabmeat puff into her mouth.

I took the opportunity to change the subject. "Have you seen Greg Samoorian? I've been looking for him all evening."

"He's around here somewhere. Over by the bar, I think. Getting soused." Jill put the plate of hors d'oeuvres down on a small side table. "You know, I'm really happy for him, getting tenure and all, but I'm sick about the rest of them. Those motherfuckers on the Executive Committee . . ."

I raised my eyebrows. I'm only thirty-seven but Jill made me feel positively middle-aged and staid.

"Yeah, I know, indiscreet again. But, jeez, Karen. From what I hear, all four of the candidates were backed by their departments. Lots of publications, good service, but they were all blackballed by the committee. Especially by that asshole, Astin-Berger."

"That's what I heard, too. That Randy opposed everyone, including Greg. But that he was especially hard on Ned Hilton."

"Yeah, so they say. It breaks my heart about Ned."

I think she meant it; she fell into an uncharacteristic silence.

Ned was a colleague in the English Department, an English Renaissance scholar. His office was next to mine, but our schedules were so different, I hadn't really gotten to know him. I'd looked earlier in the evening for his tall, stoop-shouldered figure, but hadn't seen him anywhere. Maybe he hadn't come. Prior to the tenure decision, missing the president's party would have been a fatal omission. But now . . .

"What I heard," Jill burst out, "was that Astin-Berger said Ned's work was *adequately* argued, and *eloquently* phrased, and *did* shed some new light on Milton, but it simply wasn't *exciting*, wasn't *theoretically sophisticated*, wasn't on the *cutting edge*. Jerk! Who does he think he is, anyhow? The arbiter of all true knowledge?"

I calmed Jill down and gratefully handed her over to Ralph Bottoms, the assistant chair of Sociology, her own department. "Behave yourself," I muttered, as he approached. "*You* want to be tenured, someday, don't you?" She shrugged, but turned toward Ralph sedately enough.

I took the opportunity to survey the room. Academic chitchat swirled around me like a spring snow shower: dense and blinding, but never really sticking to the ground. Miles Jewell, current English Department chair and fuddy-duddy *par excellence,* was standing by the bar, a little unsteady under the influence of what looked like some very fine brandy in the balloon glass he held in a shaky hand. With flushed cheeks and bright eyes he resembled more than ever the elderly Robert Frost, a mop of white hair, bushy eyebrows. I smiled and nodded. Miles nodded back, but couldn't get to me through the crowd. Good. I had no interest in hearing about Miles's latest exploits of the intellect.

I didn't really feel like talking to anyone. If Greg didn't materialize soon, I would leave.

Instinctively, I looked again for Randy, half-expecting to find him bearing determinedly in my direction, his mouth already open to elaborate on yet another brilliant insight. Nowhere to be seen. Good, again. I didn't think I could handle another encounter that evening with the Professor of Desire.

When I did find Greg, he was drunk. "Why not?" he demanded, with boozy smugness. "I'm tenured, aren't I?" Leaning against a nineteenth-century cherry-wood highboy, he was slightly disheveled. The knot on his sedate blue-striped tie was loosened and the tie itself hung askew. His grin, a roguish flash of white in a dark, bearded face, also seemed somewhat askew.

"You've been tenured for about four and a half hours. I'm not sure it's not revocable."

His grin faded. "It's tough, you know. I didn't think it would be so tough." The pain in his eyes was a mix of whiskey and self-pity. Heavy on the whiskey.

"What's tough? Being tenured?"

"Yeah." He appeared puzzled. "Yeah. I thought I'd be thrilled, over the top with ecstasy. But instead I feel—contaminated. This whole thing has been so slimy, you know. Why me, for instance, and not Ned? Ned's work isn't flashy, but it's interesting. I don't particularly care for Milton, but Ned's my pal so I read his book. It made me see the seventeenth century in a whole new light. He would have been tenured for certain if it wasn't for that prick, Astin-Berger. . . ." He paused, in something that obviously seemed to him to pass for deep—even pained—thought. To me it looked more like alcoholic stupor.

"You're really sloshed, aren't you?"

"Well, I should be. It's my third Johnnie Walker Black in, let's see"—he looked at his watch—"just under one-half hour."

"I think it should be your last." Children of alcoholics are often prudish about booze.

But even with his loopy grin and his inebriated self-pity, I found Greg charming. To be honest, I liked him partly because he looked so damn good to me. Oh, his vulnerability and quirky intelligence went with the package, but it didn't hurt that, burly and bearded, he looked more as if he belonged on the docks than on a college campus.

Academic men don't usually appeal to me. I go for muscle and bulk—the Springsteen type: big, tough, and complex. My former husband Fred, the truck driver—long, long ago. My not-so-very-long-ago lover Tony, the cop. It's not that I don't like academic men. I do. I just don't—well—*fancy* them.

But Greg looked good to me, and I was very careful about it. He was married. That mattered to both of us.

The string quartet segued from "God Rest Ye Merry, Gentlemen" into "What Child Is This?" and I decided I'd had enough merriment. Greg looked as if he needed a friend, a cup of coffee, and a designated driver—not necessarily in that order.

"How about coffee at the Blue Dolphin? I'll drive. Heck, I'll even buy. This is your big day."

Our coats hung in the massive walk-in closet in the alcove under the left staircase. Knowing the gossip likely to be engendered by even the most innocent actions in this incestuous little community, Greg and I agreed to meet in ten minutes in the portico outside the front door.

As Greg turned away from me, Magda Vegh sidled up to him and slipped her arm confidently into his. Greg's face lit up like a lighthouse in a hurricane. Magda was one of the few exotic features of this stark New England scene. The décolletage of her peacock blue silk dress was striking. Green malachite earrings dangled dramatically to her shoulders. A dark-brown cloud of hair floated loosely around a voluptuous, expertly made-up face.

Magda Czegledi Vegh, the celebrated Hungarian dissident poet, had come to Enfield this year from Budapest by way of visiting professorships at Harvard, Yale, and Stanford. But she sure didn't let her political commitments get in the way of her cleavage, I thought. Maybe I was just jealous. I couldn't muster up half that cleavage, even with the help of a push-up bra.

As I left Greg alone with the Hungarian Bombshell, I noticed Avery Mitchell, Enfield's president, watching me with speculative attention. *Shit*.

Avery Mitchell—Avery Claibourne Cabot Mitchell—was the epitome of certain things I had come to detest about Enfield men. He was blue-blooded, Ivy League, wealthy, impeccably attired, articulate to the point of glibness, and invariably charming. At our first meeting I had noted with smug distaste his fine-boned hands and slender, sandy WASP good looks. The slight asymmetry of his long patrician nose. The almost chilling ice blue of his eyes. A prince of privilege, I decided. Women probably fall at his feet. Since that meeting I had gone out of my way to avoid him.

Rumor had it that Avery's wife had fled Enfield four years ago with an untenured member of the

Music Department. College presidencies are hard on marriages.

My heart bleeds.

Now Avery was heading in my direction. Doing, I thought, what aristocracy is trained to do: wending his way through the adoring crowd of his subjects with a gracious word for all. No white gloves, no majestic wave. But then, this is America.

"Karen," he said, "how elegant you look this evening."

"Thank you, Avery. Lovely party." I may be a working stiff, but I know my manners.

He nodded in acknowledgement. "Have you had a good first semester here at Enfield?" He bent over me attentively, as if I were the only person in the room.

"Lovely," I said. *Lovely! Oh, God!* "I mean . . ." I was actually stammering.

He smiled. "I'm glad," he said. "If I can be of any help . . ." He moved on to his next vassal.

I glared after him. Condescending son of a bitch. Chip on the shoulder? Who? Me?

After several desultory encounters with other colleagues, I finally reached the closet. I wanted nothing more than to get out of the heat and noise of this party. My watch said 9:07. Yes, time to leave. Definitely.

I scanned the room, plotting a tactical retreat. As far as I could tell, I had an all-clear. Randy was nowhere to be seen.

The door of the closet was jammed, resisting my attempt to open it. Everything, I grumbled, seemed to be frustrating my desire to get out of this place. Odd, however, that the door should be shut quite so tightly. Some idiot must have slammed it. I grasped the ornate brass knob firmly in both hands and yanked.

The closet door flew open, and Randy Astin-

Berger found me for the last time, falling forward into my arms in a first, and final, embrace.

His handsome face was contorted and swollen. The green and gold chrysanthemums of his trendy retro neckwear no longer flowed jauntily down the front of his rumpled cotton shirt. Whoever had killed him had turned his whimsical necktie into a particularly efficient lethal weapon.

The quartet began "Silent Night."

Two

THE KITCHEN of the president's house was cheerful, high-ceilinged, and too warm. An enormous ancient combination gas and wood-burning stove dominated one side, and the walls were painted a sunny yellow. Seated on kitchen stools and on Chippendale chairs brought in from the dining room were Avery Mitchell; Maggie Maher, his housekeeper; Paul Dermott, the chief of Enfield College security; Sergeant White from the Enfield town police; and me. We were waiting for the State Police homicide investigators to tell us we could leave. Because I was the one who had found Randy's body, I'd been detained by the police when other party-goers had been released. Was I a serious suspect? I was beginning to wonder.

It had rained during the night, and the kitchen windows were nubbled with ice, distorting vision. As I sat on a high wooden stool, drinking tea from a heavy earthenware mug, the multicolored lights of the giant town Christmas tree reflected in the high window over the sink winked off. I glanced at my watch. Exactly three A.M.

The two homicide detectives huddled together at a small table in the breakfast nook, going over notes from their interviews. From where we sat at the other side of the large room, their voices were audible only as a monotonous murmur. The detectives had been conferring for forty minutes, and any feeble attempts the rest of us had made at conversation were long over.

I was trying to remain alert in the overheated kitchen but kept drifting into a kind of hypnotic stupor. My eye snagged on totally irrelevant objects: a display of Spode dinnerware behind glass-fronted cabinet doors; my own reflection in the ice-obscured window, sepulchral in the white silk dress; Avery Mitchell's ice-blue eyes, turned for a moment toward me, inscrutable. Caught in what seemed to me to be the searchlight of Avery's gaze, I unaccountably flushed. The heat of the room became momentarily unbearable, and I felt stifled, unable to breathe. I was in a very strange state, I decided; it really was time for me to get out of here.

One of the detectives, a tall, thin, dark sergeant, whose name, I swear, was Jack Daniels, came over to the silent group at the kitchen counter. "Okay, we're about to wind up here. Nobody remember anything else about the victim? He didn't seem any different than usual? Worried about something, maybe?" Daniels was looking straight at me, his hard-eyed stare designed to intimidate. It worked.

All heads swiveled in my direction.

I blinked, and thought for a minute.

"Maybe he was a little more talkative than usual."

Avery snorted with barely suppressed amusement. The lieutenant, a tall, heavy, silent man, appeared next to his colleague. Both policemen looked at Avery.

"I'm sorry," he responded, shaking his head as if to clear his thinking. "That was inappropriate. It's just that Randy, ah, Professor Astin-Berger, was nothing if not voluble."

They continued to stare at him.

"What I mean is, he talked, ah . . . a lot . . . all the time. It's difficult for me to imagine him talking more than usual."

Avery was choosing his words very carefully, but Sergeant Daniels didn't seem to notice, and the lieutenant was keeping his own counsel. Daniels slapped his notebook shut and shoved it in the pocket of his down parka. He hadn't taken the coat off, even though the heat from the big stove was oppressive. In my silk crepe dress I was warm, and Avery had removed his jacket and tie. The latter hung over the back of one of the Chippendale chairs, dark red and tasteful even in this undignified position. I shuddered. I'd had enough of neckties for the evening.

The detective capped his pen. To him, we probably all talked too much. That's what we did for a living, right? Stood in front of a room and talked. Nice neat rows of respectful students writing it all down. Long vacations. Summers off. Pretty cushy.

Enfield College clearly disgusted Sergeant Daniels. His sour attitude made it obvious he thought we were inhabitants of a world of ivory-towered privilege, sheltered from the hard realities of real life as real people lived it.

To some degree, he was correct. Enfield College was definitely a privileged institution. Founded over a hundred and fifty years ago as a light in what the Congregationalist divines saw as the spiritual wilderness of nineteenth-century America, Enfield was designed to educate the sons of the pious. Then the sons and grandsons of the industrialist robber barons and New England *haute bourgeoisie* matriculated, endowing the college copiously and enduringly. That generous endowment eased the transition to coeducation in the early seventies, at the properly enlightened moment. Now it seemed that young women in white Nikes had always, along with their brothers and lovers, scuffed the pathways between Hearst Hall and Gould Commons.

To Sergeant Daniels, I could tell, it was all pretty cushy. But the hard realities were not totally unknown even at elite Enfield. Occasionally, I mused, death climbed the ivy-covered walls. In my half-conscious daze I envisioned Death climbing a high brick wall, dressed conventionally in black robes and a green-and-gold chrysanthemum tie. He wore Randy's Reeboks. He had Randy's face.

The sand truck went by on the street in front of the house. Its revolving yellow light turned the frozen window pane opaque with amber. It cleared, and then hardened once again into an amber sheet. Cleared and—

"Okay," said the lieutenant—Lieutenant C. Piotrowski, his card said. He seemed to be in charge, but so far he'd said very little. "We're done here, at least for now. We'll call you when we need anything else. We've got your numbers."

I'll bet you do. As I jerked awake again from my near hypnotic state, I thought Piotrowski looked at me extra hard. This cop was someone I wouldn't want to tangle with under any circumstances. Big and slightly unkempt, he seemed at first impression to be a bit of a buffoon. His brown hair was cropped close in a quasi-military style. His shoulders were massive in a sloppy wool sweater whose red and green squares did little to disguise the bulk of his belly. He wore blue polyester pants and leather lace-up boots the size of some compact cars. But his brown eyes above high, flat cheekbones were cool and observant, his sparse comments astute. He had with little seeming effort secured the site of the murder, supervised the examination of the body, seen to its removal, and turned the chaos of two hundred horrified and slightly inebriated witnesses into a cool and efficient question-and-answer period.

As far as I could tell, they'd eliminated just about everyone but me. Randy, it seemed, had disappeared from sight as soon as I'd turned my all-too-eager back on him.

Did I feel guilty?

Well, yes, I guess I did. Guilty, and stunned. And more than a little sick.

I was interested to notice that my hands were shaking. Interested in a kind of detached, objective way, as if they were someone else's hands. I concentrated on steadying them by tracing with an index finger the single daisy hand-painted on the side of the brown earthenware mug. The tea was almost gone, or it certainly would have sloshed onto the scrubbed butcher-block surface of the worktable.

"Thank you, Lieutenant Piotrowski," Avery said. He *would* remember the name. He stood up to shake the policeman's hand. The same height as Piotrowski, perhaps even slightly taller, Enfield's president appeared insubstantial next to the detective's bulk. His slender, aristocratic hand almost disappeared in Piotrowski's grip. Nonetheless, with the handshake he took control of the encounter, a host bidding farewell to a visitor of ambiguous status, half guest, half plumber come to repair a nuisance leak.

"You can be certain that we here at Enfield College will do everything we can to help you get to the bottom of this unfortunate incident, Lieutenant. Call on us anytime we can be of assistance, day or night. I personally . . ."

I stopped listening. He sounded like a dean promising to look into some fairly innocuous fraternity prank. I wondered how long it would take him after the detectives left to get on the phone with Harvey O'Hara, the college's director of public affairs, to set the PR wheels in motion. Perhaps he already had.

My coat was lying on the kitchen counter. It had been retrieved from the ghastly closet by a state trooper after the closet had been checked over by technicians. I looked at it with horror, but I had no choice. It was well below freezing by now, and home was a twenty-minute ride away in a car that took forever to heat.

As Daniels and Piotrowski left, I rose to put the coat on, and was surprised to have Avery reach out a hand to detain me. "Could you stay a minute, Karen?"

He conferred briefly with the town policeman and the college security officer, who then departed together. Underage Enfield students show a disturbing proclivity to be drunk and disorderly in local bars, and it was unusual to see the two as chummy as they were tonight. I imagined Dermott and White were headed straight for Mocchio's and a couple of Buds—as far away as they could get from the high authority of the president and the staties.

Mrs. Maher had already vanished. The housekeeper and her staff had not been allowed to clear away the party debris. The police technicians had taken hours, until just a few minutes ago, to complete their investigation. Mrs. Maher had stood in the doorway of the living room the entire time, clutching a light blue hand-knit cardigan over her shoulders and watching intently. I wondered if she expected some policeman to make off with the heirloom crystal punch bowls. She'd have a strenuous morning among the crumpled napkins, discarded hors d'oeuvres, and half-emptied glasses, but at least she'd know the Waterford was all accounted for.

"Karen," said Avery, as the door closed behind the two men, "let me drive you home. You've had a terrible shock. You're in no condition to be out on these roads."

"Thank you." My reply was decisive. "But I'll drive myself. I'm fine." I reinforced my statement by sitting down hard, very suddenly and without volition. The tremor in my hands was impossible to conceal.

Avery regarded me in silence. Then he left the room, saying, unnecessarily, "Don't go anywhere." His footsteps mounted the stairs. I clasped my hands very tightly in my lap, staring at them, willing them into submission.

When he returned he was carrying a plastic prescription bottle.

"This is Xanax." He opened the container. "I think it might help if you took one."

I looked at him incredulously. Suddenly I was intensely aware that I was alone in a house where a murder had just occurred with a man I detested. And now he was offering me pills from a sinister-looking brown bottle.

"No, thank you." I spoke as politely as I could. After all, if this potential murderer turned out merely to be a concerned human being, he *was* the president of the college I would someday be petitioning for tenure.

I suddenly felt myself about to be overcome with hysterical amusement at what I saw as the irony of my situation. My hands were ice-cold and the shaking had spread to the rest of my body. Especially to my teeth, which were audibly chattering. Even in this warm room, I was shivering with shock.

Avery looked alarmed.

I stared hard at the pills. Small, oval, and salmon-colored, they certainly resembled Xanax. I knew what Xanax looked like. Believe me, I knew.

Like the heroine of a romance novel, I threw caution to the winds.

"Maybe you'd better give me two." He shook them into my hand and I swallowed them down with the rest of the tea, cold now in the bottom of my cup. The characteristic bitter flavor of Xanax lingered reassuringly on my tongue.

I gradually stopped shaking. Then I apologized—three times. It was two times too many.

I did *not* want Avery to drive me home, but my protests sounded feeble. I lived fifteen miles from the college. It was too long a trip for him to take at that hour. And besides, I would end up carless in the morning.

"You're in no shape to drive," Avery said firmly. "The roads are icy, and you're still shook up. I'll send a college car in the morning. Just let me know when."

"But—"

"Or," he said, "you could spend the night here."

"Oh."

He helped me on with my coat and into his big dark gray Volvo sedan. Infinitely classier than my gray 1988 Volkswagen Jetta. The roads had been freshly sanded. The wheels of the heavy car ground the grit into crusted ice.

I live in Greenfield, the low-rent district. Yes, I know the college owns three square blocks of prime real estate in the heart of Enfield's residential district. But the thought of bumping into my colleagues in the supermarket or over early-morning coffee at the local eatery appalls me. I'd opted instead for a cheap, shabby house in the country. One that suited both my psyche and my pocketbook.

We were turning onto Route 4 from Field Street, Enfield's main thoroughfare, when Avery shifted into overdrive, sat back in his leather-upholstered seat, and spoke.

"I didn't want to say anything in front of the police, but—Christ—as if the murder weren't enough, that scene with Margaret Smith was"—he struggled for an adequate word—"horrifying. Do you have any idea what that was all about?"

Shortly after I'd discovered Randy's body, Margaret, a member of the Religion faculty, had gone into the nastiest case of hysterics I'd ever seen. Her guttural, choking sobs and piercing screams shocked the party-goers almost as much as Randy's corpse had. Well, she was a hell of a lot noisier than the corpse.

"No. I scarcely know her. Was she a special—er—friend of Randy's?"

"Hardly." His laugh had a surprisingly bitter edge. "He liked his women young and beautiful."

"Hmm," I said.

"And as for her," Avery went on, "she's such a repressed and quiet type. I can't imagine that Astin-Berger meant anything to her. But those uncanny wails—jeez—they chilled me to the bone. Then that poor student—"

"Sophia Warzek—"

"Yes, Sophia. When she went crashing to the floor, tray and all—well, for a moment I thought I'd stepped into a grade B horror film."

"Yeah, well, I don't think she's been well." I didn't feel like talking about Sophia. How could someone like Avery Mitchell understand Sophia Warzek's life?

The conversation lapsed. We drove for five minutes or so in silence, the only sounds the hum of the motor and the soft whoosh of the fan blowing heat into the frigid interior of the car. The green lights of the dashboard glowed hypnotically in the darkness. Avery reached out and switched on the CD player, and the exquisite sound of violins flooded the confined space. Bach? Handel? Maybe. I really wouldn't know.

In my mind I was replaying the entire evening, especially my conversation with Randy. What had he been saying about a letter? "If only I'd been paying better attention," I thought, fuzzily. I think I'd overdone it on the tranquilizer. I was startled when Avery responded. I had evidently spoken aloud.

"To what?" he asked.

"What to what?" I replied, less than comprehensibly.

"Paid attention. To what?"

"To what Randy was saying. Something about desire."

"Of course," Avery said. "What else but desire? Jesus!" His tone was so abrupt I glanced over at him, startled. I couldn't read his expression. Surely that wasn't fury playing across his fine features? Noticing my glance, he made an attempt to smile. It was a rueful smile, as if we shared common insight into Randy's eccentricities.

"Wouldn't you think a topic like sexual desire would make for riveting conversation?" he went on. "But whenever Astin-Berger approached me, I felt cornered. It wasn't conversation he wanted; it was an audience. Did you ever notice that? The man was incapable of comprehending the fundamental principle of conversation: When people talk, they talk to each other. For Randy conversation was pure narcissism. Sometimes I think the most compelling desire he ever felt was the lust for applause."

He lapsed into silence. I wondered if my exhaustion and the drugs had made me fanciful. Anger of any kind, I thought, would be way out of character for this imperturbable aristocrat, let alone the powerful emotion I thought I'd seen. Certainly, when Avery began to speak again, his words were cool enough.

"He was obsessed with the mirrored reflection of his own brilliance, you know. A kind of verbal autoeroticism. All he ever wanted from anyone was a mirror to flash back an image of his own precious genius. To be frank, I found him insufferable."

I nodded agreement, too spaced out to reply. I don't know whether or not he saw me.

After another moment's silence he added, "That was very indiscreet. Please don't repeat it."

The farther away we got from Enfield, the more Avery's air of smooth competence and control evaporated. He seemed distracted and moody. Perhaps the illusory intimacy created by our isolated closeness in the car as we sped through the frozen countryside, the only sign of life every now and then a glowing Christmas display or a lighted room in an otherwise darkened house, had caused him to drop his habitual guard.

"Jesus . . ." The change of subject was abrupt. "Sometimes I hate this job. Did you hear me with those detectives? What an ass I am in full swing. *Call on me for anything, day or night,*" he mimicked, savagely. "Christ, you'd think I was a broker meeting a client."

I didn't know whether or not it was the Xanax operating, but I felt momentarily well disposed toward this man. I smiled a little loopily in the darkness, and patted him benignly on the hand, a liberty I would recall with horror in the morning. Between exhaustion and the drug I was too abstracted to speak. We drove in silence the rest of the way home, and he shone the headlights on the front door until I was safely inside.

Three

WHERE WAS Sophia Warzek? I was worried about her. She usually worked the lunch shift—serving hot food, clearing tables—but I'd been sitting at my table in the Faculty Dining Commons for more than fifteen minutes and hadn't seen her. Maybe she hadn't recovered from her collapse when Randy's body was discovered. *I'd better call her*, I thought. *That girl seems to be in a very fragile state*.

The lackluster December sun slanted through high uncurtained windows. Fat red Christmas candles flickered on every table. About the room hung the ripe odor of oversteamed broccoli. The Commons was crowded, Randy Astin-Berger was dead, and I was sitting in front of a cooling plate of chicken Tetrazzini. None of it made any sense. And where *was* Sophia Warzek?

I thought back several days to the last day of classes. Sophia had been unusually withdrawn then, too. Lingering in the classroom, shuffling papers and books, she'd come up to my desk after the other students had gone. The skin of her face seemed drawn more tightly than usual over the fine bones. Her blue-gray eyes seemed unfocused, and her normally silky blond hair was dull. She'd handed me a gift-wrapped cookie tin and muttered something about thanks for a wonderful class. Then she'd left.

I remembered staring after her. *That girl looks like she's in real deep shit,* I'd thought. Then I'd shrugged. What could be wrong? It was simply that she worked too hard. That's not uncommon with scholarship students. I knew that from experience. She'd survive. I had enough on my mind, I'd reminded myself. I didn't need to start playing mother hen to my students.

The call from the president's office had awakened me that morning at nine. Would it be convenient for the college car to pick me up at nine-thirty? By ten A.M. I was sitting at my office desk, awake but not quite conscious, staring at a pile of forty final research papers. All of which had yet to be graded. Randy Astin-Berger was dead, but final grades had to be in on time. I sighed, picked up the red pen, and got to work. Enfield students are very smart, but reading forty of anything is a little like opening your skull on its hinges and banging a rubber mallet directly on the soft tissue of your brain.

Greg rushed into the Commons, grabbed a sandwich and coffee, and plopped himself down at my table. "Karen, you all right? I hung around last night until they chased me away, but you hadn't come out yet."

"Well, the cops kept me for a while. . . ." But Greg was on to the next subject.

"This place has gone crazy," he announced. "I've been here six years, and I've never seen anything like it. Have you heard the gossip? Revenge. Intrigue.

Dark, sinister secrets. You'd think Enfield was a day-time soap opera, not one of the country's most precious little colleges!"

"Oh, come on, Greg. Revenge? Sinister secrets? Aren't you getting a little carried away?"

A hand grabbed my shoulder. I gasped and jumped straight up out of my chair.

"Jeez, Karen," said Jill Greenberg. "You're wound tighter than a sidewalk watch." She perched on the chair next to me. Today the heart-shaped face with its dark eyes held an uncharacteristically somber expression.

Jill's usually wild hair was pulled back severely at the nape of her neck and clasped with a gold barrette. Wispy curls escaped their restraint, creating endearing little tendrils across her forehead and in front of her ears. She wore turquoise jeans and a bright orange turtleneck sweater, and looked far more like a high school junior than was decent for any Enfield College faculty member—even a brand-new one. I knew Jill had to be at least in her mid-twenties. She couldn't possibly have a Ph.D. if she were only sixteen years old. Could she?

"I meant to reassure you, not *scare* you to death." Jill picked up my buttered whole wheat roll. Glancing at me for approval, she broke a chunk off and popped it in her mouth.

"I can't stay; I'm off to give an exam. But I saw you and Greg through the window and thought I'd say hi." She put the bread roll down and rose before she'd really settled into the seat. Pushing the chair tidily under the table, she stood behind it and gazed at me with solemn concern. "Karen, I just wanted you to know that I don't believe any of the rumors." Then she squeezed my shoulder again, nodded with grave sympathy, and made her way out of the room.

Rumors? I looked over at Greg. *Rumors?*

"That was certainly reassuring," he said.

"Greg? What rumors? Tell me!"

He chomped into his ham on rye. "Not to worry. Only a few people think you murdered Randy."

"Shit," I said.

"Listen, I'm telling you, don't get upset." Greg stirred sugar into his coffee. "There's plenty of sympathy for you—especially if you did strangle him." He grinned at me as he lifted his cup.

I groaned and hid my face in my hands. The only place I'd ever get tenure now was at the State Penitentiary.

Greg had finished half his sandwich. "But, seriously, what was going on with you and Randy, anyhow?"

"He was a pain in the ass, Greg. But in case you're wondering, I didn't kill him."

"I never for a moment thought you did." Greg paused. "Although I wouldn't have blamed you for trying, the way that prick kept hassling you."

"Hey, the cops don't know about that, so don't mention it."

"Well, you've been pretty discreet, Karen, but people have noticed things. This place is buzzing with gossip. The cops'll hear."

I twirled the strands of cold chicken Tetrazzini around my fork without conveying any to my mouth. The broccoli lay untouched on my plate. Randy Astin-Berger was dead, and my stomach was in turmoil. Greg reached out, serious for once, and touched my hand.

"Karen, you look sick. Maybe it would help to talk about it. What was really going on?"

"Jeez, Greg. I don't know. He seemed to have some sort of thing with me—a fixation, like."

"Like what?"

"I'm not sure. It started the first day of classes. I

was, you know, all keyed up, nervous about meeting my students. I pulled open my office door, on my way to class, and there he was, lurking in the hall."

"Lurking?"

"Well, that's what it looked like. The bulletin board is right outside my door, and he was staring at the notices, but I don't think he was really reading them. I was in a rush, and I crashed right into him."

"I bet he enjoyed that."

"He seemed to."

I pushed the limp broccoli around on my plate and thought back to my first meeting with Randy.

A dark, sinewy man, past first youth, but not by much, he'd resembled a redesigned Mick Jagger: younger, more stylish, slightly more sculpted in the facial features, a *teensy* bit feminine, as if Jagger had put himself in the hands of Michael Jackson's image consultants.

At the impact, he'd grabbed my arm, seemingly to steady me, but his grip on my upper arm lingered just a little longer than necessary.

"Welcome. Welcome to Enfield College," he'd effused, extending a strong lean hand. "I'm Randy Astin-Berger, and we are going to be great pals."

I put my fork down and looked at Greg. "It was as if the great Astin-Berger had decided I was going to be his little disciple. The first thing he did was confide in me that my new department was—and I quote—'a virtual wasteland peopled with retrograde intellects characterized by elitist, masculinist, homophobic, racist politics.' But that, together, he and I could work a radical transformation. . . ."

Greg's laugh was sardonic. "Sounds like Randy. And he was probably right, don't you think?"

"Well," I said. "It may have started out political, but it didn't stay that way. Randy made it clear—

several times—that he could do a great deal to further my career. If you know what I mean."

Greg's lips tightened. "Scum!"

"And at first I thought that was really odd. He's so well-known for his work on homosocial desire, you know; I always thought he was gay. But, God, sitting next to him at the first faculty meeting, I was thoroughly convinced otherwise."

"Well, I could have told you that. Randy's heterosexuality is—was—notorious, Karen." Greg's expression darkened, as if something more personal than college gossip was at stake. "I could tell you a story. . . ." But he let the impulse die. I was surprised; reticence was not Greg's strong point. Then he continued, "Anyhow—Randy liked to be on the cutting edge. If gay studies was the cutting edge, that's what randy Randy would be up to."

"Yeah. Right."

"Listen, I'm sorry you had so much trouble with that sleazebag. But I really don't think anyone seriously believes you killed him. Most people think he was murdered out of revenge. Probably because— well, you know—the tenure thing. Everyone likes Ned Hilton, but—"

"Not Ned!" I was appalled. Reflexively I looked around the room for him, but his lanky figure and brown cowlick were nowhere to be seen.

"I don't think so, either. I know Ned, and he's the kind who's more likely to take his disappointment out on himself, you know? He's been depressed ever since he came here, and this semester's been even worse. How someone so good could doubt himself the way he does . . ."

"You know, Greg, personnel decisions are all supposed to be confidential, but I keep hearing things."

"Like what?"

"Like—that the English Department voted to tenure Ned. That it wasn't unanimous, but he had solid support. Then the Executive Committee overturned the vote because Randy was so adamant against Ned. Do you think that's true?"

Greg shrugged. "I wouldn't be surprised. Astin-Berger liked to be cock of the walk. He probably wouldn't have taken kindly to having a young male competitor tenured in the department, someone he couldn't muscle around." Greg went to work on the second half of his sandwich.

For the first time that day I allowed myself actually to *feel*. Murder. A Xanax hangover. Abominable food. Departmental intrigue. Lurid gossip. And it was finally becoming clear to me that one of my colleagues must have committed homicide. It was a plateful, and none of it tasted good.

The small groups of colleagues at the Commons tables were beginning to disperse, leaving the room in quietly conversing pairs. None of them, for some odd reason, happened to walk past our table, even though it was directly in line with the door. My heart sank. I was already a pariah.

Miles Jewell, bulky in a conventional tweed jacket with conventional suede elbow patches, strolled out with Magda Vegh on his arm, gazing up at him attentively. She was still wearing the green malachite earrings, and her white cashmere knit dress clung provocatively to her body. Greg's head swiveled to follow their progress.

Miles was enjoying the attention. He gestured with his pipe stem to reinforce a point. His white hair flopped picturesquely over his shaggy eyebrows. A living, breathing, walking, talking stereotype— Enfield's resident curmudgeon. Now that Randy wouldn't be replacing him as department chair, I wondered if he'd stay on for another year. Or forever. That's the way Miles seemed to want it. And it looked like Magda was angling for another year, too.

At the open French doors of the Commons' entry, Miles and Magda paused. The tenor of their conversation seemed to change, to become more hushed. Miles inclined his head a little closer to Magda's, touched her white cashmere shoulder with one hand, and pointed in my direction with his pipe stem; Miles is not known for subtlety. Magda's head swiveled instantly, and for one embarrassing second we were staring directly at each other. I broke eye contact first, as if I had not been watching them at all, but merely surveying the room. But if I had needed proof that I was indeed under suspicion, I had it now. I shoved the plate of Tetrazzini out of my direct line of vision.

While Greg ate, I continued to look around. In the center of the room the wan beam of winter light from the high west windows had settled on the almost motionless figure of Margaret Smith as she sipped her coffee. Margaret certainly didn't look like a woman who had caused a hysterical scene twelve short hours before. Her thin lips were as pinched as usual, her pale skin as bloodless, her gray eyes as hedged. With her unhealthy pallor and gray-brown hair, wearing a gray sweater and skirt, she resembled nothing so much as an illuminated granite saint.

"Quick recovery," I mused aloud.

Following my line of vision, Greg snorted with suppressed amusement. "Now there's a culprit for you. Yes, I have it! She's had the hots for young Randy for years. Emboldened by a friendly word, she begins to move on him. Appalled, he spurns her lustful advances. Hurt and furious she follows him into the closet to plead her passion one final time. He laughs her to scorn, and in a purple fury she grabs

him by the necktie—an obvious phallic substitute—
and, voilà, a corpse on the coats!"

I looked at him with disgust. "Greg, you know
that's not funny."

He subsided into an apologetic slump as I went
on. "I really feel sick about all this. Since Randy and
I both work—worked—on nineteenth-century American lit, we saw a lot of each other; I was the last one
to talk to him; I found his *body,* for God's sake. This
murder feels to me like more than just an occasion
for prurient speculation. All right, so I didn't like
him. So he annoyed the hell out of me. He didn't
deserve to die. The poor bastard enjoyed his life. His
death is disgusting and needless, and I really don't
feel like gossiping about it."

"I'm sorry, Karen." He had the grace to look genuinely ashamed. "It's just my way of coping."

Two more colleagues walked past; neither bothered to greet us. Hmm. I watched them disappear
through the big doors, then turned back to Greg. "I
know that. But, listen, I want to talk a couple of
things over with you."

"I thought you didn't want to gossip."

"This isn't gossip. Through no fault of my own I
am knee-deep in this murder, and I want to do something about it."

"Do what?"

"I want to try to find out who killed Randy. If his
murderer isn't found, I have a feeling I'm going to be
under suspicion forever."

"Jesus Christ! You can't do that. It's dangerous,"
Greg responded. "There's a crazed killer out there!"
He rolled his eyes in grotesque exaggeration.

I sighed. But I was starting to feel more than just a
little panicked. People were gossiping about Ned, but
they were also leery of me. And that police lieutenant

had looked at me funny. If I couldn't talk to someone I was afraid I'd implode.

As I leaned forward to confide in Greg, however, a slim figure in a long white apron reached over my shoulder and picked up the plate of cold food. *Sophia!* I swung around with a welcoming smile. It was not Sophia.

"You're done with this, aren't you, Professor Pelletier?"

"Oh, hello, Bonnie." This was the student I secretly thought of as The Whiner—Bonnie Whiner, I'd named her. I hadn't heard her approach us. How long had she been standing there?

"Yes, I'm done. You can take the salad, too."

Bonnie balanced the salad plate on top of the cold pasta, but continued to hover.

"Professor Pelletier, I'm so glad to see you. Isn't it awful about Professor Astin-Berger? Why, just yesterday I saw him and he looked so happy. Surrounded by old books and papers and as happy as a clam. Such a brilliant man, don't you think?"

Bonnie was narrow-faced with a long thin nose and what I always think of as medieval eyes, bulgy and lacking visible eyelashes. Her real name was Bonnie Weimer. In my women's poetry class, she sat front row center, always present, always alert, always annoying.

"Yes, it is a terrible thing," I replied, as she waited, intent and unusually silent.

Another pause. Why did I get the feeling that Bonnie was listening for something in particular? Some piece of information? Some appropriate cliché? I smiled weakly, obviously inadequate in my grief. Then it hit me: she'd heard the gossip, too. She was waiting for me to say something incriminating, something she could repeat in the dorms.

When I didn't respond, she went on. "He was doing *really* important work, wasn't he? What with the letter and everything . . ." She let the sentence trail off suggestively, and I tried not to react with too much interest.

"The letter?" My voice was casual. Greg glanced over at me.

"Well, you know, the *letter*. The one he found." She looked at me sideways.

"No, I don't know." My tone was testy. I was impatient with Bonnie's prurience and her smug self-importance, but I wasn't surprised by it. Bonnie was the class nay-sayer, intently focused on what was wrong with any text or any argument proposed by me or by her classmates. I would have welcomed a straightforward dissent. But Bonnie found fault in an elliptical, sycophantic manner, protesting in a nasal whine that *really* didn't I think that Dickinson *really* didn't get the rhyme right in that poem, and didn't I think that Plath's images were more psychotic than poetic, and, *really*, Elizabeth Bishop . . .

"What letter?" I could have bitten my tongue as soon as I'd spoken. Now Bonnie was going to hoard her information in a particularly oysterlike manner. If I wanted it, I was going to have to pay dearly by answering her prying questions.

I couldn't manage that at the moment.

"Bonnie, suppose we talk later this afternoon. You still have to turn in your take-home exam, don't you?"

"Well—okay. . . ." She seemed chagrined at being put off. I smiled at her brightly.

"See you later, then."

Greg sipped from his cup of cold coffee, gazing at me over the rim. "It's not like you to be rude to students, Karen."

I sighed. "I know. But Ms. Whiner always gets on my nerves."

"Weimer, you mean," he interjected. "Bonnie Weimer."

I waved his correction away, and told him about my final conversation with Randy, that he had mentioned something about a letter. Greg listened carefully and sat in thoughtful silence for a few minutes after I finished.

Suddenly I wanted coffee. Desperately. I looked over toward the coffee urn. A slender blonde in a huge apron, her back to me, was just lifting it from its shelf. Sophia, finally. The big stainless steel urn looked far too heavy for her; I jumped up to help her. Then I saw the student worker wasn't Sophia at all. It was Bonnie Weimer. Again. I sat down. Bonnie staggered into the kitchen, removing the coffee from my sight.

Where was Sophia? When she'd fainted last night, I'd rushed over to her, but then the police had commandeered me. Mrs. Maher had called Mr. Warzek. "You'd think her father would've shown a little sympathy," the housekeeper told me later. "But, no; he snapped at the poor thing—told her to pull herself together and get in the car." Mrs. Maher clicked her tongue. "I was afraid he was going to slap her."

I would definitely call that girl when I got back to my office. Mother hen or not.

It was close to two o'clock and the Faculty Commons was now empty except for Greg and me, Margaret Smith lingering over coffee and the *Christian Science Monitor,* and a custodian in a dark blue uniform mopping the floor in the far corner by the kitchen. The smell of Lysol mixed with the residual broccoli odor.

"Can you get the key to Randy's office?" Greg startled me out of my reverie.

"Noooo," I replied, astonished by the question. "Why?"

"Well, he mentioned something to you about a letter and about his desk. Bonnie said he was excited about a letter, and she seems to have seen him in his office with it. Therefore, the logical first step would be to look for a letter. In his desk. In his office. Right?"

"That would be breaking and entering, wouldn't it?"

"Not if you had a key, it wouldn't. It would merely be illegal entry. I think. What do you want to do? Go to the cops with this information?"

I thought briefly about the intimidating Lieutenant Piotrowski and his suspicious stare. It certainly wouldn't hurt if I could come to him with some evidence of who the real killer might be. And then Jill's words about rumors came back to haunt me. Everyone knew I was the last person to admit to seeing Randy alive. But obviously not everyone was as willing to believe in my innocence as Jill and Greg were. I would be in an extraordinarily awkward position here at Enfield until Randy's murderer was caught.

"Well, now that I think about it, I could easily get into Randy's office—with the cookie key," I said.

"Cookie key?"

"Yeah. The department passkey is on a ring with a gigantic plastic chocolate chip cookie. It hangs on a board by the secretary's desk." I thought for a moment. If I pretended to have locked my key in my office, I could go into the English Department office just before closing, when it was hectic in there anyhow, and nab the cookie key. Elaine wouldn't notice if I didn't bring it back by five. She probably wouldn't even notice me take it.

I raised an eyebrow at Greg: *Let's go for it.*

Four

DICKINSON FLUSHES *her soul into the poem,* I read, and winced. With my red pencil, I circled "flushes," wrote "word choice!" in the margin, and put the paper down with a sigh. Thirty-two more essays to go. It was seven P.M., and I took another gulp of cold coffee. Between students dropping off exams and reporters seeking sensational details, I hadn't made much headway with my grading.

Greg had scheduled our little investigative foray into Randy's office for some time after nine o'clock. Irena, his wife, was due home from a couple of days in New York City, and Greg wanted to have dinner with her before he left for the college. Irena was an aspiring actress whose kooky blond beauty was suddenly much in demand. Her portrayal of one of a group of female thirtysomethings in a recent Michelob spot had led to a flurry of job offers. Earlier this week she'd had an unexpected call from her agent about a small part in *Law & Order* and had taken off immediately to Manhattan for the audition.

Irena had become a hot item, and Greg hadn't quite begun to deal with that. She didn't even know he'd been tenured, Greg told me. She was supposed to call yesterday afternoon, but hadn't. *Hah,* I thought, *that's why all the booze last night.*

I decided to read one more paper, then sneak off campus for a quick bite at Rudolph's Café. You can get a fairly decent hamburger at Rudolph's if you ignore the elaborate menu and just ask for it. And tell them to hold the Boursin.

I picked up the next paper from the pile and glanced at the title: "Emily Dickinson's Master Letters and the Language of Despair" by Sophia Warzek. Well, this should be a treat. Sophia's papers were sensational: articulate, carefully reasoned, and original.

Emily Dickinson's so-called Master Letters are not so much documents of desire, she began, *as they are documents of despair.*

She'd made this point in class recently when we'd been discussing Dickinson. Students had been fascinated by the three draft letters addressed to "Master" found in the poet's papers after her death. They listened attentively as I told of the speculation surrounding the letters' bizarre, almost shameless, appeals to some unknown beloved. *Oh, did I offend it—Daisy—Daisy—offend it—who bends her smaller life to his, meeker every day. . . .* Scholars, I told them, differ wildly in their interpretations of the letters and in naming the "Master." He's been identified as various men—and, occasionally, as a woman.

Leading candidates are the Reverend Charles Wadsworth, a distinguished Philadelphia clergyman, and Samuel Bowles, a noted journalist and editor, who was a good friend of the Dickinson family. The students looked at photographs in a Dickinson biography and unanimously chose handsome Samuel Bowles.

It was then Sophia made her comment, hesitantly and with seeming reluctance, about despair, and the discussion took a more sober turn.

The self-abasement in these texts, Sophia wrote, *is indicative of a profound sense of powerlessness and hopelessness. Despair is reflected in the peculiar use—or abuse—of religious imagery, which makes a feeble attempt at cajoling the Master, but distances and deifies him as well. "I heard of a thing called 'Redemption'—which rested men and women—You remember I asked you for it—you gave me something else—." Clearly this man who is causing the writer so much pain is associated with the remoteness and the omnipotence of the Divine. The gulf between the lowly "Daisy" and the Seducer/Redeemer is impassable.*

I finished reading the paper with a sense of gratification. If I had done nothing else this semester, I had at least stimulated this one student to some very serious thought. I deserved a good hamburger.

Before leaving for the restaurant, however, I sifted through the disorderly pile of blue books my students had dropped off this afternoon, searching for Sophia's final exam. I checked off each blue book in my class roster. What? Two exams were missing? That wouldn't be so startling, except that they were Sophia's and Bonnie Weimer's. What possibly could have happened to keep these two conscientious students from turning in their final exams? I riffled through the exams again, then closed my class book. I was too tired to make any phone calls tonight, but i'd give both girls a ring in the morning.

Eight-twenty. Time to get some supper or I'd never survive the evening. As I stood up from my desk chair, stretching, and arching my back to relieve the tension, the telephone rang. Immediately, as if in response, there was an imperious knock at my office door. Startled, I hesitated, ridiculously paralyzed into indecision.

I picked up the phone and asked the caller to hold. Then I went to the door. Lieutenant Piotrowski stood in the corridor wearing a baggy gray polyester suit with a rumpled white shirt and a crimson tie, loosened at the collar. He looked a little like Babar the Elephant. Down at the far end of the hall I could see that the door to Randy's office stood open. Inside, the light was on.

"Lieutenant—" I glanced reactively toward my desk where the cookie key lay. Fortunately, it was hidden by the pile of exam books.

"Miss Pelletier," the policeman said.

"*Doctor* Pelletier," I countered, in what I immediately realized was an obnoxious manner. But I hate to be intimidated, and this man's very bulk in my doorway intimidated me.

"*Doctor* Pelletier." Piotrowski drew the title out patronizingly, with the stress on the first syllable. I hadn't gained any points with that move. "*Doctor* Pelletier. I wonder if I might request the favor of your assistance for a few moments?" Very formal. Very polite.

Equally formal, I replied, "Certainly, Lieutenant. What can I do to help you?" What indeed? I didn't have a clue.

Standing back from the doorway, he gestured toward the open door of Randy's office. To say that my heart sank is too empyreal a metaphor; weighed down with guilt, my heart plummeted. I could almost feel it squoosh as it hit the polished oak floorboards of Dickinson Hall. My illegal entry plan had been found out!

Was he going to arrest me? Was "the favor of your assistance" some kind of euphemism for giving me the third degree? I could feel the blood drain out of my cheeks.

This was the last time I would listen to anything Greg Samoorian suggested. I was ready to kill him.

Wait.

Not a good choice of words.

I stood rooted in my doorway until the lieutenant motioned me once more toward the rectangle of light that was all I could see in the dim corridor. In Randy's office I noticed nothing at first but the usual welter of books and journals, blue exam books, stacks of papers. On one corner of his desk a Styrofoam coffee cup teetered crazily atop a copy of *Genders,* which had been thrown on top of the most recent *Critical Inquiry,* both of them surmounting a pile of at least a dozen copies of *American Literary History*.

Then my eyes focused on Randy's leather bomber jacket hanging from a coatrack in the corner. I shuddered. He'd been wearing that jacket the last time he'd waylaid me in the coffee shop and treated me to a short dissertation on theories of narrative encryption. The soft, expensive leather had given my handsome colleague an exceedingly becoming military air—even though the distinctive yellow-and-red divisional patch on the sleeve probably signified nothing more martial than Banana Republic.

It was only after wrenching my gaze from the jacket that I noticed the uniformed trooper seated at the computer, dark eyes in a lean black face focused intently on the screen. Evidently the cop and Piotrowski had been going through Randy's files.

"Dr. Pelletier," Piotrowski said, "we thought you might be able to help us here."

Really? Maybe I hadn't been found out after all.

"In examining Professor Astin-Berger's computer files we've found something that we think might relate to you. What's your middle initial?"

My middle initial?

"A. For Ann. Why?"

"Well, there's a file titled KAP that we have reason to believe is addressed to you. Will you take a look at it, please?"

I turned my eyes to the computer screen. On it was a short poem. At least I think it was a poem. The amber letters read:

Karen   dark heat and distance
my hands in all that beautiful hair
what I wouldn't want to do
that white throat where the pale pulse leaps
those eyes   yes
yes   those eyes
yes   *yes*

I blushed. Piotrowski noticed; I could tell by the stillness of his eyes and the deliberate lack of response in his expression.

"Did you have any reason to believe that the victim had, ah, special feelings for you?" The lieutenant's face was inscrutable.

"No," I responded, automatically. Then I thought better of it. Certainly the campus was rife with gossip.

"Well, yes. I guess I did. Professor Astin-Berger had been very—attentive."

"Were his attentions welcome, Doctor?"

"No. Not at all." Vehemently.

"I see. Had he been making a nuisance of himself?" Very smoothly and quietly.

"I didn't murder the man because he wanted to play nooky with me, if that's what you think."

The officer at the computer snorted. Piotrowski

whipped around and scowled at him fiercely. The young trooper stared at the monitor, blank-faced again, engrossed in the scrolling files.

"There's no need to be so defensive, Doctor." The lieutenant turned back to me and raised his sturdy hands in a gesture of appeasement. Now he was going to lay it on thick with the "Doctor," and I couldn't very well tell him to cut it out. "I'm not accusing you of anything. As a matter of fact, I wouldn't blame the professor for being, ah, enamored." One raised eyebrow. A conciliatory smile.

I didn't return the smile.

The policeman registered my coldness. *Stuck-up bitch*.

"Doctor, I just want to get the lay of the land here. Do you have any particular, ah, boyfriend at the moment?"

"No, I don't." An image of Avery Mitchell flashed into my mind. *What the hell?* I suppressed it immediately.

"No. And if I did, it wouldn't be someone who would strangle anyone."

He waited for me to go on. When I didn't, he pulled a small notebook out of his jacket pocket, flipped through several pages, read something with close attention, and changed his line of questioning.

"According to some of your colleagues, you're the person around here who would be most likely to know what's what with Professor Astin-Berger's scholarly work. Can you give me some idea of what might be significant in his files?"

I told him that Randy and I both worked in nineteenth-century American literature but from very different perspectives. My specialization was gender and class. His was sex. He was doing a study of homoerotic troping in sermon discourse.

Piotrowski rolled his eyes. "What does that mean—in English?"

"Well, Randy was reading sermons, both published and unpublished, for evidence of either homophobic reaction or repressed homosexual desire. What he was doing was actually much more complex and specialized than I can explain. But it was very important work. Professor Astin-Berger was highly regarded in the scholarly community."

Piotrowski looked first disgusted, and then puzzled.

"But he wasn't, it seems, qu—ah, gay, himself?"

"It wouldn't seem so."

He was silent while he digested this information. Then again he took his inquiry in a different direction.

"Do you have any new thoughts about this letter the victim mentioned to you?"

"No. I'm still baffled."

"Might it relate in any way to this, ah, work he was doing?"

"Could be. But I don't know why he'd think *I* would be so excited about it. *Thrilled,* he said."

"Yes, so you told me." The lieutenant's face was impassive again. "What about this, ah, document on the computer? Do you think that might be the letter? A letter that he thought might *thrill* you?"

I felt myself blush again. "In his dreams!" I snapped, then bit my lower lip. Antagonizing the police wasn't going to do me any good.

"Listen, Lieutenant, I'm sorry. I know you have to ask these questions. But I really hardly knew Randy. He talked so much that I never listened to him when I could avoid it. Whatever fantasies he had were his alone. Believe me, Lieutenant, I never gave Randy any reason to think he could thrill me in any way. Now, I'm exhausted. I'm upset. I'm starving. I don't think I can be of any further help. Can I please go home?"

"Certainly." With another shrug. "You're under no restraint. Just keep yourself available for more questioning. And let me know if you're going to leave town for the holidays."

He turned back to the officer at the computer. As I went down the hall I heard Randy's printer start up, most likely printing out that embarrassing little poem.

By the time I returned to my office and remembered the telephone, the caller had, of course, hung up. It was well after nine. Greg, thank God, hadn't shown. I called his house and got no response. That puzzled me. When he didn't appear by nine-thirty, I gathered up the exams and papers, stuffed them in my briefcase, pulled on my heavy gray wool jacket, and started for home.

Hunger and exhaustion have never been good for my brain. As I headed toward my car I realized how confused I really was. And—was it possible I hadn't told the detective the whole truth? Was there something I'd forgotten? If there was, what was it? Well, I'd stop at the McDonald's out on the miracle mile and get myself a Big Mac. And fries. Maybe a massive infusion of calories and fat grams would jolt my memory into gear.

My thoughts began to revolve again around my final conversation with Randy. What *was* it he had been saying to me? *Why* hadn't I been listening?

Unexpectedly, a wave of pity engulfed me; Randy was dead, horribly dead, and I was treating his death merely as a puzzle. For the first time he became real to me as a human being, rather than as a nuisance to be avoided. This was a man—an *odd* man, maybe even a *nasty* man—but a fellow creature.

It seemed to me now that whatever he was saying

at our final encounter had been immensely important to him. Was I fantasizing, or did I truly recall that he had produced his information as if he were playing a trump card of some kind?

The Queen of Hearts, probably, knowing him.

Five

I ARRIVED HOME in a state of weariness unparalleled in my adult life. I hung my jacket on a hook in the foyer, eased out of my boots in the hallway, nudged the thermostat up to sixty-eight degrees, dropped my sweater and skirt in a heap at the foot of the bed, turned off the telephone bell, and hit the mattress in my old sweats. Then I slept for more than twelve hours, a dead, dreamless sleep.

The answering machine message light was blinking as I stumbled into the kitchen late Saturday morning. The machine whirred back through yesterday's voices and clicked as it replayed the first message.

"Mom, it's me. Friday afternoon. It's five-thirty. They're talking about Enfield College on the news. An English professor strangled to death. Until they said his name, I thought it was you. Why didn't you let me know?" Click. Whir.

Oh, shit! I hadn't called Amanda.

"Mom? Me again. Are you there?" Silence.
*"Mom. Call me. It's after seven. I'll stay in the
dorm."* Click. Whir.

*"Mom? I'm worried. It's after ten and you still
haven't called."* (As if I didn't know.) *"Where* are
you? Don't do this to me." (To *you?*) *"Call whenever
you get in. I'm waiting."* Click. Whir.

Oh, God. How could I have forgotten to call her?
Now it was the middle of finals, and she was getting
hysterical. Well, I'd call, but I wasn't about to let my
daughter know just how closely I was involved in
this murder. She had an active enough fantasy life
already; she didn't need to picture dead bodies falling
out of closets on top of her hapless mother. As the
only child of an only parent, she worried about me
far too much anyhow.

Pause. Click. Whir.

Why was I hearing the click? There hadn't been
another message. I rewound the tape, but after
Amanda's previous message there was only a brief
silence, an intake of breath, and a hang-up. The tape
continued to roll, and the next voice startled me. The
dulcet tones of Avery Mitchell.

*"Karen? I'm calling at, ah, eleven-oh-seven. I just
wanted to check in and, ah, make sure you were
okay. Sorry to make it so late, but, ah, it's been an
insane day."* Brief silence. *"As you can imagine."*
Longer silence. *"Well."* Silence. *"I'll touch bases
with you tomorrow."* Click. Whir.

Bemused, I turned the rewind knob and sent the
tape back to its beginning. It wasn't his words that
mystified me quite as much as it was the silences.
What did the silences mean? And, then, what did the
words mean: *touch bases with you tomorrow?* On
the one hand it was a nice sports metaphor, implic-
itly accepting me as one of the gang—or the team, so
to speak. On the other hand, wasn't "touch" a par-

ticularly loaded word? And *"bases"*? I didn't even
want to think about it.

God! I must be sick. Only someone with a truly
sick mind would think such a thing.

I had set the coffee dripping and was halfway
through my shower before I remembered Amanda's
calls. *I am an appalling mother,* I thought. *Obsessing
over a perfectly casual phone call from a man and
forgetting all about my only child.* The phone was
ringing again when I stepped out of the shower.
Amanda! I snatched up a thick white bath towel and
sprinted into the bedroom.

"Hello!" My tone was brusque. Guilt does that to
me. It wasn't until the word was out that I remembered it might be Avery Mitchell. "Hello," I said
again, immediately, in a different tone of voice.
Friendlier.

But it wasn't Avery. It was Darien Cromwell, the
college physician, calling to tell me that one of my
students had tried to kill herself and was in guarded
condition in the intensive care unit at Enfield Re-
gional Medical Center.

It was Sophia Warzek, and she was asking for me.

I pushed open the double doors of the ICU at about
one-thirty. A chubby man wearing a white cotton
jacket and pants stopped me at the desk.

"May I ask where you're going?"

Since medical personnel all dress alike nowadays, I
didn't know how intimidated I should be. I looked at
the black lettering on the white plastic badge. Robert
Martin, R.N., Head Nurse, ICU. Plenty intimidated.

"Yes," I said. "I got a call from Dr. Cromwell. I'm
looking for Sophia Warzek? She wanted to see me?"

"Oh, yes. Well, she's not available to visitors at
the moment—"

"But I'm not just a visitor. Sophia tried to commit suicide. She's in crisis. She's asking for me."

"I'm aware of all that. But you'll have to wait. You'll find other college officials in the lounge." The nurse gestured to a small room just inside the doors of the ICU and bustled off.

"But . . ."

Earlene Johnson, the Dean of Students, sat in the lounge with Darien Cromwell. Next to Earlene, who is black, chic, and energetic, Darien's tall, stooped body and sallow face looked enormously unhealthy. A network of broken capillaries webbed his prominent nose, and the whites of his pale eyes were tinged ever so slightly with yellow. He fidgeted with a pack of cigarettes, even though a No Smoking sign in neon-orange and black occupied a place of honor on the wall.

"What happened?" I asked, looking at Earlene. She was dark-skinned with a long, thin, arched nose, high cheekbones, and, right now, a deeply concerned expression. As she opened her mouth to respond, Darien broke in.

"It seems the kid slit her wrists and OD'd on Valium at the same time. If her mother hadn't heard her fall off the bed about five this morning she sure as hell wouldn't have made it. Brought her in, pumped her stomach, stitched her up, and it looks like she'll pull through. They just called us an hour ago. Her father wanted us to know she wouldn't be taking her final exams, for chrissake. I came to check up on her medical status. Earlene here came along to talk to the parents. Kid'll only talk to you, she says."

He crossed his arms over his hard, round little stomach, nodded his head once, firmly, and abruptly stopped speaking. All had evidently been said.

I thought about Sophia's thwarted attempt to speak to me the night of the party. I thought about the missing blue book. I thought about the impulsiveness of youth. And I didn't know what to say. This could be as much my fault as anyone's. Why hadn't I insisted that she talk to me, then and there? Tears came to my eyes.

Earlene was on her feet with her arm around my shoulder before I even knew I was crying.

"It really sucks, doesn't it?" She led me to the orange vinyl couch, sat me down, and supplied tissue—all in a series of practiced, compassionate moves.

"She was—is—the neatest kid. All those privileged crybabies on that campus, and that brilliant, beautiful child, working her fingers to the bone—I just can't stand it!" Earlene, too, had tears in her eyes.

Darien looked at us as if we were some sort of inferior species, then immersed himself deeply in a *Newsweek* with a picture of Dan Quayle on the cover. We were all relieved when the head nurse, obsequious now in the presence of a physician, came to take Darien into Sophia's room.

"So, Earlene, what happened?" I demanded. "I mean, what *happened*? Do you know?"

"Karen, all I know is that her mother heard the thud when she fell off the bed, ran to her room, found the door locked. Then she heard moaning and called Sophia's father. He took the door off its hinges. Found her covered with blood and her eyes rolled up inside her head. No note. Mother's practically catatonic. Father's a cold son of a bitch. Pissed as hell that she's not gonna finish the semester." The slip into the vulgar showed how shaken Earlene must be. Her usual manner was controlled and elegant.

"Have you seen her?"

"Just from the doorway. She looks terrible. Won't talk to me. Won't talk to her mother. Sure as hell won't talk to her father, and I don't blame her; that's one scary dude. Won't talk to anyone but you. Why's that?"

As I began to tell her about our aborted conversation at the party, Nurse Martin returned to escort me to Sophia's bedside.

"Only five minutes, at the most. And, remember, she's a very sick young woman. Don't say anything to upset her."

Sophia did look terrible. Her eyes were sunken, each surrounded by a deep, unhealthy purple, like an old bruise. She lay thin, flat, and immobile under white sheets. The monitors danced and beeped, ceaselessly reminding her that she was still alive. Both wrists were heavily bandaged. Her eyes were closed when I entered the room. She didn't seem to know I was there.

An equally thin and pale woman, an older, worn, version of Sophia, stood up from the bedside chair and slipped out. She didn't introduce herself or acknowledge my presence. Just vacated the room silently, as if she were used to removing herself unobtrusively from the scene. Any scene.

I walked over to the bed and sat in the chair. Sophia's eyelids flickered; her eyes opened when she saw me. She reached out, feebly, attempting to take my hand. Surprised, I took her hand in both of mine and bent toward her.

"Sophia, I'm so sorry. . . ." But she shook her head almost imperceptibly, and I shut up.

"I tried to call you," she whispered. The words were raspy, and painful to hear. "Last night. I thought you'd . . . understand."

"Me?" But as soon as the word was out, I realized she desperately needed me to understand, or at least to seem to understand. I nodded.

"About the Master," she said. "You see, I loved him."

I nodded again. She began to sob, softly at first, and then with increasing volume. I stroked her hand, and nodded, although she couldn't see me for the tears.

The Master?

The head nurse came bustling in, his round face rosy with irritation.

"I told you not to upset her. I'm afraid you'll have to leave."

"But she wants to tell me something. I can't go now."

"Look at the state you've got her in. You certainly aren't doing her any good. Now, please go."

"Sophia, I'll come back. You get some sleep, and then I'll come back. Okay? I'll stay right here at the hospital until you can see me again."

She nodded faintly, her eyes already closed.

In the lounge I found Darien ready to depart and Earlene trying—fairly unsuccessfully—to talk to Mrs. Warzek. I leaned on Darien and persuaded him to tell the nurse to let Sophia talk to me. The best thing they could do for Sophia, I insisted, would be to let her unburden herself of whatever was causing her such distress that she wanted to end her life.

"That's what we have a social work staff for," Nurse Martin said, tartly. "And the clergy." Obviously life was slopping over into his routine again, and he didn't like it. Not one bit.

"Fine." I was trying hard not to lose my temper. "I'll talk to the social worker. I'll talk to the priest. I'll talk to anyone. But Sophia will only talk to me. If she'll talk to me with the social worker there, that will be fine. Or the priest. But I really don't think she will. Especially not the priest."

Not given the little she'd told me already.

So I said good-bye to Earlene when she left and,

along with the phantom mother, settled in for the long wait until Sophia woke again.

After about two hours, during which I had thoroughly perused the Dan Quayle magazine and every other piece of printed material in the waiting room, Mrs. Warzek finally began to respond to my gentle advances.

In a soft, hesitant voice she said, "I didn't know anything was bothering Sophia. She seemed just the same as usual. She's such a good girl. Never gave us any trouble before this. Always did what she was supposed to."

"Oh," I said. "That's nice."

"Of course, her father would never stand for any nonsense. Not even when she was real little. He's real upset at Sophia. It's not like her to do anything to get him so upset."

"Where is he?"

"Now? Well, at work, of course."

"At work? But Sophia . . ."

"He doesn't want to lose his job. He just started as a custodian at the college. It's not what he's used to. But the cement plant . . ."

Her faint, uncertain voice trailed off. Another tragedy of the failing northeast economy.

Although I could see traces of Sophia's delicate beauty in her mother's face, Mrs. Warzek was a ruin of a woman. Her skin was pale and papery, her eyes a dead blue. It was difficult to tell how old she was, but her dull hair was still blond. I thought she probably wasn't more than forty-five.

Talking to her was like entering some alternative universe presided over by a deity referred to as "Sophia's father" or "he." As with most supreme beings, the penalties for transgressing divine rule seemed a little vague. But then, perhaps transgression had never been attempted. Until now.

Poor Sophia.

And now she was looking to me for help. She had tried to call me, she'd said. I remembered the telephone call in my office the night before, from which I'd been distracted by Lieutenant Piotrowski. I remembered the hang-up on my answering machine. I began to feel inadequate; people tried to talk to me, and I was never there for them.

Then they died.

I jumped up from the yellow vinyl chair. *Oh, my God! Amanda!*

She was grouchy when I reached her in her Georgetown dorm room. "Where have you been, Mom? I've been worried sick."

"Isn't that supposed to be my line, honey? Listen, let me tell you what's been going on." And I did.

"Tell Sophia to—to chill out," Amanda advised, as I was about to hang up from our half-hour conversation. "Everything will be okay. You'll help her, won't you, Mom?"

Oh, yeah. That'd be real easy. But I was pleased by my daughter's faith in me. Amanda's the best thing in my life. I wouldn't have believed anyone who told me that in my senior year at Lowell High, though, when I skipped a monthly period, ignored it, and then skipped two, then three. So, I did what I thought I had to do: got married the day after graduation and blew my full scholarship to Smith.

Fred was a truck driver, and his job kept him on the road for long stretches of time, five or six days per trip. In a basement apartment in North Adams, without friends or family, I retched my way through a long, sick pregnancy, surviving largely on saltines and secondhand Regency romances, both of which I bought in bulk.

If I'd retained a shred of self-respect in face of my mother's shame, my father's fury, Fred's resentment, and the hypocritical sympathies of my high school classmates, Amanda's birth rendered me totally docile. I was nineteen. I had no money, no skills, no confidence. If I displeased this volatile, moody man to whom I seemed to have bound myself forever, how could I care for the child I had been careless enough to bring into the world? It was my fault; I was the one with the uterus. I'd been told that often enough to remember it very, very well.

For two or three years I merely functioned. I washed my face, combed my hair, went through the nightly obligations of the marriage bed. I took abuse passively. But when Fred started backhanding Amanda, I scooped up my daughter, walked out, got a job waitressing at a truck stop, started evening classes at the state college. Read better books.

Grew up. Went to graduate school. Got the job at Enfield. Had a dead man fall into my arms.

Sophia woke around eight P.M. A young Pakistani nurse explained in English so meticulous I knew it wasn't native that she'd been directed to stand in the doorway while I talked to the patient. This, I thought, was Nurse Martin's revenge, even though he was now off duty. Mrs. Warzek was asleep, slumped uncomfortably in a yellow vinyl armchair, covered with a hospital blanket. I whispered to the nurse not to disturb her.

When I saw Sophia, propped up on pillows for my visit, even I wasn't at all certain I should be talking to her. Her eyes, sunk deep in their discolored sockets, were lackluster. She looked as if she wouldn't have energy enough to speak.

But she managed a wan smile when she saw me and mustered sufficient strength to begin apologizing immediately for causing me any trouble. I took her hand in mine and squeezed it gently to silence her.

"Sophia," I said. I found myself tempted to call her "honey," as if she were Amanda. If ever a young woman needed some mothering, it was this one. *You are only her teacher,* I reminded myself firmly. *You are not her mother. You have enough on your hands. Do not get yourself too deeply involved here.*

"Sophia," I began again, "I'm only sorry you're hurting so badly. Is there anything I can do to help?"

"I'm such a fool." She began sobbing convulsively. I glanced over at the nurse in the doorway, but she smiled ruefully and turned her back on us.

"We're all fools, sweetie," I told Sophia. "Honey, it's part of the human condition." *Such* wisdom. But she needed to hear it.

She stopped sobbing.

"Not you." Her voice was weak.

"Sophia, if I counted up the times I've made a complete, blithering idiot of myself, in a major way, I'd run out of fingers and toes."

"Really?"

"Yes." I paused to think about it. "Well—maybe I'd run out of fingers."

I couldn't quite believe it, but I think she smiled. At least, I took the weary upward curve of her lip on the right side and a momentary glint of life in her blue-gray eyes to be a smile.

"Would it help you to talk a bit?"

She sighed, a sigh that came from somewhere deeper than the lungs.

I shouldn't have been surprised at the story she told me. It was a very old story, perhaps the oldest: a story of seduction and betrayal. I shouldn't have been surprised but, of course, I was.

Over the course of the fall semester, very slowly and with cool calculation, Randy Astin-Berger had seduced her. After several weeks of intrigue, he had tired of her enthralled devotion and, somewhat abruptly, dumped her.

Sophia, of course, had been brokenhearted. His attentions had been so unexpected, and he had seemed so godlike to her, that she had seen herself as being at fault, unworthy. His death had devastated her. It was as if the sun had set forever. Nothing remained for her but the murky emotional twilight of her family life.

Of course, she couldn't stand it.

Her story, as she told it, had been more halting and fragmented—and confused—than that. When she finished, she looked enormously debilitated, but her face had relaxed somewhat, as if she had achieved a temporary peace.

I talked with her for a while, trying, clumsily, to give her what little reassurance I could. What can you say to someone who feels so deeply betrayed that the foundations of life no longer seem to hold? I promised I'd come see her tomorrow and sat with her until she fell into what looked like a genuine sleep.

As I walked to my car, I thought back to this fall's fierce debates about sexual harassment, remembering that Randy Astin-Berger had taken a prominent part. The college was trying to define a consistent policy about sexual relationships between faculty and students. Those who opposed sex between professors and students felt such liaisons were irresponsible and exploitative, that they constituted a blatant abuse of power. The other side felt guidelines would be repressive and puritanical. Astin-Berger—the prick—had given an impassioned faculty-meeting speech against "incarcerating the body in a pernicious web of moralistic regulation."

Greg declared he'd never heard such frenzied polemic in all his years at the school. It was the most divisive college issue he could remember. The faculty was split right down the middle, and each side had defended its position with the high moral passion of the righteous. By the end of the semester, the issue hadn't been resolved, other than for a fuzzy provisional statement that satisfied no one, infuriated almost everyone—and never once mentioned the word "sex."

All the way home from the hospital I fumed about that bastard, Astin-Berger. A sexual predator if there ever was one. Putting the make on a vulnerable child like Sophia. I wanted to kill him.

But, then, someone had beaten me to it.

Six

AT LUNCHTIME on Sunday the Blue Dolphin diner was packed with Christmas shoppers and students letting off steam between exams. Although it was after noon, people were still ordering the enormous breakfasts for which the place is famed. A waitress went by, carrying a tray heaped with omelets, home fries, and sausage. The odor of potato, onion, and grease was irresistible. American ethnic food. I stood in the doorway of the battered chrome-and-steel diner—an original '40s eatery, not one of the trendy reproductions—and waited for Greg and for a booth. The intense cold had relented a bit, and the outside steps were covered with muddy slush. I stamped my feet to shake the melting mess from my boots.

As a couple in matching purple hand-knitted mittens, hats, and scarves brushed by me, zipping up their identical navy blue down jackets, a fiftyish waitress with improbable blond hair offered to show me to my booth.

"I'm waiting for a big man with a dark beard," I told her.

"Sounds good, honey," she responded promptly. "So am I."

I had tried, with no luck, to reach Greg by phone three or four times after he'd failed to show up Friday night for our planned raid on Randy's office. By Sunday morning, however, Sophia's suicide attempt had driven my worries about our broken sleuthing date back into a very dim corner of my mind. I was grading papers, huddled in front of the wood stove in jeans and a ratty Boston University sweatshirt, rushing through the essays at warp speed so I could make time to get over to the hospital. When the phone rang, I grabbed it immediately.

"Yeah?"

"Karen? Karen, I want to apologize."

"Greg? For what?"

"For not showing up the other night."

"Oh. Right. I've been worried about you. What happened?"

There was a silence. Then, "I don't want to talk about it on the phone. Could we get together?"

Shit, I thought. *Irena.*

I glanced fatalistically at the scarcely diminished stack of papers, took a deep breath, and offered to meet him at the Blue Dolphin for lunch. That would give him time to pull himself together a bit, and I could get through another five papers. If I was ruthless. After lunch I could go on to the hospital.

I followed the blond waitress to a table in the back of the diner. Avery Mitchell was sitting in the next booth. Well, it's a small town. Sometimes much too small.

He was with a couple of trustee-type middle-aged men—burly, balding WASPs in Sunday leisurewear of brightly colored Eddie Bauer sweaters. Most likely they were holding a damage control session. Funny, I would have expected him to host such important guests at the Enfield Arms or the new Biscotti Café. Someplace with original prints, overgrown orchid plants, and risotto. But he looked quite comfortable with the aqua vinyl of the Blue Dolphin decor and a half-eaten bagel.

Avery nodded when he saw me and after a moment excused himself to come over to my table.

"Karen, how *are* you?"

My hands went cold. Tall, lean, suave, patrician: There was no denying it now, this man looked terrific to me. So much for my working-class erotics.

"I'm fine, Avery." *I'm cool. I'm smooth. I'm totally unruffled.* "And you?" *Brilliant conversationalist, too. And still, oh God, wearing the B.U. sweatshirt.* "How are you?"

"Okay." His right hand made a that's-of-no-concern gesture. A slender, well-manicured hand. Beautiful. "But you? You've recovered from the shock?"

Shock? Was he implying I had been in shock?

"I'm fine," I replied. With a little distance.

The waitress returned, carrying my coffee and followed by Greg. She raised an eyebrow at me in approval. Avery seemed startled to see Greg; God knows what he thought. And Greg looked positively disconcerted to see Avery. Which I could understand. Here he is ready to spill his guts, and who's standing in the aisle but the big boss. The one who had just granted him tenure.

The waitress gave me a second knowing glance as she put down the coffee. *Two* good-looking men. Some girls have all the luck.

I didn't feel very lucky at the moment, however. Just damn awkward. What I really wanted was for everyone to vanish—Greg, the waitress, the trustees.

No one would remain but Avery and me. Preferably in a dark, smoke-filled club with a moody piano in the deep background. I would reach up and with the tips of my fingers slowly stroke that elegant hand. Just once, beginning at the wrist and moving down to the tip of the little finger. Once would be enough. . . .

"Well, I'll leave you folks to your breakfast, ah, lunch," Avery said, after a few seconds of uncomfortable silence, and returned to his trustees. I was left with Greg and a fairly grimy menu. I ordered a Wisconsin cheddar omelet with herb sausage, home fries, and buttered whole-grain toast.

The omelet came. Involuntarily I gave the waitress a complicitous smile. Then I turned my attention to Greg, who was brooding over his coffee.

"Here," I said, cutting the cheddar concoction in two pieces, "take half of this. I'll never eat it all, and you look as if you could use a little nutrition." And truly, if anyone as hefty as Greg could looked malnourished, he did. I thought I detected a slight hollowness in his cheeks even under the beard. As I lifted the half omelet onto the plate with his abstemious order of toast, thick yellow cheese dripped onto the Formica tabletop. I dabbed at it absently with my napkin.

"So," I said. "What's up?"

Greg stared at the table and mumbled.

"What?"

He looked up at me abruptly. "Irena never came home." He spoke louder than he intended to, then winced. He looked over at Avery, and lowered his voice.

"You remember Friday night, I was making bouillabaisse? To celebrate? Well, she doesn't come home by six, when she's supposed to." Greg was slipping into the narrative style of his Brooklyn youth. "And by eight everything's cold, the champagne's flat. And *then* she calls." Greg paused, overcome by indignation.

I sipped my black coffee and waited for him to continue.

"She's been delayed, she says. Isn't going to make it home tonight. Doesn't even ask whether I got tenure. So . . ."

"Yes?"

"So, we had the mother of all arguments, Karen. And then I jumped in the car and went to Manhattan to talk some sense into her." He stirred cream into his heavily sugared coffee.

"Did it work?"

"She's not coming home."

Oh, God. "Ever?"

"I don't know." I think it was only the presence of Avery Mitchell in the next booth that kept Greg from dissolving in tears. I'd never seen a man look so despondent.

That was all Greg would say. I was quite certain he thought Irena was involved with another man. It wasn't inconceivable. With her bouncy strawberry blond curls and eyes the color of sherry, she has just the kind of peachy beauty that would prove irresistible to any show-biz Lothario. A good ten years younger than Greg, she had married young, and life in a stuffy academic town might well have begun to chafe.

Greg was by now completely lost in gloom. After a few minutes of one-sided conversation, I changed the subject. I told him about Lieutenant Piotrowski's visit to my office, the poem on Randy's computer, and Sophia's suicide attempt. For some inexplicable reason all this misery seemed to perk Greg up.

He knew Sophia, he said. She'd done an independent study with him the previous year on the anthropology of American ethnicity. "Her parents are from Poland," Greg said. "And she was fascinated by ethnic novels, tales of assimilation. You know, where the protagonist struggles with personal identity? What does it mean to be an American when your parents live the old-world ways? She wrote a paper for me on *Bread Givers*—have you read that?"

"Oh, yes. The novel with the horrible father, the one who tells his daughter she's not a person."

"Yeah. She wrote a truly brilliant paper. I'm no therapist, but I think that's Sophia's battle. She wants to become a person, an American person. But she's so loyal to her family." He shrugged. "It's not a new problem."

As he talked about Sophia, Greg began to work his way through his half of the omelet, and then finished up what I had left of mine. "Maybe I could help," he said when he was done. "Could I come with you to the hospital?"

"Sure." I began to feel more hopeful. Perhaps I'd pulled Greg out of his slump, for now, anyhow. Maybe I wouldn't have to play Miss Lonelyhearts any longer. And maybe I'd enlisted someone to help me out with Sophia.

When the waitress reappeared to refill our coffee cups, she winked at me. The big man with the dark beard was displaying feeling. Way to go, girl. And another guy waiting in the wings.

I glanced over Greg's shoulder. Avery was evidently laying out a plan to his companions. With his right hand he was outlining details, some on the tabletop, some in the air. It was like a ballet, I thought; his hand moved so elegantly. When he saw me looking in his direction, he gave me a barely perceptible nod. I immediately dropped my gaze. My face grew hot.

No matter how it may have appeared to our waitress, I am no sophisticate as far as men are concerned. Listen, when you come from where I came from, men are a luxury. For most of my adult life, I have been working much too hard to have any time for them. I started out way behind everyone else, and I've had a hell of a time catching up.

Since my disastrous marriage I'd really only had one long-term relationship. Tony and I had been together for over six years but, when I insisted on taking the Enfield job and moving more than four hours away from where he works as a state police narcotics investigator in Manhattan, we had separated. He couldn't live like that, he said. He needed someone to commit to him, marry him, start a family. He *needed* that, he said, and I believed him. But, after fifteen years of combining full-time mothering with full-time studying, balancing poorly paid adjunct teaching jobs with enough part-time waitressing to keep food on the table, and then laboring anonymously in a factorylike city university, it was no contest. I wouldn't, even for Tony, contemplate turning my back on an offer from Enfield College.

Separating from Tony was a little like ripping out my heart, to borrow a simile from one of my romance novels. But his conditions were absolute: If I went away from him, that was it. No retreat, baby, no surrender.

He has another girlfriend now. They're engaged. The wedding is next summer.

Amanda, who still sees Tony, the only father she wants to remember, insists his fiancée looks like me.

She teaches nursery school.

So there I sat with my good job and my slowly mending heart, sneaking peeks over Greg's shoulder at the eloquent hands of a man who was in a position to pulverize me completely, good job, healing heart, and all.

Someone should tell me to wise up.

When we got up to leave the diner, Avery was still deeply engaged with his trustees. I inadvertently brushed his arm as I put on my coat in the narrow aisle. He looked up at me and smiled.

I left the waitress a ridiculously large tip.

Seven

MY FEET swooshed with almost reverential silence over the deep pile of the burgundy carpeting in the main corridor of Emerson Hall, Enfield's administration building. Emerson's oak wainscoting and paneled doors with their elaborately ornamented brass knobs had presided with somber elegance over the education of generations of elite New England youths while my illiterate ancestors were hoeing potatoes in the rocky fields of eastern Canada. I never entered this building without the sense that someone might well hand me a soft cloth and a bottle of brass polish and tell me to get to work. That I was actually a professor on my way to submit grade sheets to the Enfield registrar seemed to me to be nothing short of miraculous. The ghosts of the college's former presidents obviously agreed. They frowned down on me from massive gilt-framed portraits lining the high walls of the corridor.

Monday, long before dawn, as I finished calculating my students' final grades and was about to enter

them on the registrar's grade sheets, I realized Sophia
was not the only student whose work was incomplete: Bonnie Whiner's—excuse me, Weimer's—final
exam was also missing. Sophia's crisis had driven
Bonnie from my mind.

At nine A.M., when no one answered my calls to
Bonnie's dorm room, I loaded all the papers and exams in the car along with my grade sheets. I couldn't
wait to be rid of the detritus of this semester, and it
annoyed me to have to deal with loose ends. In Emerson Hall I stopped at the Dean of Students' office
to inquire about Bonnie. I wasn't the first. Her roommate had just come by, uneasy because she hadn't
seen Bonnie all weekend. And Bonnie's parents, unable to reach her, had called Earlene first thing this
morning.

When I reported Bonnie's missing exam, Earlene's
expression grew even more concerned. "Stacey, Bonnie's roommate, said Bonnie stayed up all Thursday
night because she wanted to get your final in on time.
And Stacey knew she'd finished it because the printer
woke her up about six A.M. She says Bonnie isn't
always considerate that way. Karen, are you *sure* you
don't have her exam?"

"I saw her briefly at lunch Friday, but she didn't
give me anything. And she never came to the office.
I'd have remembered, because she was going to tell
me something—" I paused as the significance hit
me "—about—about Randy."

"That does it!" Earlene reached for the phone.
"This is not the type of young woman who just takes
off without telling anyone. And if Randy was involved— I'm reporting her missing."

The feeling of unease that I had been trying all
weekend to exorcise began once again to rattle its
spectral chains. What could have happened to hyper-
conscientious Bonnie? I marked *I* for Incomplete in

the slot for her final grade and left the grade sheet with the registrar. Maybe nothing else was resolved, but my grading, at least, was complete.

"Karen? Can I offer you a cup of coffee?" Earlene caught me on my way out of the building.

"Sure." Not only did I like Earlene, I also enjoyed spending time in her office. She had decorated it with African masks and sculptures and large handwoven reed mats from Kenya. It was the most distinctive office I had seen at Enfield, where people seem to think nondescript shabbiness is a mark of intellectual merit.

"I wonder what those old presidents out in the hall would think of your decor, Earlene? Or your outfit?"

Today, perhaps in celebration of the upcoming holiday, Earlene was togged out in African fashion, wearing a purple batik dashiki over black leggings. With her close-cropped hair and the hammered silver hoops dangling from her ears, she looked stunning.

Earlene laughed. "It really doesn't matter, does it? They wouldn't approve of yours, either."

I had made a real effort this morning to avoid my usual dishevelment. Wearing tight black jeans, a form-fitting black turtleneck sweater, short black leather boots, and my hair pulled back in a purple scrunchy retrieved from among Amanda's rejects, I had left the house feeling . . . well . . . baaaad. But now, next to Earlene, I felt positively dowdy.

Earlene wanted to talk about Sophia. "I saw her this morning and she seems to be doing a little better," Earlene said, seating me in an armchair by her desk and pouring a cup of fresh-made coffee. After refusing food for two days, she said, Sophia had begun to eat again. She'd also agreed to talk to a hospital social worker.

I had noticed a slight improvement on Sunday

when Greg and I visited. Greg's half-solicitous, half-teasing banter had even elicited a hint of animation. Sophia's hair had been washed and brushed and lay on her pillow in an ashen profusion. Her blue-gray eyes, although pained and guarded, held their usual depths of intelligence and irony.

"I've known Sophia since she was a freshman," Earlene continued. "She grew up in Enfield, on the north side, over where the mills used to be, and she still lives at home. She's a terrific student, but Enfield isn't the best place for a kid on scholarship: all these yuppie puppies with their designer jeans and their designer drugs."

"Did she ever talk to you?" I was fishing to see if Sophia had confided in Earlene, too, about her involvement with Randy.

"Only about her schedule and her work-study. Stuff like that. She never seemed comfortable talking about herself. Why? Do you know something I don't?"

I shrugged my shoulders, but she didn't pursue the matter. She'd just remembered something. "Wait. About a year ago she came in one morning, obviously in distress. She wasn't crying, but she had been. I remember thinking that her eyes had that kind of washed-out look to them. In my job I see too much of that. It was the only time I ever remember Sophia being less than completely composed." She paused. "Do you want more coffee?" I nodded.

It was good coffee, dark and full-bodied with a hint of nut flavor. While I sipped, Earlene leaned back in her chair and chewed on her upper lip as if she were trying to recover a memory. Sunlight from the tall, uncurtained windows slanted across the sculpted masks adorning the walls. Split between light and shadow, the stylized faces brooded ambiguously over our silence. Earlene leaned forward with a sigh.

"I see so many students, and a surprising number of them are in crisis. After a while they all blur together. I may bitch about how privileged most of these kids are, but they've got problems you wouldn't believe. I'm dealing with stuff that's not too different from what's happening on the streets of Cleveland where I grew up—drugs, pregnancies, incest, date rapes. It can be a real zoo. I guess when someone is as self-contained and responsible as Sophia is, I just breathe a sigh of relief and let her go her own way."

"But you remembered something?"

"Yeah. She came in that morning as distraught as I've ever seen her. She wanted to know if it was possible for me to get her a room on campus. I looked into it but had to tell her that her financial aid covered only tuition, not room and board. I remember how disappointed she seemed. I asked if I should call her parents and see if we couldn't work out some kind of delayed payment program. She went a little pale when I suggested that, jumped up from her chair and said, 'No. Don't do that. Things are fine just the way they are.' "

In repose, her face shadowed in the sunlight, Earlene looked older than I had thought, her features more careworn. Her heavy eyebrows grew straight, without an arch, above the dark, deep-set eyes, and her dark skin gleamed in the sunshine as if it, like the African masks, had been carefully polished. She seemed lost in her reflections. I thought, not for the first time, *This woman is really beautiful.*

When she didn't pick up the conversation after a minute or two, I spoke. "At the hospital you said her father was 'a scary dude.' "

"Did I?" She laughed, fully present again. "Well, he sure is. Have you met him?"

"No. But I've met his wife." I remembered the pale ghost of a woman at Sophia's bedside. "So I think I know something about him."

"Yeah. A cramped-up, constipated type. But domineering. And *big?* Whew! You know, the hell of it is, if Sophia hadn't been so damn stoic about it, if she'd only confided in me, if I'd had any indication she was in such a state of crisis, I might have been able to work something out for her. There are ways . . ."

"You're not clairvoyant."

"No, but it would sure help. Well, I'll keep an eye on Sophia as best I can. But it seems you're the one she trusts."

"Yeah." I reflected for a minute. "Well, when I teach poetry, I'm dealing with some pretty elemental feelings—love, hate, self-loathing, despair. It's heavy stuff and students tend to think I've got a handle on it. If I don't watch out they use me as a mother confessor." I sighed. "Well, if there's anything I can do . . ." My resolve to stay uninvolved seemed to be evaporating fast.

"I'll let you know. And you let *me* know. And, by the way," Earlene added as I got up to leave, "I wish I could wear black the way you can." She looked at me appraisingly, her eyes narrowed. "Today you look positively feline." She nodded, raising her eyebrows in approval.

I always knew this was a discerning woman.

The talk with Earlene had given me some insight into Sophia's state of mind. She'd probably built a separate emotional world for herself, one where school, books, and ideas took on the affectional weight of mother and father. After a while, I imagine, she felt herself to be adequately protected by her intellectual armor, merely walking through the daily motions of her family life.

No wonder she had been so vulnerable to Randy.

I decided to drop in on her later. I'd take along some light reading: murder mysteries, maybe. Death, mayhem, and general social corruption: just what she needed to get her mind off her problems. Hey, I mean it. But now, to clear my head, shake this oppressive uneasiness, and celebrate the end of the semester, I was going swimming.

The gym was almost deserted. Those students who weren't either taking exams or studying for them had already left for home. I was relieved to see that I didn't have to strip in front of any of my students. For a woman staring forty in the face, there is nothing more disconcerting than having a naked twenty-year-old inquire earnestly about your syllabus as you emerge, saggy and dripping, from the shower.

The woman's locker room is a cavernous and dreary place, smelling of a particularly noxious combination of air freshener and damp feet. Enfield seems to spend a great deal of money, especially alumni money, on athletics, but not much of it is thrown in the direction of women's sports.

At the moment the locker room was empty, and, except for a gym bag sitting open on a bench just under the high, opaque glass-block windows, there was no sign of anyone having been there at all that day. A fairly threadbare white towel was thrown over the bag, and a worn pair of duck boots sat lined up neatly under the bench.

On my way to the pool I glanced into the Nautilus room and was surprised to see Margaret Smith working out on the biceps machine. Dressed in sweat shorts and an Enfield T-shirt, deep in communion with her mirrored image, she looked nothing like the pale, nondescript scholar of the Faculty Commons or the hysterical woman of the fatal Christmas party.

As I opened the door to the pool and nodded to the lifeguard, I wondered for the first time about Margaret. How old *was* she? Was she married or partnered in some way? Did she have children? Was she really a human being with hopes and fears like the rest of us? But that was going a little beyond the scope of my imagination.

I dove into the pool and forgot all about Margaret—and suicide, and murder, and final grades. For thirty minutes I knew nothing but the motion of my muscles, the intake and exhaling of my breath, and the flow of the cool, clear water over my body. The preoccupations of the past few days scattered and then vanished, and I thought fleetingly of Amanda, and Christmas, and how I could prepare a sumptuous holiday dinner for two when one was a vegetarian and the other wasn't. I thought about Avery, and the presidential portraits, and the fact that his was nowhere to be seen in that imposing corridor. My response to him in the diner the day before, I decided, had been just a momentary erotic aberration. But what a stupid thing! My boss! I must really be hard up, I thought. I must really be desperate. Then I stopped thinking altogether. I swam my usual half mile, threw in five additional laps for good measure, and emerged from the pool renewed and ready for another go-round with life.

Margaret Smith was in the locker room when I entered, drying her short gray-brown hair in front of the long mirror. The threadbare towel and worn duck boots were hers. I still wore my bright yellow swim cap and had wrapped myself in a large chartreuse towel with a hot pink palm tree on it. The towel was a gift from Amanda, who is delighted that her mother is, as she puts it, "finally doing something for your body." I looked, I know, as frivolous as I was certain Margaret had always thought me to be.

Margaret appeared startled to see me and nodded in her customary wary manner. Dressed now in a saggy brown wool crewneck sweater and brown tweed pants, equally shapeless, she had regained her customary persona of faded British don. Except for a faint color in her cheeks, she looked middle-aged and not particularly healthy.

I unzipped my gym bag to get my shampoo and conditioner. "How are you, Margaret?" I can do the social thing when it's necessary. "Have you finished grading your exams yet?"

Her response was slow in coming. "Why do you ask?"

Jeez. "No reason. Just being polite."

"Oh. Well. In that case, yes. Yes, I have."

"Great," I responded inanely, and escaped to the shower room. I took a very long, very hot shower.

When I came back into the locker room, Margaret was gone, and I was alone with the scarred benches and battered lockers.

Eight

JILL GREENBERG was getting off the hospital elevator as I came out of the gift shop with a paperback mystery.

"Hi," she said. "I just saw Sophia. She's better than I expected. She actually smiled when I asked permission to seduce her social worker. What a hunk!"

Jill was in rare form today, hair flamboyantly loose, curling in profusion around her heart-shaped face. Her cowl-necked jersey was hot pink, a shocking contrast to the orange tones of her wild curls. The gigantic plastic bananas dangling from her earlobes were a shade of purple not to be found anywhere in nature. Her jeans seemed to have been grafted onto her body, and with dark red lipstick she had shaped a stylized 1950s mouth over her own delicate lips. Somehow this outrageous conglomeration of colors and shapes combined to create a charming image. I doubted she had any idea just how very young and innocent she looked.

"I'm really glad I ran into you, Karen. Can we talk?"

"Sure," I replied. "I haven't had lunch. Do you want to get something here?"

In the coffee shop I took off my jacket and flung it over the back of a chair. Jill reached across the table and stroked the sleeve of my black sweater. "Soft. Cashmere?"

"No. It's probably some synthetic. I don't think I've ever owned a cashmere sweater."

"You don't like cashmere?"

"Can't afford it."

"Oh." She looked slightly mystified, as if that were a concept alien to her. "Anyhow, it's neat. Makes a person want to touch you."

"Well, I guess there could be advantages to that."

Jill grinned, and turned to the waitress. The grilled cheese and bacon on rye she requested sounded to me like certain death. I ordered it too, and added coffee. I'd drink the coffee black.

"What's up, Jill?" This sudden intimacy surprised me.

"You do know people are talking about you." It was a statement, not a question.

"Yes. So I surmise."

"Randy was so hot for you these past few weeks—"

"Was it that obvious?"

"He made it obvious. I really felt for you. What a creep. You know, he *looked* so cool. When I first saw him I thought—that's something I could go for. So I hit on him."

"You *what!*"

"Well, you know—I made sure I went where he'd be. Sat at his table at lunch. Said flattering things. Made myself approachable . . ."

"Oh," I said, swallowing hard. Anything further

from my own response to an appealing man, I couldn't imagine. My usual reaction to the stirrings of sexual attraction is to go undercover, do covert surveillance, check out his credentials as a human being. Is he smart? Does he have a sense of humor? Does he seem kind? And then, maybe . . .

No wonder there haven't been all that many men in my life.

"But, anyhow," Jill went on, "he did *look* great. Terrific shoulders, neat clothes, great buns. And he was a bit of a celebrity, too. But then he opened his mouth . . ."

"Yeah. Right."

". . . and he never shut it. I'd imagined engaging in quirky stimulating conversations—among other quirky stimulating things—but I must have been doing something wrong. I never got a word in."

"You weren't the only one."

"So I dropped him, and started looking at Avery Mitchell." She grinned.

"Jill!"

"What's the matter? You look horrified. You don't think he's attractive?"

"Of course he's attractive. But, my God, Jill, he's the president." *And probably twenty years older than you, for God's sake. Maybe more.*

"Yeah, well . . . Don't worry about it. I asked him out but he turned me down."

I gulped. She asked him out? I had been chastising myself simply for breathing infinitesimally faster when he smiled at me, and this—this *teenybopper*—had asked Avery Mitchell out!

Jill must have interpreted my appalled look to mean I couldn't believe he had turned her down, because she elaborated on his reasons.

"Said he was flattered"—she made a solemn face and dropped her voice to its deepest tones—"*deeply,*

deeply flattered." Her voice rose to normal pitch. "But he doesn't believe it's ethical for him to date untenured faculty members. He actually said *date;* can you believe that, Karen? What I had in mind was jumping his bones, and he says *date!* Watch out for him, Karen. I know he's got *nice* bones. But watch out. I think that man is trouble. I think he's actually—well"—she leaned toward me, confidentially—*"repressed."* She brought the word out reluctantly, with a bit of a hiss over her bottom teeth, as if she were accusing him of a truly regrettable perversion. And maybe, given where she was coming from, she was.

To me "repressed" sounded okay. Actually, it sounded fine. I was really rather comfortable with "repressed."

Then, without giving me a chance to respond, Jill laughed. "I know. You think I'm being indiscreet." The ceiling light shone through her fine curly hair, causing an intriguing halo effect, a bright red aureole surrounding the delicate face with its vivacious red mouth.

"I am, aren't I? But, hey, I don't care. Everyone around here's so stuffy and uptight. You're different. You seem so—well—cool, in a reserved, sophisticated sort of way. I hope we can be friends. And, hey—what's the use of living if you have to watch every word out of your mouth?"

"How old are you, Jill?" I knew it was a patronizing question, but it just popped out.

"I'm twenty-four." At having to admit to such extreme youth, she looked chagrined.

"But how . . . ?"

"I'm a bit of a whiz kid, you know. Graduated high school at fifteen, Columbia at nineteen. Got my Ph.D. at twenty-three."

"And you'll be tenured before you're thirty."

"Yeah, but not here if I can help it. This place is the pits. I want to go back to New York. NYU is looking at me. I have an interview there next week."

She brushed off her truly impressive achievements as if they were hardly worth mentioning.

She's only six years older than my daughter, I thought. God, she made me feel ancient.

And I'd be over *forty* before I was tenured.

But Jill clearly didn't want to chat about careers. She wanted to get down to the important stuff. Men. "I hope you don't think I'm a ditz about men. It's just that I don't want to settle down yet. I'm too young. I just want to have fun. Is that wrong?"

"No," I said. "No, not at all." A Cyndi Lauper refrain lilted through my head: *Girls just want to have fu-un!*

If *I get tenured,* I thought.

"But I'm getting away from what I wanted to talk to you about, Karen—I really hope you don't think I'm a ditz—but like I said, people are talking about you. Mostly they're talking about Ned Hilton, but a little bit about you. 'Still waters run deep,' that type of thing. *You* know. I thought I should tell you so you would know where you stood. So you'd understand if anyone was treating you weird. *Do* you think I'm a ditz?"

"Thanks, Jill. No, I don't think you're a ditz at all." *Just younger than I ever was in my entire life.* The waitress, a middle-aged hospital auxiliary volunteer with a comfortably plump body underneath her pink uniform, delivered our grilled cheese sandwiches. With fries. The fries looked great, big slab-cut things. I took one, salted it, and popped it in my mouth. Ummmmm.

Jill bit greedily into her sandwich, and began talking again with her mouth full of bacon and cheese.

"And did you hear that now there's a student missing? Ronnie or Lonnie or Bonnie something?"

"Bonnie Weimer. Yeah. She's in my poetry class. I saw her Friday at lunch, but she never showed up to turn in her take-home exam that afternoon. And nobody's seen her since."

"God! Now I'm starting to get nervous. No wonder I want to get back to Manhattan: It's safer there!"

"But you're sitting here talking to me. So obviously, in spite of what other people are saying, you don't think I killed Randy."

"Hell, no! There's a hundred people more likely. I heard he wasn't above banging students. Maybe one of them got angry. Or a boyfriend. Or"—again she lowered her voice—"maybe Avery Mitchell, you know."

I should simply have stopped the conversation right then and there, but I found myself responding.

"I find that very difficult to believe. What on earth possible motive could Avery have to murder Randy?"

"You haven't heard the rumors?"

"What rumors?"

"That our beloved president hated Randy. Something about his wife—Avery's, I mean. I didn't get the details. People were being extremely discreet." She raised her eyebrows to underscore the significance. "Or, maybe it *was* Ned Hilton. But I'd hate to think so. He's really kind of *nice,* isn't he? And 'nice' is not a word I usually like to use about anyone. But Ned *is* nice, genuine, and kind of shy." She shrugged her shoulders and stopped talking. Maybe she'd finally been overtaken by a fit of discretion.

"He's married," I said.

"I *knooow!*" She sounded just like Amanda.

• • •

Sophia was asleep when I finally got to her room. I stood in the doorway, my hand on the cool stainless steel door handle, and marveled at her paleness, the almost bloodless complexion, the pale yellow of her hair. Her thin body curled loosely under the white sheets suggested a kind of tenuous resignation. *All right. I'll stay alive. If you insist. For now.*

I left the paperback novel at the nurses' station along with a brief cheerful note. As I waited for the elevator I thought about what I'd really like to say to her. *Sophia, sweetheart. Don't let your life weigh so heavy on you. Dye your hair bright red. Buy purple plastic earrings. Get young. It won't last long.*

The elevator disgorged a tall blond man in a short gray zip-up jacket. His expression was severe. Cold blue eyes passed over me without taking notice. An involuntary shudder vibrated through my body. He turned left, toward Sophia's room. I stood, irresolute, while the elevator doors closed. Then I shrugged and pushed the button again. What could I do? He had a right to visit her. He was her father, after all.

That night I dreamt that Randy, dressed in sober nineteenth-century clerical garb, had escaped his confinement in the heavy gilt frame on the high wall of Emerson's central corridor. As if I were the viewer of a private film in which I was also the starring actress and the character she played, I watched him stalk the halls in search of me. It was midnight, of course, and on my knees I polished a brass doorknob. Over and over again I rubbed the brass knob with my soft cloth. Closer and closer he came on his ghastly errand. I was all too aware of his muscular body, which gleamed almost phosphorescently now with a haze of ghostly sweat. "He's dead," I tried to tell me—or was it Sophia? Or maybe Bonnie Weimer? Whoever I was, I paid no attention, idiotically intent on getting the blood off the doorknob. When he found me he knelt beside me. With one hand he cupped my left breast; with the other he handed me his bloodstained letter. But it was no good, of course; I couldn't read.

Nine

AMANDA WAS coming home for Christmas. I was to pick her up at Bradley International in Hartford at four that afternoon, and I spent the entire day being happily domestic. I vacuumed and polished and scrubbed. For the first time in months the old wood floors felt the loving touch of a dust mop. My random collection of tag sale furniture gleamed with a patina of lemon oil. I took out holders I hardly remembered I owned and fitted them with bayberry candles. I twined princess pine stolen from the woods behind the house around the candles on the mantelpiece. Then I baked: shortbread, cherry crisps, date pinwheels, sour cream cake, and one enormous gingerbread man.

The air was redolent with the scent of molasses and spices, and the final pan—the one with the annual gingerbread man—was just coming out of the oven when I heard a knock on the door. I turned down the volume on the Emmylou Harris Christmas carols and pulled aside the living room blind to check out my visitor.

Lieutenant Piotrowski.

"Jesus Christ," I muttered. "So much for Christmas." I switched off the tape player resentfully as I went to open the door. My holiday spirit had deflated abruptly, like a punctured foil balloon.

"I like Emmylou." Piotrowski walked in as if he assumed he were welcome. "You didn't have to turn her off."

"What can I do for you, Officer?" I was in no mood for niceties.

"Baking, are you?" The detective craned his thick neck to get a look at the kitchen where the spicy odors were coming from. "Smells just like my mother's house at Christmas. Gingerbread, right? And, what else? Date squares?" He looked hopeful. "I haven't smelled anything this good since she died, oh, about ten years ago now."

Today over his festive red-and-green sweater Piotrowski wore an elderly royal blue down jacket. The pocket flaps were grimy, the zipper tab hung at an unnatural angle, and a few errant feathers peeped out of the seam at his left shoulder. His nose and cheeks were red with the cold. Give him a white beard and a stocking cap, I thought, and he could be Father Christmas. Well, maybe Father Christmas with a bad wardrobe and an attitude.

I was feeling just mean enough to ignore his hints. I sat him down in the living room, facing away from the kitchen.

He sighed.

"So, Lieutenant," I repeated, "how can I help you?"

The nostalgia in his expression vanished instantly, replaced by cool detachment. He leaned forward in his chair, his large, square hands resting on his knees.

"I think, Dr. Pelletier, that perhaps you know more about the odd goings-on on the Enfield campus than I thought you did."

"Just what do you mean by that, Officer?" I, too, was an expert at coolness.

"Weeell," he replied, leaning back in his chair and placing his hands together, fingertips at his lips. Very thoughtful. "A couple of interesting pieces of information have just filtered up to me from the town police. Very interesting."

He looked at me silently for a few seconds, as if waiting for a reaction. Then he nodded. "Yes, very, very interesting."

"Lieutenant, let's not play cat and mouse. I don't have the slightest idea what you're talking about."

"I'm talking about an attempted suicide and a missing person report. You know, I always get suspicious when odd events happen in clusters. I watch for those clusters. And this is a real odd set of events, Doctor: one murder, one attempted suicide, one missing person. And all occurring to people from Enfield College. In particular, all occurring to people who have some connection to you."

My annoyance turned suddenly to cold terror. "What the hell are you getting at?"

"Well, let's look at it, okay? The last person known to have seen Randy Astin-Berger alive: you. The last person known to have seen Bonnie Weimer: you. The first person requested by Sophia Warzek after her suicide attempt: you. Odd little clump of coincidences, don't you think?"

I did think. Hard and fast. He'd heard those wretched campus rumors. He thought I was the killer. Oh, my God! I'd be arrested, dragged away from home in handcuffs before the cookies had time to cool. Amanda would be left stranded at the airport. She'd spend Christmas day alone in a dank green prison reception room with the families of murderers and thieves, just waiting for fifteen precious minutes with her incarcerated mother. Tears began to fill my eyes.

"Dr. Pelletier, you look a little stunned. Didn't you think about how odd this all was?"

"Well—no. You see, I've been so . . . preoccupied. With grades, with housework, with Christmas . . ." My voice trailed off.

Piotrowski waited for me to go on.

"I just haven't had time to think about anything."

He waited some more. I didn't say anything. Then rationality prevailed. I wasn't guilty, was I? No, I wasn't. Shock turned to anger.

"I don't know what you're thinking, Lieutenant." I had my feelings back under control. "But I assure you I haven't strangled anyone, or disappeared anyone, or driven anyone to suicide. I think you know that."

"Dr. Pelletier, I assure *you* that I wasn't thinking anything of the sort. I merely—er—conjecture that all unconscious you may have stumbled into the middle of something you don't know anything about. I thought if we could have a little conversation, open and honest, without you being so defensive, we might be able to get a few ideas on what's going on here."

I didn't respond. When you grow up in the neighborhood I grew up in, trusting the police runs counter to all your instincts. All right, so I slept with one for years. He was an exception.

"Look, lady." It seemed that Piotrowski's patience was beginning to fray. "Let me spell it out. I don't suspect you of anything. Your movements at the Christmas party check out. You were with one or another person from the time Professor Samoorian saw the victim walk away from you until you opened the closet door. And Professor Jewell saw you do that; he saw the body fall out just as you opened the door. All right? Unless we find out something new, you are not a suspect. All right? So now can we talk? Like a real conversation? Like maybe over a cup of coffee?"

I thought about it. "And a plate of cookies, right?"

"A plate of cookies would be very nice," he replied with dignity.

As I ground the coffee, boiled the water, and placed the warm cookies on a Santa Claus platter, I wondered whether or not this could be considered police extortion.

Or, on the other hand, maybe what I had here was merely a hungry human being, nostalgic for something that reminded him of his childhood. Was it possible that I simply needed to lighten up?

I smiled tentatively at Piotrowski as I placed the platter of cookies and the pot of Colombian decaf on the coffee table in front of him. After all, it was Christmastime. To my surprise he returned the smile tenfold, an enormous, delighted smile that transformed his entire person. He was no longer a stolid, phlegmatic policeman but a human being with unexpected feelings. Suddenly, he was a *man*, almost handsome in all his bulk.

I must have looked startled because his face shut down again immediately as he bent to pour coffee into his mug and stir in enormous helpings of milk and sugar. He swallowed about a third of the cup in one gulp and devoured a date cookie while I poured my coffee (black, no sugar) and took my first sip.

Then he looked up at me, smiled more moderately and began to ask questions, questions about how long I'd been at Enfield, how I had happened to come there, how things were going for me. They were innocuous queries, no doubt carefully designed to lull me into a sense of security. In spite of the fact that he was still very much the detective, something shifted between us. I began to feel that we were engaged in a joint endeavor, an endeavor to set things right.

As I had known from the beginning: This man was good—very, very good—at his job.

Piotrowski's questions began to focus on my relationship with Randy: how I felt about him; what kind of moves he had made on me; what his work was all about. I told him all I knew, holding back nothing because, really, I had nothing to hide. Randy had disgusted and bored me, and in spite of his prominence in the profession, his power in the department, and his trendy good looks, I had barely been able to tolerate the man. I think that had been clear to him. Perhaps, perversely enough, my evident distaste had fueled his interest in me.

I told Piotrowski what I knew about Randy's current research, although I couldn't imagine what relevance that could possibly have to his murder. "He was reading the sermons of Henry Ward Beecher, for God's sake. That pompous, self-important, womanizing little twerp!"

"Who?"

"Who what?"

"Who was a womanizing little twerp? Astin-Berger?"

"Well, yes he was. Not so little, but a womanizing twerp. But I meant Beecher."

"Who is he?"

"Who *was* he, you mean. He was probably the most prominent minister in nineteenth-century America. A charismatic figure by all accounts, abolitionist, public speaker, novelist, and at the center of one of the most publicized sex scandals of the century."

"Oh, yeah? Tell me more."

"Why do you want to hear this? The man's been dead for a hundred years."

"Just tell me, would you? Chalk it up to my pressing desire for a higher education."

So I told him what little I knew about the Libby Tilton case. How the very married Reverend Mr. Beecher had spent long afternoons with this wife of an influential parishioner, supposedly reading her his novel-in-progress. How her husband had sued him for alienation of affections. How the ensuing trial had been reported by just about every newspaper in the country. How it had been followed avidly by readers with both religious and carnal interests.

What Piotrowski thought of all this was not clear. But he did say it was interesting that Randy should have been attracted to the work of this particular man, who in so many ways seemed to resemble him.

I hadn't thought about that, but it certainly was true. Both men were brilliant and incessant talkers, both seemed to have attracted feminine attention, and neither seemed to have been overly scrupulous about exploiting that attention. This thought led me instantly to Randy's brief affair with Sophia. I had completely forgotten about that as I was responding to Piotrowski's queries. However, she had given me that information in confidence, and I had no intention of sharing it with the police. I reached for a cherry crisp to give me something to do with my mouth.

"What?" said Piotrowski.

"What do you mean, 'what'?" I responded, still chewing and reaching for another cherry crisp.

"You just thought of something. What was it?"

"Nothing, really." I tucked a second cherry crisp in my mouth. Whole.

"Indulge me. I'll decide if it's nothing."

This man was too smart. I decided to pacify him with at least a partial truth. Still chewing, I responded, "It's just that I remembered hearing that Randy was known for sexually harassing students. That bit about the womanizing reminded me."

"Students like Sophia Warzek?"

Shit, I said to myself. Was I that transparent? But, as it turned out, it wasn't me; the churning Enfield College gossip mills had conveyed that titilating piece of information to the lieutenant's receptive ear. I surmised he had some notion that, perhaps in retaliation for Randy's dumping her, Sophia had killed him. Then, in a state of profound remorse, she had attempted to take her own life. She *was* at the party, after all, Piotrowski reminded me.

"No way!" My usual powers of articulate persuasion had deserted me. "No way could she resort to that kind of violence. She simply doesn't have it in her."

"You'd be surprised, Dr. Pelletier, what some people have in them."

"Don't patronize me." I was furious not only at his remark, but at myself for having trusted him, if only for a few minutes.

"You're very protective of Miss Warzek." Piotrowski put his empty cup down on the coffee table. "Did you have any particular relationship with her outside of class?"

"No, I didn't have *any particular relationship with her outside of class.* Whatever you mean to insinuate by that. However, she did turn to me in her trouble and I've seen a good deal of her since, enough to know that while she may be a human being in an enormous amount of pain, she isn't a killer. Besides, I've been teaching for years, and I have a daughter almost exactly Sophia's age. I know young women, and this one is decent, through and through."

"Dr. Pelletier." Piotrowski sighed. "Please don't snap at me. I'm not out to *get* anyone. I just want to clear this matter up. In the process of doing that I have to pursue every possible line of inquiry. Is there anything more you can tell me about Miss Warzek and Professor Astin-Berger?"

But there wasn't. There wasn't anything more I could ever tell him about anything, the bastard. As I showed him out, he palmed one last date cookie, perhaps to console himself as he drove back down the winding country roads to wherever it was he was pursuing inquiries next.

Ten

AMANDA CAME THROUGH the arrivals gate to the strains of "Have a Holly, Jolly Christmas." Carrying an enormous navy blue duffel bag in her left hand, her brown suede backpack flung casually over her right shoulder, she looked terrific. That's not just a mother's partiality. In her own peculiar stripped-down style, Amanda is genuinely beautiful, tall and lean with dark-lashed hazel eyes, a long narrow nose, and slender, mobile lips. Even with her shiny chestnut brown hair cropped short and her face, as usual, innocent of the slightest trace of makeup, she's eye-catching. In her grungewear of jeans, green plaid flannel shirt, and heavy Timberland boots, she resembled a scale-model lumberjack, tough and delicate at the same time, ready for action.

"Mom!" Amanda broke into a run as she spotted me in the crowd. "Hey, Mom!" Dropping her duffel bag, she jumped at me and hugged me hard. Almost as hard as I hugged her. Then I held her out at arm's length to see her better and she said, "You look gnarly."

"Yeah?" I wasn't quite sure how to take that.

"Yeah, that red sweater looks terrific on you. And the leggings. A whole new image. Fairly hot."

"Hot, yourself." I grinned and ruffled her hair. Then I picked up her duffel bag and we made our way through the holiday crowds to the tune of "Rudolph the Red-Nosed Reindeer."

Strong, vibrant, free: This kid is the embodiment of all I never was at her age. I had spent most of my eighteenth year in secondhand maternity clothes, nibbling saltines, vomiting bilious froth. Immobilized by notions of femininity I'd picked up from *Reader's Digest* and *Woman's Day,* the domestic bibles of the American working class. Amanda, on the other hand, was born spouting Steinem and Friedan. For her the feminine mystique was a somewhat amusing cultural artifact dimly remembered from the incomprehensible distant past. Something like Jell-O molds.

The parking lot was hazardous. The previous week's snow and ice had turned into filthy slush and then frozen again in the current frigid temperatures. By holding on to each other and sharing the weight of the duffel bag we managed to get back to the car without falling. The Jetta bumped out of the parking lot and headed back up Interstate 91 toward home.

I had news for Amanda, and I wasn't sure how she was going to take it. Earlier that afternoon, as I sat brooding over cold coffee and recovering from Piotrowski's visit, Earlene had called with a request. Sophia was recovering sooner than expected, and the hospital had informed her she could go home for Christmas. This news had precipitated a crisis. Sophia had gone dead pale, turned her face to the wall, and refused to speak. A savvy social worker, cued by her responses to her parents' visits, had coaxed Sophia into admitting that she didn't want to go home, couldn't bear to go home, not even for Christmas.

Especially not for Christmas.

When queried by the social worker as to what she did want, she begged to be allowed to stay in the hospital until after the holiday. Then she wanted to go live at school. If she could. If they'd let her. No, she didn't want a conference with her parents. Please, no. That wouldn't help. She became distraught at the suggestion.

The social worker, fearing a serious setback if Sophia were forced to return home, called Earlene. There was no problem with getting Sophia on campus. Earlene could find a dorm room for her when she got back from her own holiday trip to Cleveland. Her suggestion for the interim was that, rather than stay in the hospital, Sophia come spend Christmas with me. How could I say no? A kid who'd rather celebrate the holiday in a hospital ward than at home in the bosom of her loving family.

"I'd take her in myself, Karen," Earlene told me, "but my mother'd have a fit if I didn't come home for Christmas. And if I came dragging a bandaged white girl—well—I just can't do that."

"This the kid you went to the hospital to see?" Amanda asked when I'd told her the story. As if she weren't a kid herself. "Sure. Why not?" But her expression lacked enthusiasm, and there were unspoken depths of reserve in her voice.

Well, what could I expect? For as long as she could remember there'd only been the two of us for Christmas. And Tony, of course. But then, she loved Tony, and once again we were reduced to having holidays without him. Through no fault of hers. And now some emotionally unstable stranger was about to replace him by the Christmas tree? The unspoken reproach was almost palpable. It was clear to my daughter that her mother was becoming truly unreliable.

As we approached Enfield, I suggested we stop in at the hospital. I wanted to speak in person to Sophia about staying with us, in hopes that I could make her feel welcome. Also, I thought it would provide a good opportunity for the girls to meet. On neutral territory, so to speak. Amanda didn't think so.

"Geesh, Mom. She's not gonna want me to see her in the *hospital.* She'll be too embarrassed. Like, she'll think I'm thinking all the time about the *bandages,* you know? And besides, you're not a *person* in the hospital. You're just a bod in a johnny coat. She'd *really* be embarrassed, you know? That's a *really* bad idea. Geesh, Mom." She looked at me askance, appalled at my lack of sensitivity.

"Okay. Okay." I was properly admonished. "So it's a lousy idea. But I've got to see her. Do you mind if we stop for a few minutes?"

"No, go ahead." Amanda set her jaw bravely and looked straight ahead down the long hospital driveway. "*I* don't mind. I'll just sit here in the car and finish reading this fascinating in-flight magazine." From her duffel bag she pulled a four-color glossy periodical featuring a cover photo of Disneyworld. "I'll be fine," she continued as I turned off the ignition, her tone just one shade this side of martyrdom. I gave her a sharp look, but she smiled at me seraphically and buried herself in the magazine.

Sophia was alone in a double room. When I arrived she was sitting in an armchair watching CNN. Some battle was happening somewhere. On the screen a woman and her children huddled in a makeshift shelter, in exile from home and kin. A U.N. relief worker ladled noodles into enamel bowls while one child gazed back at the camera, dark eyes opaque with incomprehension. The voice-over intoned a detailed record of the ancient hostilities behind this private suffering.

Seeing me, Sophia clicked off the TV and smiled tentatively, clearly uncertain as to how I felt about having her foisted on me for the holidays. She had become so thin in the days since her suicide attempt that in the white hospital gown and robe she gave the impression of translucence. With her long blond hair hanging down her back and the snowy robe, she could almost have passed for a Christmas-tree angel. At least, she could have if it weren't for the pain in her eyes. Gauzy bandages braceleted each wrist, mystic symbols of survival.

"Hey, Sophia." I hugged her gently. "So, I hear I'm going to get to take you home with me?"

She nodded. Also tentatively. She looked at me with wary eyes.

"Great!" I said. A hearty buffoon. "You'll get to meet Amanda."

"Is Amanda your daughter?"

"Yes. I just picked her up from the airport. She's home from her first semester at Georgetown."

"Oh." Silence. "Will she mind . . . ?"

"No," I lied. "Not at all. She's never had a sister, or cousins, or anything. She'll love it."

This poor, poor kid. I'd have a good talk with Amanda on the way home. She'd damn well better love it.

I knew I'd have only about ten minutes before she'd begin to freeze in the Jetta, so I tried to cut my visit short. That was easy. Sophia was not in a talkative mood, and I despise the kind of hearty babble that was all I seemed capable of producing at the moment.

I arranged to pick her up the next morning, the twenty-third. As I took my leave I asked if there was anything I could bring her. She looked embarrassed. "Well, yes, there is. . . ." She fell silent.

"What?" I queried when she didn't say anything more. "What is it?"

"Well." Silence. "Well, my father . . ." More silence. Whatever it was, it seemed to be more than she could articulate.

"What, honey?" I put my arm lightly around her. Her shoulder blades felt like fine steel knives.

Sophia refused to meet my eyes. "My father is so angry. He won't let my mother bring me anything. Not even clothes. He says . . ." She stopped, head drooping, overcome by the hurt and humiliation. "He says if I don't come home for Christmas I'm no longer his daughter and he has no responsibility for me. My mother wanted to bring me some things, but he won't let her. He won't even let her come. She called me when she thought he wasn't listening, but he heard her and hung up the phone. I hope . . ."

She fell silent. I prompted her. "What do you hope, Sophia?"

"I hope—he didn't hit her. . . ."

I winced. Sophia was openly sobbing. "Sweetie," I said, hugging her again, "you can't do anything about it. You just can't. Going home wouldn't help your mother at all. It wouldn't. You can't be a hostage to her weakness. Believe me, I know."

She looked up at me. "You do?"

"Yes, I do." Then I changed the subject. Fast. "And about clothes, don't worry about them. I'll bring you stuff. Just don't worry about it."

Suddenly her expression changed. Her eyes sparking blue fire, she spoke with more passion than I would have thought her capable of. "You know what makes me so goddamn *furious?*"

I shook my head wordlessly. This was a new Sophia, with an edge of violence to her.

"I bought all those goddamn clothes myself. I've been working ever since I was twelve, baby-sitting and stuff. I paid for all my own clothes. He hasn't bought me anything in years. That goddamn *motherfucker*." She clapped her hand over her mouth, and stared at me, eyes wide, amazed by her own outburst.

"You're really angry, aren't you?" *Good,* I thought, *hang on to that anger, sweetie. You're going to need every ounce of fury you can muster.*

"You have every right to be angry." I tried to model myself on the only therapist I had ever consulted, the public health social worker who had gotten me through my separation and divorce. "But don't worry about clothes now. Maybe we can get them back for you. But right now, just don't worry about it. I'll take care of it."

She slumped again, her anger spent, then said miserably, "I don't want to be an expense." What little energy she seemed capable of calling up had evidently dissipated. "I'll pay you back for everything when I get better. I *will.*" She fell into a deep silence.

Oh, the pride of the poor. How well I remembered it.

"Do you like blue?" I felt a little desperate in the face of all this emotion. "Maybe a blue sweater, the color of your eyes? And jeans? And some other stuff? Underwear and stuff?"

She nodded, her head hanging again, looking up at me with only her eyes, a brokenhearted little girl promised a new dress for a party she didn't particularly want to attend.

Five minutes later, as I walked past the nurses' station, deep in thought, a strong hand grabbed my arm. Hard. I jumped, and looked up, startled. Piotrowski was staring past me down the corridor.

"Who's that?" he demanded.

I turned to look, but too late to see anything other than a brown blur disappearing through the stairwell door.

"I couldn't tell. Why?"

"Oh, probably nothing. Only they were just slowing down to look into Miss Warzek's room when you came out. Then they saw you and speeded up to get by fast. But you seemed lost to the world. Did you notice anyone you knew?"

I couldn't remember. And I wasn't about to tell Piotrowski that I had been deep in the contemplation of something as frivolous as sweaters and jeans. "You said 'they,' Lieutenant? Was it more than one person?"

"No. I just couldn't tell if the individual was male or female. Medium height. Medium weight. Brown hair. Brown pants and jacket. Who could tell?"

"And what are you doing here, anyhow, Piotrowski?" I looked down meaningfully at the big hand that still gripped my arm.

He released me, sheepishly. "Sorry."

"Well?"

"Official business." All of a sudden he was all business. Very official.

"Lieutenant, you are *not* going to harass that poor girl."

"It's none of your business what I'm going to do, Dr. Pelletier."

"It certainly is. I'm her temporary guardian."

"What?" His response was incredulous. "I thought she had parents. And besides, she doesn't need a guardian. She's twenty-one."

"Well—unofficially." I explained our holiday arrangements. Piotrowski listened, head cocked to one side, hands in the pockets of his shabby blue jacket.

"Dr. Pelletier," he said, "I know you're concerned about this girl—"

"Young woman," I interjected, and then dimly recollected that I had just called her a girl.

He nodded and continued, ". . . young woman. But I have to talk to her. A murder has been committed and she may well know something about it." As I started to interrupt again, he held up his hand to silence me. "No matter what it may look like, Doctor," he gestured at himself with a look of wry self-deprecation, "I am not a brute."

I started to protest, and the hand came up again. "I understand Miss Warzek is emotionally vulnerable right now, and the hospital's counseling staff knows I'm here. She will be well looked after. Now, why don't you go home? I saw a very cold-looking young woman sitting in your car. I assume that's your daughter? Amanda, is it?"

"Yes," I replied with some asperity, turned on my heel, and headed for the elevator. *Know-it-all.*

Amanda was waiting for me in the lobby, standing with her hands clasped behind her back as she read the dog-eared notices on the community bulletin board. She turned to look at me, expressionless, when I touched her on the shoulder. "I was getting cold," she said flatly.

As we walked to the car, I tried to convey to her some of the pathos of Sophia's life: the poor kid at the rich school; the heavy workload; the brutal father. I wanted to tell her about Randy, but, of course, I didn't. Amanda remained expressionless. All she seemed to respond to was Sophia's lack of clothes.

"God!" she said, with obvious feeling.

It was enough. I'd use it.

We pulled into the mall just outside of Enfield, circled the parking lot until a space opened, and plunged into the chaos. Loudspeakers blared "O Little Town of Bethlehem" as we pushed our way through the crowd. A short man with a hockey stick plowed into me and let loose an astounding string of profanities. Directly into my ear Amanda sang, "the hopes and fears of all the years . . ."

At The Gap I asked Amanda to choose jeans for Sophia. This turned out to be a momentous decision requiring consultation on numerous aspects of Sophia's life and taste ranging from hair color to academic major to favorite musicians. Once chosen—properly dyed, properly faded—the jeans had to be complemented with sweatshirts and tees. After three shirts I remembered my credit card balance and called a halt.

"But, Mom, she's got *nothing!*" Amanda was genuinely horrified.

"Well, honey, now she's got jeans and three shirts."

Amanda stared at me as if I had revealed unpardonable moral ignorance.

"That's what I said, *nothing.*"

"Listen, after Christmas there'll be sales."

Amanda subsided, perhaps mollified by visions of heroic postholiday shopping adventures.

From a shelf I grabbed a cotton sweater, the rich azure of a cloudless August sky, checked the price tag, shuddered, added it to the pile, and headed for the cash register.

Well, she needed at least one Christmas present.

Amanda trailed behind me, for once uttering noises of approval. I didn't know whether it was my taste in clothing that was improving, or my morals. Or then, maybe, really, there was no difference.

Eleven

THE ANSWERING MACHINE message light was on when we arrived home. In the dark living room it blinked eerily, as if it were some diminutive beacon of disaster. But when I turned on the overhead light, the couch and chairs sprang into visibility, and the illusion of danger vanished.

The first call was a hang-up. So was the second: silence on the other end, then the soft thunk of a receiver being recradled. The pause before the hang-up was so prolonged it made me uneasy. I wondered if this was a crank caller. I'd had to deal with one in New York: a perverse oppression—*I know who you are; I know where you are. And now you know that I know.* I decided not to worry about it. Probably a student angry about a grade. He'd get over it.

The third call was not a hang-up. Definitely not. "*Karen. Avery Mitchell calling at four thirty-five. I wanted to let you know the college is planning a memorial service for Astin-Berger. It'll be in mid-*

January, when everyone's back on campus. Maybe the seventeenth. I have Lonnie calling around to put it together, but I wanted to let you know myself." (Brief silence.) *"Because of the, ah, circumstances, I mean."* (Another silence.) *"His wife is coming."* (Pause.) *"Did you know he had a wife?"* (Silence. Then briskly):* "Well, sorry, I'm meandering. I'll be back in touch when things are finalized. Good-bye, Karen."*

Before I had a chance to collect my thoughts, Amanda emerged from the kitchen nibbling a date pinwheel. "Nice voice," she commented. "Who's that? New boyfriend?"

Children can be so irritating.

"Hardly," I responded. "That was my boss, the college president."

"Oh." She raised her eyebrows at my tone. "Nice voice." She threw herself down on the couch. "Is there anything to eat?"

It was destined that I should run into Avery the next morning. On the way to pick up Sophia, I allowed myself an extra hour to stop by campus and do a few things: collect my mail, drop off papers and exams, clear off my desk. As I rounded the corner from the mail room, Randy's office door opened slowly. Half expecting to see his ghost emerge, I almost dropped my armload of manila envelopes and publishers' catalogs. Avery Mitchell walked out carrying a stack of file folders. When he saw me, his eyes widened. "What are *you* doing here?" he demanded.

"I *work* here."

His strained expression lightened and he laughed. "You do, don't you? Guess you should be asking what *I'm* doing here." Then, without giving me a chance to respond, he went on. "It's just that the secretaries are all on vacation. That's why I came over myself—to pick these up, I mean." He gestured with the folders. "I didn't expect to see anyone here, so close to Christmas."

"I stopped by to get my mail." I knew as I said it that an explanation was totally unnecessary. But, then, why had Avery felt compelled to offer me one? And such a detailed explanation, too.

"Curriculum revision," he said. Once again the folders came into play. Avery's blue eyes were shadowed with something resembling exhaustion.

"Oh."

"Astin-Berger was working on a plan. But now . . ."

"Right."

"College-wide. Someone's got to get on it."

"Sure."

"Did you get—?" The hall door opened, and Ned Hilton entered with a bulging briefcase. When he saw us, he looked spooked, as if he wanted desperately to turn and run. Avery nodded at him gravely. Uncomfortable situation all around. Then he glanced back at me. "Well—Merry Christmas, Karen." He tucked the file folders under his arm and strode away. Ned stared at Avery's retreating back until the heavy wood door slammed behind it. Then he ventured a tentative nod at me and scooted into his office. Awkward—but understandable.

But it wasn't like *Avery* to be so awkward. And it wasn't like me to be tongue-tied around a man. What the hell was going on here?

A light went on behind the thick, translucent glass panel in Ned's door. All the other doors remained dark: No one was in the secretary's office, as Avery had said; even Miles's office appeared vacant—and he practically *lived* in the department.

My office smelled stale; it had been almost a week since I'd been back. I left the door open to air the room. Being there reminded me forcefully of the disquieting poem on Randy's computer. His murder seemed to hang in a diffuse fog over my holiday needs and desires. A little like acid rain. I kept trying to forget his contorted face, but the memory polluted most of my waking thoughts and just about all of my dreams. *Merry Christmas, Karen,* his ghost seemed to sneer. *Merry, merry Christmas.*

I cleared a space on one of the shelves and stacked student papers, arranged alphabetically so I could find them easily when the students returned in January. Then I remembered Sophia's paper on Dickinson's Master letters. Warzek: It should be on the bottom of the pile. Yes, there it was. I pulled it out from among the others, thinking briefly that I would return it to Sophia when I picked her up. Thinking, stupidly, that the A+ would hearten her. When I glanced at the first page, however, I realized just how insensitive that would be. I should look at this again, I decided. Maybe it would give me some insight into what was going on in Sophia's mind.

As I took the paper over to the window seat, I heard Ned's door close; then the heavy building door slammed. I was alone in the department. Eerie. Sitting in the window, I put my feet up on the cushion, and read Sophia's paper for the second time. With this perusal the subtext was clear. On one level, the essay had been an attempt to provide some insight into Emily Dickinson's experience, but, more to the point, it had also been a desperate attempt to understand her own. In the poet's letters Sophia had read her own heartbreak. No wonder her insights had been so acute: Over a chasm of one hundred and thirty years, pain had responded to pain. I put the paper down and sighed.

The window behind my desk is one of those nineteenth-century treasures Enfield abounds in; tall, wide, and deeply recessed, with green plush cushions on the ledge, it commands a view of the entire campus quad. I sat curled up in the window seat with Sophia's paper in my lap, staring out at the snow that had begun to whirl through the leafless trees and thinking about this troubled young woman. Then I found my thoughts turning to the encounter with Avery Mitchell. Curriculum revision? Why would that necessitate a personal visit from the college president? And how would he have known where Randy kept his files?

When I looked up, a man was standing in the office door staring at me. He was big, wearing the dark blue uniform of a college custodian, and his bulk filled the doorway. It was the man from the hospital elevator, the one I had decided must be Sophia's father.

"Yes?" I queried, shuddering involuntarily. How long had he been standing there, silently watching me?

"Are you Professor Pelletier?" The man's voice betrayed an edge of suspicion.

"Yes, I am." I smiled at him politely. "And I think you're Sophia's father. I saw you at the hospital."

"Oh, yes?" His response was not friendly. My smile died of malnutrition. "Well, I want to talk to you." A faint accent betrayed his Eastern European origins. He pronounced "want" *vont*.

Although not heavy, Mr. Warzek was broad across the shoulders and upper arms, muscular, a tall man, blond and severe. He was in his mid to late forties, handsome, I suppose, with a long, pale, rigid face, high cheekbones, and icy blue eyes. His hair was cut severely short in a very out-of-date brush cut. He looked like a man who held himself in a state of strict physical and emotional discipline, and expected everyone around him to do the same.

"Certainly," I responded. "Won't you come in?" I'm usually not so formal, but this man's rigid expression did not encourage a casual response. I rose from the window seat, feeling oddly vulnerable there, where he had watched me without my knowledge. I sat behind my desk. I seldom used the desk when I was talking to students, but a solid oak barrier between Mr. Warzek and me didn't seem like a bad idea.

"Have a seat." I gestured at the green vinyl armchair by my desk. But Sophia's father didn't sit down. Rather, he strode over to the bookshelves and stood with his back to me, perusing the titles. After a brief hesitation he pulled down a book. I could tell by the cover that it was *Extravagant Love*, a recent history of female homoeroticism. He leafed through the pages for a moment, as if he knew what he was looking for. Mr. Warzek paused, seemingly at one of the illustrations, then slapped the book shut and slammed it down on the table. He turned toward me, his face tight with disgust.

"What're you teaching them here? Filth and perversion? Sophia brought that book home and I made her get it out of the house. Was it you assigned it?" Anger intensified his accent. He was at my desk now, looming over me. I immediately regretted my seated position. I nodded. I'd assigned the book as optional reading.

Warzek's look of loathing intensified. "I shoulda never let her come to this school. This place ruined her. She usedta be such a good kid. I thought maybe you'd learn her to be a teacher. Take care of herself. Help the family out. But no. All you did was spoil her for anything useful." He braced his hands on my desk and leaned toward me.

Earlene is right, I thought, *he is a scary dude*.

"And now she got crazy notions. Wants to be a

writer. No goddamn money in that. How's she gonna live? Huh? Am I supposed to support this kid for the resta her life? Tell me that? How's she gonna live?" The sleeves of his blue shirt pulled tightly across the muscles of his upper arms. Red stitching over his shirt pocket identified him as "Stan." He was glaring at me as if he actually expected an answer.

I shrugged. His manner was angering me. "People do. Live by writing, I mean. I didn't know Sophia was thinking about that, but she might succeed. She's got a great deal of talent."

"Fuck—talent." He pounded a large fist on my desktop, twice, emphasizing each word. I jumped with each crash of his fist and thought about calling Security. He must have seen from my expression that he had overstepped the line. He straightened and moved several inches back from the desk. His Adam's apple bobbed up, and then down.

Then he pivoted away from me and walked over to the bookshelves again. I wondered what other perverse or obscene texts he might find there. *Lady Chatterley's Lover? The Catcher in the Rye?* I wondered, briefly, if someone had told Sophia's father about her affair with Randy.

Warzek mustn't have been looking at the books, however, because when he turned toward me and spoke again his voice was tightly controlled. He had obviously used the time to collect himself. And he didn't seem to have Randy on his mind; it was me he was thinking about. "The hospital told me you was taking Sophia home with you. Is that right?"

I nodded.

"Why?" It was not a question, but a challenge.

"She needed a place to go."

I hadn't asked for this hassle. In my younger days I'd taken a lot of shit from abusive men, and this was beginning to feel like an all-too-familiar encounter. Power and control. Nothing that belonged to this man was going to be taken away from him, by God. Not his daughter. Not her clothes. Not her life.

"She needed a place to go," I repeated. "So I told her she could come to me."

"She's got a place to go, dammit! She's got her own home." His voice was low now, but impassioned, each word expressed through clenched teeth.

I'd had enough. I got up slowly from my seat, walked around the desk with measured steps, and stood confronting him. I'm tall, and sometimes in dealing with obnoxious men I find that useful. Bullies don't operate well when they're looking a woman in the eye.

It didn't work this time. Warzek must have been about six three; he had at least six inches on me.

I drew myself up to my tallest, nonetheless, and squared my shoulders. A tiny muscle in the corner of Warzek's left eye jumped. He was in danger of losing control again.

"I'm not taking her away from you, you know, Mr. Warzek. She simply doesn't want to go home. *I* don't know why, but maybe *you* do. Do you treat her like you're treating me? Do you bully her? Well, goddammit, maybe *that's* why she doesn't want to go home. Did you ever think of that? Maybe she's simply not well enough to handle being tyrannized!"

With each sentence I advanced on Warzek a step or two. And for each step I took, he took one backward. His eyes widened, just a little, and he looked surprised. It occurred to me that he was used to bullying women, but that having one browbeat him in return was a new experience.

By the time I had backed him all the way to the door, he had recovered his composure enough to glare at me one last time. His voice was venomous.

"What're you gonna do with her? Teach her to be a dyke?" Then he turned on his heel and departed.

His accusation stunned me speechless. Not because he thought I was a lesbian; that didn't bother me. But the loathing in his eyes was a different matter. It terrified me, and for the first time I understood the kind of irrational hatred my homosexual friends face on a regular basis. I thought about reporting this encounter to someone in authority at the college. Then I realized it might cost Warzek his job. It wouldn't do Sophia any good for me to get her father fired.

"Shit." I think I said it aloud. "Shit. Shit. Shit. Shit. Shit."

Furious, I stalked back to the window seat, retrieved Sophia's paper, and replaced it at the bottom of the pile. If she wanted it she would ask me for it.

I somehow didn't think she would.

Through my office window I could see Warzek walk across the snowy quad toward the staff parking lot. His shoulders were squared. His back was unnaturally straight. When he had vanished from sight, I sat down in the window seat and began to debate the wisdom of taking Sophia home with me. Perhaps she'd be better off in the hospital rather than all the way out there in the country with no one around but Amanda and me. Reaching over to my desk for the phone, I called Earlene's extension. Her voicemail told me she'd left for the holiday. For several minutes I sat motionless in the window seat while snow tapped lightly against the pane. Then I sighed. Sophia was expecting to come home with me. I couldn't disappoint her. Especially not at Christmas.

I shrugged my shoulders, but couldn't rid myself of the anxiety I carried there like some kind of appalling cosmic backpack.

Since I already had the phone in my lap, I tried

Greg's number again. I'd been calling him sporadi-
cally for the past couple of days but hadn't been able
to get him. Maybe he'd gone to New York again. As
I sat there in my office, holding the phone to my ear,
absently listening to it ring eight, nine, ten times, I
saw Greg walking across the quad through lightly
blowing snow, hands shoved deep in the pockets of a
slate gray parka. It seemed hallucinatory: the phone
ringing unheard in the empty house; the object of the
call passing before my eyes.

I reached up, unlatched the window, and pushed it
open. "Samoorian!" I yelled. Greg looked up, waved
half-heartedly, and veered toward me.

"Hey, how ya doin'?"

"Okay. And you?"

He shrugged.

"Can you come in for a minute?"

"What for?" he replied, after an uncharacteristic
hesitation.

Whoa, I thought, *something wrong here.* This
from a man who was willing to drop everything,
even at semester peak, for a cozy little gab.

"Just a chat. I've been wondering how you're doing. With Irena. And all that."

He shrugged again, dislodging flakes of light snow
dandrufflike from his shoulders, turned from the
window, and headed down the path that led to the
front door of Dickinson Hall. As I closed the window a miniature whirlwind of snowflakes whipped
through the opening onto the green plush of the seat
cushions. For one ephemeral moment each flake
stood out on its verdant ground, individual and exquisite. Then—specks of damp on the upholstery.

The weather did not look promising for my drive
back home from the hospital. Snow was, of course,
preferable to an ice storm, but then neither was
much to be desired by anyone on wheels.

"Irena," Greg said, standing in my doorway, "isn't coming home for Christmas."

Ouch, I thought. Greg is a big Christmas freak. He'd been planning the holiday for weeks. The day after Thanksgiving he'd plunked down an outrageous sum at a tree farm near Greenfield. This reserved him a huge blue spruce, to be cut on demand. The tree had now been sitting in his garage for a week, awaiting its transformation into the tree of light and life. He'd had his homemade fruitcake wrapped in a rum-soaked tea towel since October, replenishing the rum twice a week, and had ordered his fresh, free-range turkey at least ten days ago.

"Oh." I didn't really know what to say. "Where will she be?"

"She's going to her parents in Connecticut. And I'm not invited." Greg plopped himself down in the green armchair. "I've never been particularly welcome in Greenwich, anyhow, and now even less than ever. Now that it is obvious that I am overbearing and restrictive, that is. Treating her like a child. Her mother always said I was wrong for her—too old, too *overdetermined*."

"Overdetermined?"

"Too Armenian, I think. You know. Loud. Unrestrained. Emotional."

"Jeez." Now I was really at a loss for words. "Jeez."

He crossed his legs and leaned back in the chair. Evidently he had overcome his reluctance to talk. "Yeah, *jeez* is right. They haven't liked me from the start. We got married on the spur of the moment after living together for a few months. Cheated them out of their elaborate formal wedding. We had a big bash in the house we were sharing out on Saddleback Road. My family all came. Lots of friends from Enfield and elsewhere. Everyone brought food and wine. We had a student rock band and danced like maniacs on the grass. It was great.

"But Irena's folks didn't come; two weeks, it seems, wasn't sufficient notice for them to plan and prepare for a trip of one hundred and fifty miles. Since then they've turned down every invitation to visit us, on one pretense or another. When we go there I am clearly *persona non grata*. I make a joke and her mother looks politely puzzled. I talk about sports and her father discreetly changes the subject. I end up mute in the corner feeling big-nosed and sweaty and crass, smiling like an idiot whenever anyone looks my way. Which isn't often."

We sat in silence. I didn't want to ask the obvious question: *Did this mean a formal separation?* And what else was there to say?

"So, what are you doing for Christmas, then?" I had the glimmerings of an idea. "Are you going to your folks'?"

"You kidding? They'd kill me if I came without Irena. They're crazy about her, Karen. It's possible they like her better than they like me. My mother calls her a sunbeam. Me: I'm a big moody klutz who thinks too much. If they thought I'd done anything to screw up this marriage they'd . . . they'd . . ." He paused, open-mouthed, incapable of articulating his dire imaginings. "Well, let's just say I can't go home without Irena."

"Do you still have that tree?"

"Tree?"

"Yeah, *tree*. It's Christmas, isn't it?"

"Oh. Yeah. It's in the garage. Why? You think if I put the tree up Irena will come home?" He looked hopeful. This brilliant scholar, this nationally renowned cultural analyst, this modern skeptic: grasping at straws like any superstitious pagan.

"Well—that's not quite what I was thinking."

"Yeah. Right." He blinked his eyes: rational again. "What were you thinking?"

"Why don't you spend Christmas at my house? Sophia will be there, and she seems really comfortable with you. It would be a good thing for her, and for Amanda and me, too. Kind of take the edge off a crisis situation." He started to object. Something about imposing on me. I held up my hand to silence him.

"Listen, I've just had a rather nasty encounter with Sophia's father, and it's made me nervous. So I could use some muscle." Greg grinned; the image of himself as a hired goon seemed to cheer him up. "Besides, I don't have a tree yet—and couldn't afford a gorgeous one like you got, anyhow, Samoorian. So you'd be doing me a favor."

After a few token protests, he agreed to come to dinner that night and bring the spruce. We'd have potato-and-leek soup, trim the tree, and—if the anguish level seemed muted enough, what with Amanda's pique, Sophia's slashed wrists, and Greg's broken heart—maybe we'd even sing a carol or two. *God rest you merry, gentlemen, / Let nothing you dismay.*

What was I getting myself into here? This was not a promising situation, a Yuletide gathering of the hurt, the lost, and the unwanted: a real festival of waifs.

Twelve

SOPHIA AND I had a fairly mute trek from the hospital back through Enfield and Greenfield in the deepening snow. Never a confident driver in bad weather, I concentrated intently on steering my way through the late December afternoon gloom as the snow fell heavy and wet on the unplowed country roads. Emily Dickinson's words came to my mind talismanically, as they often do in times of stress—and bad driving. *It sifts from Leaden Sieves—,* I chanted to myself, staring into the onslaught of snow. *It powders all the Wood.* Bowed down by the dense whiteness, the trees bent together, forming a chill tunnel through which we were the sole travelers. Once, when I touched the brake quickly to avoid a bewildered deer, the car skidded sideways but straightened out as I held my breath and, going against all my instincts, steered into the skid. *It fills with Alabaster Wool / The Wrinkles of the Road—* Through it all, Sophia sat silent, white-lipped, staring straight ahead. She was desperate already. What terrors could a mere automobile accident in vicious weather in a desolate and remote area hold for her?

I knocked—kicked, really—on the front door of the house, my arms loaded down with groceries and a plastic bag with Sophia's pathetic few possessions. My stomach was knotted with anxiety—from the trip, yes, but more in anticipation of Amanda's reception. From her room I could hear, through a loud grid of percussion and guitar, a melancholy male voice bemoaning the isolation of human consciousness. *"I fear nothing besides myself. Please don't touch me."* Sophia stood right behind me, a little closer than was absolutely necessary, like a frightened, big-eyed colt sidling up to the mare.

Amanda opened the door and the music blared out, annoying me with its inappropriate racket. *"I feel nothing besides this pain. Please don't watch me."* I frowned at Amanda and stood back to let Sophia enter ahead of me. As she did, she smiled faintly at my daughter and said something incomprehensible, something that made me fear momentarily for her psychological stability. She said, "Toad the Wet Sprocket."

To my astonishment Amanda flashed her a thousand-watt grin. "You like them?"

"The best," replied Sophia. "The absolute best."

"Aren't they hot?" Amanda reached out her hand. "Let me take your bag. I'll show you where you're gonna sleep. Back here, with me. Did you ever hear anything sadder than . . . ?" They trekked off, Amanda chattering away. The bedroom door shut and the decibel level diminished.

I relaxed. I guess I've done something right in my life; Amanda's one okay kid.

• • •

Christmas Eve, the following day, continued snowy and cold, with the thick hush that envelops country houses when the flakes fall fat and fast, obscuring sound and vision. The world was all interior, ending at the windows. In the swirling storm, even the woodsmoke from the chimney vanished. With the lights from the tree, the fire in the wood stove, the spicy smell of the *tourtière* baking in the oven and the steam from the pierogi Sophia was boiling in a pot on the stove, we three seemed cut off from the cosmos in a warm, fragrant, cozy isolation.

The plow had gone by in midmorning, but as the snow continued to accumulate, traffic diminished, until by midafternoon the road was completely deserted, enhancing our seclusion.

Afraid that Greg wouldn't be able to make his way through the storm for Christmas morning, I called and suggested he come for supper that evening and spend the night. A slight hesitation greeted my invitation—in his present unsettled state "spend the night" must have sounded ambiguous—followed by a half-joking: "So, what exactly are you suggesting, Pelletier?"

Being friends with a man is not always easy. And with Greg the relationship, on both sides, has never been totally free of a certain—shall we say—wistfulness. Immediately I pictured him in my bed, conjured up his embrace, imagined the warmth and the weight of his body. For one brief second I didn't quite have control of my breathing.

"I'm suggesting you sleep on the couch, Samoorian."

"Oh, tooooo bad." He sounded disappointed as convention required, but also, slightly to my pique, he sounded relieved. I could just hear him thinking: *That's all I need in my life right now—another woman.*

Greg arrived around five, just after dark, with his turkey, his fruitcake, and a shopping bag full of packages wrapped in white tissue paper with green and red curlicue ribbons. In one arm he held a long florist's box. This he presented with a flourish to Sophia and Amanda. "Beauty to the beautiful," he said with comic fatuousness. A dozen long-stemmed red roses, so fresh you could almost see them quiver, met their delighted eyes.

"Flowers!" Sophia seemed somewhat stunned. I could swear there were tears in her eyes, but she immediately occupied herself with finding a vase and arranging and rearranging the flowers in their thicket of ferns.

"Well, girlie, it won't be the last time some guy buys you roses; I can guarantee you that." Greg was still playing his role of comic uncle.

"So, what about me?" I feigned petulance; I've never been quite comfortable with sentiment.

"You have not been forgotten." Greg returned to his car and came back with an oddly shaped, bulky pasteboard florist's box, which he handed to me with a bow. It contained an orchid plant with two lush blooms in a purple so deep it was almost black. Exquisite.

"That's the second time today you've taken my breath away, Samoorian," I said after a moment, and reached up, half unwittingly, to pat his cheek. "Thanks."

"Oh, yeah?" Greg responded, and gave me a funny twisted smile. "You're very welcome." He intercepted my hand, squeezing it gently and kissing the palm before releasing it.

Definitely a complicated relationship.

Our idyllic mood was shattered a couple of hours later by a completely unexpected knock on the door. The storm hadn't let up, and the road looked all but impassable. The girls were in Amanda's room listening to something called Smashing Pumpkins, and Greg and I were finishing up the supper dishes.

"Who's that?" Greg asked.

"Who knows?" I wiped steam off the kitchen window, trying to get a glance at the vehicle in the driveway, thinking immediately that it was probably Piotrowski come to harass me with more questions. Outside the snow was so thick in the air I couldn't see a thing.

Drying my hands on a dish towel, I opened the door as far as its chain would allow, a reproach ready on my lips: Damn cops, couldn't let good Christian people alone even on Christmas Eve. However, it was not the familiar figure of the lieutenant standing there. It was Sophia's father.

"Yes?" My voice must have sounded strained because Greg came from the kitchen to stand behind me. Snow swirled through the partially open door, scattering across the mat and the hardwood floor.

"I'ff come to see my daughter." Warzek's accent was intensified by the alcohol I could smell on his breath.

I hesitated, then opened the door. Leaving him out in the storm wasn't going to help Sophia any.

As Warzek stepped inside he noticed Greg for the first time. An expression of befuddlement crossed his stolid face. He clearly hadn't expected to find a man at my place. After all, I was a dyke, wasn't I? He paused for a moment, then seemed to gather resolve.

I noted for the first time that his left eyebrow was bisected by old scar tissue on which no hair grew. It looked almost as if he had three eyebrows, one long, two short. In the ludicrous way odd details have of eliciting an emotional response, this feature seemed to me to be imbued with menace.

I immediately regretted letting him in, and Greg

seemed to empathize because he moved closer. Out of the corner of my eye I could see his hands. They were clenched into fists, beginning to strain white across the knuckles.

This time I didn't invite Warzek to sit down. Instead, I left him standing by the door as I turned toward the bedroom where Sophia, as if she were any carefree young person, was grooving to the latest in contemporary music.

"I'll ask her if she wants to see you."

"It don't matter if she wants to see me or not. I want her out here now." He took a step as if to follow me. As cold as the weather was, his heavy gray jacket was unzipped. I wondered wildly if he were carrying some kind of weapon. Greg smoothly placed himself in Warzek's way, impeding him from moving. I'd have to ask Greg some close questions about his past. He certainly had all the defensive moves down pat.

Sophia did *not* want to see her father. Pale already, she turned ghost white, the blood draining visibly from her lips when I told her he was in the living room.

"Get me the car keys, Mom." Amanda grabbed her jacket off the upholstered slipper chair. "I'll take her out the back door."

I gave my daughter a startled look. Where had *she* been hanging out? "I don't think that will be necessary, do you, Sophia?"

"Is he drunk?" Sophia was clearly ashamed to have to ask.

"I think he probably is. He's been drinking, anyhow."

"Is Professor Samoorian still here?" Another question embarrassing in its implications, implying as it did cowardice on her father's part.

"Yes."

"Then I don't think you'll have much trouble with him." Her face and body were stone still, but her hands moved, unconsciously it seemed, the right hand winding a thin blue satin ribbon tightly around the fingers of the left. In and out it wound, around and around until her fingertips assumed the color of the snow on the windowpane behind her. I motioned to Amanda with my eyes, and she nodded. As I turned to leave the room, she took Sophia's hands in hers, reclaiming the ribbon she had been about to tie on the braid in Sophia's pale hair.

Warzek and Greg were in the same positions when I reentered the living room as they had been when I left. I imagined them standing there, practically eye to eye, not speaking a word the entire time I was in with Sophia. I was reminded of something extremely primitive, like stags in a standoff. Since, of course, I'd never actually seen stags in a standoff, I guess it would be more precise to say I was reminded of a *picture* of stags in a standoff—for some reason done in needlepoint, in somber tones of brown and gold, framed, rustic style, in intertwined varnished branches. Somewhat of a cultural icon, I thought. The elemental male aroused.

For once I was glad I had one around.

"Sophia does not wish to see you." I sounded like a prissy headmistress.

"What?" Warzek moved toward me, attempting to sidestep Greg, who blocked him again with his body.

"Perhaps if you were to call in a few days and make arrangements, she would change her mind. Right now she isn't feeling well enough."

He stared at me for a prolonged moment, the blue rage of his eyes not unlike that of his daughter's at the one moment of anger to which I had been privy. I was reminded of encounters with Fred, my ex-husband, whose eyes could transform themselves from sultry blue seduction to murderous rage within seconds. My left wrist throbbed where Fred had once broken it, close to twenty years earlier.

"I think it would be a good idea if you left now." The boldness I'd felt dealing with this man yesterday was gone. I was trying hard not to look terrified. He already knew where my office was, and now he somehow knew where I lived.

He glared wordlessly, and then took another step toward me. "It's Christmas Eve, goddammit. I'm taking my daughter home." His hands moved, almost involuntarily it seemed, up from his sides. Then he looked over at Greg, who stepped toward him, fists clenched. Warzek hesitated, then dropped his hands. When he turned back to me, his eyes were blue slits in a face contorted by hatred.

"Fuck you."

Each word was an act of violence, a savage explosion of frustrated rage. He threw open the door with a fierce gesture and went out, leaving the door wide open behind him. If his presence had been menacing, the manner of his departure was an implied threat. A whirlwind of flakes blustered across the room before I managed to get the door closed and bolt it shut.

Greg's eyes met mine. *What would have happened if I hadn't been here?* I chose not to respond to the unspoken question.

Together we watched Warzek's headlights recede, miniature cones of swirling snow in the darkness.

With cookies and hot rum toddy we coaxed Sophia back from the psychic fortress to which she retreated after her father's visit. She even joined us, in a sweet high soprano, in the last chorus of "Silent Night," Amanda banging away lustily on the old piano and Greg singing in Motown falsetto. *Slee—eep in heavenly pee—eace. Slee—eep in heavenly peace.*

At bedtime she kissed me on the cheek, as if she were Amanda, and then hurried away to bed.

Santa Claus came early that night; I went to bed with my eyes full of tears.

Thirteen

THE DAY AFTER Christmas I curled up in my battered black leather recliner with an afternoon cup of English tea. The storm had subsided, and thin winter sunlight haloed the bright roses on the table by the window. Sophia had recovered enough strength to leave the house, so the girls were out for a short walk, and I was reveling in the silence. I sipped at the strong hot tea. With its clear, uncomplicated flavor, it seemed like an elixir of peace.

The wrappings and ribbons were swept up, the gifts had been gloated over, and Greg had gone home to find a repentant Irena awaiting him. He had called this morning, dazed and happy, to report her return. Tea, sunlight on roses, the prospect of holiday leftovers for dinner—life was good.

Then the phone rang. When I said "Hello," no one responded. "Hello," I repeated. "Hello?"

No one there. Another crank call?

I hung up. Immediately, the phone rang again.

"Hello!" I snapped.

This time it was Piotrowski.

"Dr. Pelletier?"

"Yes?" I knew immediately that my fragile peace was about to be snatched away. "Yes? What's the matter?"

"Could I come see you?" I noticed that he hadn't responded to my question.

"What's the matter?" I repeated.

"I'm not far from you. I could be there in ten minutes."

"Is it important?"

"Yes," with a slight tone of impatience, probably at the implication that he would call me for anything trivial.

"I'd rather you didn't come here. I don't want Sophia upset. Where can I meet you?"

"Right now I'm at Bub's Coffee Shop over on One Thirty-eight. Do you know where that is?"

"Yes," I responded. "I'll be there. Ten minutes. How're the roads?"

"Okay." He hung up without giving me a chance to ask any more questions.

I had driven by Bub's Coffee Shop numerous times, but would never have thought of stopping in. The parking lot was always full of cars, but the place itself looked shabby and uninviting. Inside, however, it proved to be clean and functional, if somewhat dull in decor. The walls were blond wood paneling and the floors asphalt tile, brown with white striations. Each table featured a milk-glass bud vase holding a bunch of artificial daisies.

Piotrowski sat in a booth toward the back, chowing down on a hot turkey sandwich and mashed potatoes, just what I was planning on having for supper. Both the bread and turkey were thick, fresh, and hand-sliced. The dressing looked homemade and the

gravy was lumpy with giblets. I was instantly raven-
ous, and had to remind myself that I had leftovers at
home. I ordered tea. Wonder of wonders, it came
steaming in a china pot. I poured tea into the thick
brown mug and sipped. Prince of Wales. I sipped
again, then put the mug down. I was not here for a
culinary experience.

"What's up, Piotrowski?"

He pushed his plate away. "Dr. Pelletier, do you
remember Bonnie Weimer?" He was watching me
closely.

"Yes, of course." I had almost completely forgotten about Bonnie and about her disappearance; subsequent events had proven to be so much more
pressing.

My look of mystified apprehension seemed to satisfy Piotrowski. "The body of a young woman has
just been found not far from here. There is a possibility it is Miss Weimer. I wondered if you would be
willing to come look at her. We'd like to see if we can
make an identification before we take her into the
morgue in Springfield. Otherwise we'll have to wait
to get a positive ID until we can get her parents up
here from New Jersey. And there's no sense in disturbing them if it isn't her."

I swallowed hard. I had not seen many dead people in my life, and only once—and very recently, at
that—had I seen a victim of violent death. I certainly
had no desire to set eyes on another. But it seemed to
be my duty.

"Where . . . is she?"

"Do you know the hiking trail at Pioneer State
Park?" His gaze, once again, was disturbingly intent.

"Not really." I vaguely remembered having driven
a few times by a green road sign with an arrow
pointing to the trail.

He told me where it was, about a fifteen-minute

drive south of Bub's, in the direction of Williamstown. As far as I could recall there wasn't much on that road but mountain vistas, rocks, and trees. And, evidently, a state park with corpses.

"Who found it, uh—her?"

"A pair of snowshoers. Idiots were trying to cover a ten-mile section of the trail today and almost froze their ass—er, themselves. Came across the body in one of the trail shelters—seems they got some sense and were trying to get out of the cold. Young woman, about twenty years old, same height and hair coloring as this Weimer girl. Hard to tell from a photograph if it's the same girl, but could be. . . ."

I could feel my lips go cold. It was as if I had stepped without warning into some alternate reality where the assumptions of daily living were weirdly and permanently suspended, where colleagues and students tumbled quite routinely from closets and shelters. My mind conjured up a fantasy image of Bonnie with Randy's tie knotted around her neck.

"How?" I croaked, surprised my voice worked at all.

"Strangled, it would seem. With her wool scarf."

Piotrowski went on, something about no evidence of sexual molestation, at least initially. About the body being fully clothed, wearing a jacket, mittens, wool hat, and boots over jeans and a sweater. And the fatal scarf. About the initial estimate of the time of death. But I wasn't hearing much all of a sudden.

"Are you all right, Dr. Pelletier?" His voice faded; my mind seemed to have migrated to some far distant zone. "Here. Here, drink this." The mug of tea was an intrusion at my lips. I resisted. "Drink." It was an order. Obediently I sipped, and then sputtered, fully conscious again.

"Dammit, Piotrowski, you put sugar in it! Yuck."

"Yeah. You gonna be okay with this? You don't have to do it, you know."

An image of sunlight on roses flashed into my mind.

The roses were the color of blood.

By the time we arrived at the state park, the afternoon light was almost a memory. Piotrowski was driving a Jeep, and we covered the short distance from the main road to the site where the body had been found without any trouble, even over a trail that had just recently been broken in a foot or more of snow. Ahead, revolving amber and blue lights confirmed that we were headed in the right direction. In the distance, a two-way radio crackled.

Piotrowski stationed me outside an area marked off with yellow crime-scene tape. The area inside the tape looked no different from the rest of the woods. Evergreens and maples interspersed with birch. Deep snow, pristine in some sections, trampled down and soiled in others. Starkly delineated in the harsh white spotlights of two state police cars, the shelter was a fairly primitive structure: three sides of rough boards and a peaked roof that overhung the open front. The shelter's protection had not been sufficient to keep the body from being almost entirely covered in snow, Piotrowski had told me, but the snowshoers could hardly ignore the red boot sticking out of the drift.

Visualizing the lieutenant's blunt image—that homely boot, like a splash of blood on the snow— had affected me oddly. Emily Dickinson's words again floated through my mind, made this young woman's death real to me. Real—and final. *Looking at Death, is Dying— / Just let go the Breath— / And not the pillow at your Cheek / So Slumbereth—*

But the boot wasn't visible now. "Wait here. The technicians are almost through." Piotrowski stepped over the tape and approached two uniformed troopers standing by what looked like a stripped-down hospital gurney. In the deepening twilight the dark bulk on the gurney resembled nothing so much as a row of half-filled trash bags.

It was Bonnie Weimer. In the near dark of a late winter afternoon, before I even saw the corpse, I knew that in my gut. The gurney bumped over the packed, lumpy snow. The officer pushing it, an athletic-looking blond woman not much older than Bonnie herself, brought it to a halt in front of me, and unzipped the black plastic bag. Bonnie's eyes were wide open, in death even more protuberant than usual, and her mouth was agape in final petulant complaint. *Looking at Death, is Dying*— I stared for a few seconds, not really seeing much other than that it was indeed Bonnie and that her jacket sleeve was dirty and ripped open at the shoulder seam. I nodded at Piotrowski and turned away.

"It's her?"

"It's she." Then I hated myself for being persnickety at a moment such as this.

"It's Bonnie Weimer?" The lieutenant was persnickety himself.

I nodded. "May I go now? Please?"

"Yes, of course." Piotrowski was suddenly solicitous. He looked at the trooper, and made a "take it away" gesture with his gloved hand. "Why don't you go sit in the Jeep for a minute while I finish up here, and then I'll drive you home."

"My car . . ." I could hear the faintness of my voice.

"Don't worry. Someone will get it for you."

By the time he returned to the Jeep I was sobbing quietly into some "man-size" tissues from a pack I'd found on the dashboard. He glanced over at me once and then turned the key in the ignition, looked over his left shoulder, and began to back the vehicle down the rutted lane.

When I could speak again, I said inanely, "She would be so upset about her jacket."

"What do you mean?"

"It's all dirty, and she took such good care of it when she came into the classroom, hung it on her chair just so, so the sleeves wouldn't touch the floor. The other kids just fling their stuff around, but she—" A graphic memory replaced the image of Bonnie in class—Bonnie in a white apron standing by my table in the Faculty Commons the day after Randy's death. The memory came flooding back so vividly I could almost hear her nasal whine: *Isn't it awful about Professor Astin-Berger . . . he looked so happy . . . with the letter and everything. . . .*

"Ah—Lieutenant—did I happen to mention to you . . . ?"

The whole time I was telling Piotrowski about talking to Bonnie in the Commons, what she had said about Randy and the letter, I was thinking, *Ohmigod, ohmigod, ohmigod. Why didn't I tell him right away? If I had gone right to the police, maybe she'd still be alive. Ohmigod, ohmigod, ohmigod.*

"I don't know why you didn't tell me about this sooner. . . ." His exasperated eruption was what I expected. What I deserved.

I dropped my head into my hands and shook it slowly from side to side. My eyes burned. "I simply forgot. I've been on such overload. First the murder, then that crazy note on Randy's computer, and then Sophia's suicide attempt—everything else just flew out of my mind. . . ."

"Well, it probably wouldn't have made any difference." He sighed. "You say she didn't show up to turn her paper in?"

"Right."

"And that wasn't like her?"

"Right. She always had everything done on time."

"Well, then I'd say, whatever happened happened shortly after you left."

"Again?"

"Again," he said, and clicked his tongue. "Again." The look he gave me was straight and serious.

The rest of the way home we talked about what exactly Bonnie had said, how she had behaved, who else had been there, about Bonnie's personality, her annoying little traits, her performance in class, about other students and teachers and how she had gotten along with them, about the course itself, what we had studied, about Anne Bradstreet, Emily Dickinson, Sylvia Plath . . . Piotrowski was a skilled questioner, and the words just seemed to flow.

By the time we pulled into my driveway, I felt in control again, although I had wandered far afield from the subject of murder. I realized later that that had probably been Piotrowski's intention. I was telling him about Sophia's brilliant paper on the Master letters as he turned off the ignition and started to open his door.

"Oh, but you're not interested in that. . . ." I was babbling. "I'm sorry."

"Don't be." He pulled his door shut again and settled back in his seat. "It's fascinating stuff. I always enjoy getting educated." Was he being snide? I didn't think so. He was silent for a moment and then went on, "Sounds like the nineteenth century was a pretty hot time in spite of its reputation: You know, lie back and think of England. And all that."

I glanced over at him, surprised.

He looked straight ahead, silent and thoughtful for a minute. I could see Amanda peering out at us from the kitchen window, trying to scope out the unfamiliar vehicle. If I sat out here much longer she'd go looking for a baseball bat. My hand went to the door handle, and Piotrowski spoke, almost as if he were thinking out loud.

"You know, this doesn't smell like sex to me."

"What?" My expression this time was undoubtedly one of pure astonishment. My hand dropped back into my lap.

"Sorry." He looked a trifle shamefaced. "Talking to myself. What I mean is that I've been operating on the assumption that this case was somehow related to Astin-Berger's, er—copious—sex life. But, now I don't know. . . . I don't quite . . . That just doesn't feel right to me anymore. I have a hunch. . . ."

He ceased speaking and sat in silence another minute or two. It had just popped into my head that maybe I should tell him about my two visits from Sophia's father when he shrugged, opened his door, got out into the snow, and crunched around to my side of the car. By the time he reached my door I had it open and was halfway out. I decided not to say anything. Poor Sophia had enough trouble without me siccing the police on her father.

It was not absolutely necessary that Piotrowski help me over the icy spots, but he did it anyhow.

"Take care," he said at the door. And for an instant I feared it was more a warning than a conventional farewell.

Fourteen

A SMALL COLLEGE like Enfield never really lets you get away: classes, department meetings, faculty meetings, damage-control meetings, secret strategy conclaves, gossip sessions, encounter groups and, worst of all, dinner parties. At times I found myself actually yearning for the anonymity of my former teaching job in New York. There, in that city of infamous repute, I'd never had to deal with the violence that seemed to be hounding me on this bucolic little campus.

The day after my ghastly visit to the state park, I decided not to show my face at the college. Nonetheless, all morning I had to handle curiosity calls from colleagues, people as varied as Miles Jewell and Magda Vegh. With them I was evasive and vague, qualities I had developed during a wary childhood and mastered during my brief but treacherous marriage.

One call I couldn't fend off, however, was from Avery Mitchell. He called around noon and asked if I could come in and meet with him, "about the, ah, difficult situation we seem to be finding ourselves in at the moment." From his subdued tone I couldn't really tell what kind of a session this was to be: gossip, strategy, or damage control. Or something more personal and much more to be desired.

Dream on, little dreamer.

I dressed with self-conscious nonchalance in my best jeans and a black scoop-neck sweater. I didn't want my clothes to suggest in any way that I had dressed to impress. On the other hand, I wanted to look fantastic. I must have changed a half-dozen times. Go figure.

I dropped the girls off at the mall. Amanda, slender as she was, looked almost hefty in her plaid jacket next to Sophia, frail in a loden three-quarter coat Amanda had outgrown when she was fourteen. Amanda had my credit card, and they were headed for the postholiday sales. I made a valiant attempt to rein in the spending. "Remember, a three-hundred dollar limit. Right? And mostly for Sophia. Right? Underwear. Socks. Sneakers. Boots. Right? *Practical* stuff." The gleam in Amanda's eye did not bode well for my MasterCard balance.

As I walked down the corridor of Emerson Hall, I noted once again how the ranks of the departed dominated this center of college power. President after president, from Amos Pratt Hamilton in 1819 to Wesley Buckman in 1985, brooded over the long and gloomy space. Dead white males all: How ironic that from the power brokers of their own times they had become the power clichés of this era of pseudoegalitarianism.

Bucky, as he had come to be known, was the most recent to be hung—so to speak: President of Enfield College, 1970–1985. Portrayed in his presidential robes, the velvet hood of his Harvard doctorate framing a pale, heavy face with only a trace of the pendulous jowls that show up in yearbook photos, Wesley Buckman looked complacent and in control. Who could have expected the suicide that would end his tenure as president, and the subsequent financial disclosures that would send shock waves through the entire extended Enfield community of students and alumns? Avery had succeeded him and, I'd been told, had done a brilliant job pulling the school out of the period of anxiety and self-doubt—and, it was rumored, something approaching financial collapse—that had followed Bucky's demise. How nice that the solidly comfortable should find themselves solidly comfortable once again, I thought snidely, and pushed open the door leading to Avery's outer office. How very, very nice for them.

The main office was deserted. Neither Lonnie, Avery's secretary, nor Anne, his administrative assistant, was in. The window drapes, ecru-and-green chintz, were drawn, the thick green carpet had been freshly vacuumed, and the computers wore their plastic covers. Of course. College staff was on vacation the week between Christmas and New Year's; officially, the school was closed. I'd forgotten about that. It was so quiet in this usually bustling building that the silence was beginning to give me the creeps. The door to Avery's inner office stood open. I walked over and looked in. Empty. I knocked on the door frame, remembering my hiring interview, the only other time I'd been here.

I'd arrived at two P.M. for that meeting, and was ushered in immediately. Part of Avery's charm, I'd heard, was that he made an effort never to keep anyone waiting, no matter how lowly. If he did keep you waiting, I was told, it was for a purpose. And you knew it. I had evidently been allotted a half hour, because until precisely two-thirty we had a delightful and very cultivated chat by a softly crackling wood fire, a conversation ranging from Emily Dickinson to the new cultural criticism to New York City performance artists. Then, without having addressed any of the issues for which I had so assiduously prepared, I was ushered out, a little bedazzled and totally bewildered as to the purpose of the meeting. Whatever it was, evidently I passed, because the call offering me the job came the next day. Passed as what? Cultured and elite, I guess.

If only they knew.

Now I was standing in the doorway of Avery's empty office wondering if I had hallucinated his call. It was a beautiful room, richly furnished with Persian rugs and maroon leather chairs and sofas. A polished mahogany desk featured a gold picture frame and matching pen holder. Other than a green blotter with tooled leather corners, nothing but a small stack of neatly arranged file folders—the folders he had taken from Randy's office? I wondered—indicated that an important educational institution was run from this very room.

It was difficult to tell whether the elegant furnishings reflected Avery's taste, or whether they were standard ambience for Enfield administrators. The Hudson River landscapes that covered the walls probably belonged to the college. But the dozen or so stark black-and-white nature photographs dominating the alcove by the desk must have been Avery's; they were just a little out of sync with the rest of the decor. I recognized three or four Ansel Adamses and an Eliot Porter and walked over to look at them more closely. Absorbed in contemplation of a Grand Canyon scene, I heard nothing when Avery entered the room, the sound of his footsteps muted by the thick rugs. When he placed a hand on the back of my neck, I jumped, a little wildly. Not only had he startled me, but his hand was ice cold.

"Karen, I'm sorry." He stepped back from me, biting his lower lip and looking contrite. Charming, as usual. "I shouldn't have surprised you like that. You've been through a great deal these past two weeks. No wonder you're jumpy."

"I am not jumpy." My reply was given with some asperity. "But when a person comes up behind another person in a totally empty room, he should be a little more considerate than to grab her by the neck!"

"Okay. Okay. *Mea culpa. Mea culpa.*" He backed farther away, laughing a little and raising his hands placatingly.

Why was I so attracted to this condescending son of a—patrician?

Avery motioned me to the love seat by the cold fireplace and sat in one of the matching armchairs across from me. He even sat gracefully, I thought resentfully, his long, lean body sideways in the chair, his left arm resting on his crossed knees, his chin resting on his right hand, forefinger at his lips. I wasn't used to seeing him in jeans and a sweater—but it occurred to me I wouldn't mind getting used to it. The jeans fitted him well and emphasized the long, slender lines of his legs. *A very nice-looking man,* some still-objective part of my consciousness summed him up.

Okay. So I was attracted. But I'd be damned if I'd ever let this—this—genteel lady-killer know how he'd gotten to me. I sat up a little straighter, not an easy feat on the soft leather couch, and initiated the conversation.

"So, Avery, just what did you wish to discuss?"

His wry smile flashed fleetingly. "With two murders discovered at the college within ten days, what do you think I want to discuss?" Then he raised a hand to ward off a response. His blue eyes grew clouded and his face suddenly seemed drawn. "Karen, I don't exactly know why I asked you to come in. But you seem to be so, ah—embroiled in this situation I thought maybe you might find it helpful to talk openly to someone about it, and I certainly would. I've been doing nothing all day but spouting bullshit: to the press, to trustees, to parents, to alumns. I'm very good at that. It's my job. They pay me well."

His voice lowered to a self-mocking mellifluous bass: "Yes, it certainly is a tragic situation, but we are cooperating fully with the police. They have it well in hand, following every possible lead. Well—yes, a student *has* died. But there is nothing to fear. Everything is under complete control. Students need have no concern about returning in three weeks. Blah, blah, blah."

He paused and studied me. I wasn't certain what it was he wanted. Sympathy? If so, he wasn't about to get it. In spite of the fact that he looked so tired and strained. So truly drained and exhausted . . .

He went on, "Then I had a little visit from Lieutenant Piotrowski. You remember Piotrowski?"

"Oh, yes."

"Yes, of course. Well, it was a sobering little discussion, and what hit home to me most was that there's a good deal more at stake here than the usual crap that falls to my lot: preparing a pretty face to show to the world, pacifying the trustees, appeasing the alumns, securing a diverse financial base, blah, blah, blah, blah, blah."

At this point the phone on the table by his chair rang. His hand instinctively moved toward it and then stopped. "I'm not answering that damn thing again today. The press is relentless, and I can't be rude to them because I have public relations to think about."

When the ringing continued unabated, I rose from the couch and picked up the receiver. Avery looked at me, surprised. I raised my eyebrows at him. Then, in a gross approximation of the clipped public school accent of his English administrative assistant, I intoned, "Enfield College here, president's office."

It was the *New York Times*. They had a reporter on her way to Enfield and would like to speak to someone about setting up an interview with President Mitchell.

"President Mitchell is out of the office for the rest of the day. He is not granting interviews. He will have a prepared statement for the press within a day or two. Thank you so much. Good-bye."

As I put the receiver down Avery began to laugh, and I could see some of the strain leave his face. When the phone began to ring again, almost immediately, we both began to howl.

But when it finally stopped, we sobered up. I rooted in my bag for tissues to mop my teary eyes. Avery wiped his with the knuckle of his left forefinger. Then we sat back and gazed assessingly at each other for a moment, apparently on a new footing.

"Avery, it's very difficult for me to know what to say to you. I seem to be caught in the middle of something about which I haven't got a clue. I could moan and groan to you about my anxieties and my sleepless nights, but you're my boss and I'm not about to do that. Otherwise I have nothing to say that you don't already know. So maybe it's you who should do the talking."

"Well—you really do dispense with the bullshit, don't you? Good. I'll be frank with you. I'm worried sick about what's going on here. When Astin-Berger was killed it was easy to see his death as an anomaly, something that happened to *him* alone, something *personal* to him. Oh, it occurred at the college, all right, but it could have happened anywhere, at the airport, at the Modern Language Association convention. But now, with a student dead, too, it seems like a much more dangerous situation, clearly connected to the college. Clearly unresolved. Maybe even unfinished."

Avery reached over to a wooden rack on the table next to him and selected a pipe. He filled the bowl with tobacco and without lighting the pipe put its stem in his mouth. He sat in silence for a minute or two, sucking on the pipe stem, then removed the pipe from his mouth and put it down on the table. I watched the whole procedure closely, fascinated. Then, having given himself some time for thought, he spoke again.

"You were unfortunate enough to be on the scene for the first, ah—body, and doubly unfortunate to be the person Piotrowski settled on to identify the second. You've suffered from this more than anyone—except the victims, of course—and I'm extremely sorry about that."

I bit my upper lip, torn between self-pity and wariness. I still had no idea what he wanted from me.

"But what I am, even more than sorry, is concerned." By the time I'd untangled his syntax, he'd gone on. "Karen, you are just a little too close to all this, and I'm worried about you. I don't want a third corpse showing up at Enfield College, and I especially don't want it to be you." He leaned forward and touched my hand lightly. Then he sat back again.

How very sweet, I thought, but the sarcasm couldn't mask the chill that passed through my body.

"Do you have any idea at all what this is about?

Any inkling?" He was leaning forward in his chair now, hands clasped at his knees, paying close attention to my words and looking at me with what truly did seem to be concern.

"If I did, Avery, I'd tell Piotrowski, not you. That's *his* job. He's a smart guy. He knows what's what." Then I snorted a little as I remembered what the lieutenant had said to me the previous evening.

"What?" Avery's gaze was intent. He seemed deeply interested.

"Oh, nothing. Just that our stalwart investigator is thinking things through in a very sophisticated manner." And I related Piotrowski's comment about the case no longer "smelling like sex."

"Intriguing." Avery sat back with a grin, one long slender finger tapping at his lips. A fleeting expression of relief crossed his elegant features, and I remembered Jill's tidbit of college gossip: something about Randy and Avery's wife. Smoothly, he went on to turn what had started as a serious conversation into a kind of witty tête-à-tête. "I wonder how many 'smells' murder could have. Rudimentary motives, I mean, such as, well, say, sex."

"Well," I responded, "anger, envy, greed . . ."

"Self-advancement, self-aggrandizement."

"Pride, shame."

"Whew." Avery shook his head with a mock professorial sagacity. I remembered that in his teaching days he had been a medievalist, a historian I thought. "Add sloth and gluttony and you'd have the seven deadly sins." He laughed softly. "With all those possibilities, it's a wonder *anyone* at Enfield College is still alive. Anger, envy, vanity, greed, lust, sloth, gluttony." He ticked them off on his fingers. "This place is a hotbed."

We talked awhile longer, about the murders,

about Randy, Bonnie, Piotrowski. We speculated about how it would be possible to live for any length of time with the knowledge that you were associating with a killer, perhaps even on a daily basis. That someone you nodded to in the hall or sat next to in committee meetings was so alienated from the implicit contracts of human community that he or she could choke the life from a fellow being.

"It would almost be comforting," Avery mused, "if we had a crack epidemic or something like that going on here, and we could blame the murders on that. Massive social problems, human beings gone mad under the influence of the drug, personal responsibility somehow suspended. But . . ." He spread his hands wide in bafflement.

When the light from the windows began to fade and Avery reached over to turn on the table lamp, I remembered the girls, who would probably be waiting for me in my office by now. I said good-bye with a handshake. Maybe I was closer to trusting this blue-blooded scion of the American aristocracy. Just maybe. But I was a good deal further than ever from trusting my own feelings about him.

Avery's comment about Enfield being a potential "hotbed" of murder motives ran through my mind as I walked by Randy's office windows in the gathering darkness and noticed a light. Assuming the police had returned, I passed his door on tiptoe and entered my own office. The building, indeed the entire campus, was deserted and quiet to the point that it gave me a sort of comfort to think the minions of the law were so very close by. Amanda and Sophia showed up shortly thereafter, and I took them for burgers— tofu, in Amanda's case—and drove home. It wasn't until the next day that I learned from Miles Jewell, our erstwhile department chair, always on the job, especially where scandal was concerned, that Randy's office had been entered sometime the previous day and thoroughly rifled. Odder still, all the files on his computer had been systematically erased.

Fifteen

I STOOD in the doorway of Randy Astin-Berger's office and stared. It was a disaster. Randy's office always had been a disaster, but this was a disaster of catastrophic proportions: Every book had been pulled from the shelves; every file cabinet had been rifled, its contents strewn across the thick beige carpet. His beautiful leather jacket had been pulled off its hook with such vehemence that the coatrack had fallen across Randy's desk. The jacket lay in a heap in the corner where it had been flung, pockets and sleeves pulled inside out. The Styrofoam cup that had teetered on a pile of journals during my last visit had been toppled, splashing coffee over the contents of the desktop and the open drawers. The computer monitor was on. Its cursor blinked on a nearly blank screen.

It was a scholar's nightmare: a life's work trashed.

Piotrowski, of course, had picked on me as the world authority on Randy Astin-Berger. As I'd hung up from Miles's call, the phone had rung with his.

"Dr. Pelletier? I'm at the college. I just overheard Professor Jewell informing you of events here, so I'm aware you know about the break-in."

"Yes?" I said warily.

"Since you seem to be familiar with Professor Astin-Berger's work, I wonder if you would mind coming down and looking over the scene? You might be able to give us some real useful insider stuff on what the intruder was searching for."

"Piotrowski, what is this? Am I on a per diem contract with the state police or something? I do have a life outside your investigation, you know. And I've got work to do."

That gave him only momentary pause. "Dr. Pelletier, it's no fault of mine that you're mixed up in this situation, so please don't take your frustrations out on me. This is no frivolous request I'm making. The sooner we can clear these homicides up, the sooner you'll be . . ." He hesitated, but I could swear he had been about to say "safe." "Er . . . *uninvolved.* So, I should think you would be happy to give what help you can."

"Right." My reply was subdued. "I'll be down as soon as I can get there, Lieutenant."

"Thank you, Doctor." He hung up without saying good-bye.

I threw on jeans and a maroon Georgetown sweatshirt of Amanda's, pulled my hair back in a loose bun, told the girls something had come up at work, and headed out into the cold.

The road into Enfield was clear for the most part, but covered with glare ice in places where the wind had whipped snow across it during the night. I drove cautiously; if I was going to be a fatality, I didn't want it to be through my own carelessness.

Piotrowski, wearing his rumpled gray suit, stood by the bookcase on the window wall, taking notes in what I assumed was an evidence book. His expression when he saw me was impassive. "Thanks for coming in, Dr. Pelletier. Look around, will you, and give me your impressions. Anything not here that should be? Anything here that shouldn't be? Whatever strikes you. The technicians have just finished up, but I'd appreciate it if you didn't move anything. I want you to see it exactly as we found it. Just eyeball what you can. If you need to see something close up, let me know."

With his large hand he made an expansive gesture, indicating that the entire disgusting mess was all mine.

I shook my head, hopelessly, then walked over to the computer, trying to place my feet on islands of oak floorboards in the ocean of paper. The computer monitor—dusted, even on the screen, with fine, dark fingerprint powder—displayed Randy's work directory, which indicated the date and the time, and listed zero files.

"Where are the backup disks?"

"Gone." Piotrowski's tone was acerbic.

"Had you copied anything when you were here before?"

"Yeah, bits and pieces. But we were working with different assumptions."

I knew what his assumptions were then, but didn't have a clue as to what they were now.

I wandered around the room, noting folders pulled from the file cabinets and strewn on the desk, chairs, and floor without any seeming pattern. Carbon copies of library call slips, photocopies of letter and sermon manuscripts, three-by-five note cards, handwritten notes on lined yellow sheets, and printouts of essay drafts traced Randy's work through various stages.

Glancing at Piotrowski for permission, I picked up

a yellow call slip carbon, handling it by the edges. It was from the Houghton Library at Harvard. I looked at it closely, but all the slip told me was that Randy had requested manuscripts of sermons by a number of nineteenth-century divines. And I already knew that. I asked Piotrowski if I could sit at the desk. From there the view looked no different; the search had clearly been indiscriminate.

"Well, Lieutenant," I said finally, "I don't think I can help you at all. What I see in this chaos is just exactly what I would have expected to see. Astin-Berger was doing research into nineteenth-century American sermons. He'd visited research libraries in the Northeast on a regular basis, and a few at a greater distance. There are call slips here from—"

"Call slips?"

"The forms you fill out to request a book or personal papers."

Piotrowski nodded.

"And he's got them here from a number of libraries: Yale's Beinecke, the New York Public, the Stowe Center in Hartford, the Houghton at Harvard, the Alderman Library at Virginia, the BPL, the AAS. These are all major scholarly collections, archives of manuscripts. If you needed to see letters, sermons, or personal papers of important nineteenth-century clerics, these are the places you would go."

This all seemed obvious to me, but Piotrowski was writing everything down in his little notebook, as if it were relevant information. Could it be evidence?

"The BPL? The AAS?"

"Oh, sorry. The Boston Public Library. The American Antiquarian Society. That's in Worcester."

He wrote it down.

"Now I'm going to say something totally off the wall. No matter how incredible it may seem, it's possible that these murders have something to do with Randy's work, with his research and writing."

"Humh," Piotrowski grunted, but I didn't wait for him to speak.

"How it could be, I don't know. His work was interesting, but only in a limited way, for a very limited audience."

I paused, thinking about the delicious scandal these murders must be causing at the Modern Language Association convention, being held that very moment in San Francisco. This was Astin-Berger's real constituency—ten thousand scholars of the written and spoken word. Only among these people would you find anyone who could possibly conceive of Randy's work as being "to die for."

I thanked whatever angels might be hovering over me that I'd decided not to go to the MLA this year. The literate tongues wagging, the articulate horror, the morbid theoretical badinage: I shuddered at the thought, and went on.

"The fact that his computer—"

"Can I help you?" Piotrowski's gruff voice tore through my meditations. I looked up, surprised. Ned Hilton was standing in the doorway, his face the color of the three-day-old snow on the campus quad.

"I thought—I thought—" he stuttered. Then he swayed and grabbed the door frame. The lieutenant caught him before he fell, and began to steer him toward one of the black-lacquered Enfield College captain's chairs with which all college offices seem to be furnished. Ned resisted.

"I'm all right," he said, making a visible effort to pull himself together. "I don't want—to go in there. I'll be okay. It's just that . . ."

"What?" Piotrowski's brusqueness with this distressed man irritated me.

"It's just that . . . when I saw the door open and

the light on . . . Oh, God—I'm such an idiot." He shook his head, as if to clear his thinking.

"What?" Clearly Piotrowski hadn't taken any of the sensitivity training courses Tony had talked about.

"I thought—for a second—that—that—he was back."

"Who?"

"Randy. . . . I thought Randy was back." Ned rubbed his eyes with a broad, pale hand. "But I'm all right now. What a stupid thing. I don't know what you must think. . . ." He hefted his fat briefcase from the hall floor where he'd dropped it and wandered off toward his own office.

The lieutenant stared after him. "Hmm." Then he turned to me. "Do you know this young man at all?"

"Hardly." I was still pissed at his abrupt manner with Ned. "His office is next to mine. I see him around once in a while. That's all."

Piotrowski gazed at me pensively. Then he nodded his head once, seemingly having made a decision. "You ever see him in the victim's office?"

"No."

"You have any idea why his prints would be on Astin-Berger's desk? Two complete and distinct sets, right in the center of the desk? Like he was leaning forward facing the victim?"

"Noooo."

The lieutenant registered my taciturnity. "Just trying to get things straight, here, Doctor. Don't get upset. And, for your information, I figured I'd get more out of the guy if I didn't coddle him. And he'd be better off, too. He's not—er—unbalanced, is he? Thought he saw a ghost! Jeez!"

I remembered only too well my own spooked reaction a week earlier when Randy's door opened and Avery came out. Prudence cautioned me to keep that little incident to myself. "No," I said, "as far as I know, he's not—unbalanced."

Piotrowski shrugged. "Okay, Doctor, go on."

"Go on? With what?"

"With what you were saying—about the scene here."

"Oh." I shifted in the desk chair, thinking back to the moment before Ned's appearance. "I was going to say . . ." It was difficult to pick up the thread.

"You said, 'The fact that his computer . . .'"

"Oh, yes. The fact that Randy's computer was totally erased suggests to me that his work was of some—what?—threat?—value? to someone. The intruder didn't have the time to go over everything, so he took the backups and destroyed the main files."

"He?"

"He. She. Whatever. So, I would think that what the intruder was looking for might have been on the computer, and I assume that, like most active scholars, Randy used his computer almost exclusively for his research and for the articles he was working on."

Piotrowski removed a sheaf of papers from the captain's chair. The sheets were held together with a large paper clip, but were fanned out as if they had been shaken vigorously. I recognized row after row of Randy's bold, left-slanting scrawl. Piotrowski looked at the writing closely, and then placed the cluster of pages on a pile of journals on the floor. He sat in the chair. It creaked audibly as his weight settled in.

"You confirm my hunch," he leaned back, his hands clasped behind his neck, "that the motive for these killings could be a scholarly one. And that baffles me. Not that scholarship should elicit murderous passion. That doesn't surprise me. I've seen everything under the sun do that—from a jug of Thunderbird in a fleabag motel in Springfield to a corner office in a Fortune Five Hundred executive suite. So why not scholarship? *Nothing* surprises me, Doctor.

"But what stymies me is how I should go about investigating this, when the subject is so obscure that there's, from what you tell me, only a handful of specialists in the world."

He looked at me. It was a hopeful look.

"Oh, no, Piotrowski." I jumped up from the desk chair, and tripped over a large bound volume. A closer look revealed it to be *The Annals of the American Pulpit* by Dr. W. B. Sprague. "I'm no expert here."

"You know . . ." He ignored my disclaimer. "The first thing that struck me when I saw this mess is that it's not finished."

"What's not finished?"

"Whatever this is all about. A custodian found the office in this state on her six A.M. cleaning rounds. She called campus security and they contacted us. When I got the phone call, it gave me a cold shiver, because this break-in tells me it's still going on, whatever it is, and I have no idea where it's going to hit next."

I experienced a cold shiver myself as he was speaking.

"Lieutenant, were you or your officers here yesterday afternoon? Say, around five P.M.?"

"No." He was suddenly doubly attentive. "Why do you ask?"

"Someone was. When I walked by the window on the way to my own office, there was a light in here. I assumed it was you."

"You don't say? And you on the scene again, huh?"

"What do you mean by that, Piotrowski?"

"I don't mean anything, Dr. Pelletier. Other than that you can't seem to shake loose of this, can you?

What were you doing here? You're on vacation, aren't you?"

I told him about the call from Avery, and about waiting for the girls in my office. He wanted to know what Avery and I talked about. He asked pointed and specific questions. He wrote in his notebook for a long time.

"And you were in your office when this was going on, were you?"

"I don't know if anything was 'going on' when I was here. A light was on, that's all I can testify to. Not that anything was 'going on.' "

"Right. There was no light at six A.M. And the door was locked." He wrote some more. Then he glanced up from his evidence book, cocked his massive head, and said, "Your office is so close to this one—ya ever see anyone hanging around here, shouldn't be?"

"Only Avery." Then I wanted to bite my tongue. Shit! When was I going to learn to keep my mouth shut around cops?

"Mitchell?" Piotrowski's tone was sharp. "Mitchell was here—in this office? When?"

"Oh, last week sometime. I don't remember exactly. Maybe a couple of days before Christmas."

"Yeah? And what was he doing here?"

I decided to omit mention of the files Avery had been carrying—especially that I had seen a similar stack on the desk in his office. They were his business, not mine. And, besides, all file folders look alike. "How would I know? I'm not in President Mitchell's confidence."

The lieutenant squinted at me, as if to get a better bead on whether or not I was lying. "You sure?"

I stared back at him, innocent as sin. "I'm sure."

I could see him weighing whether or not to press the issue; he decided to let it go.

"Well, okay." The notebook came into play again. Scribble. Scribble. Scribble. Avery would be receiving visitors shortly.

For some reason, Piotrowski must have decided he could trust me, because he went on. "You know, I don't think this intruder found what he was looking for. The disorder here is too general. There's no one place where it stops. He kept looking until he had looked everywhere."

"He?"

"Or she."

He got up from the chair and walked over to the window, gazing out at the frozen quad with its piles of lumpy snow. In the full morning light the planes of his face were impressive. Wide, flat cheekbones and a strong jawline defined a countenance whose individuality was not lost, even with the amount of weight Piotrowski carried. His mouth was wide, with attractively full lips, but was set, at this moment, in a fairly grim line. His brown eyes stared out at the common, seemingly without seeing either the denuded trees or the occasional faculty member wandering to an office or library research carrel. His gray suit jacket hung a little loosely across his shoulders, as if it had been made for an even larger man.

He turned away from the window and looked down at his notebook while he spoke. "And since he hasn't found what he's searching for here, he's gonna look somewhere else. Where will that be? Astin-Berger's house? We've got someone there now. No sign of entry."

"What about Randy's carrel?"

"His carrel? Where's that?"

He called security and then asked me to accompany him and the security guard with the keys to the library. Randy's narrow, fusty research carrel was practically empty. Four books on the history of

American religion were stacked neatly on the shelf over the desk, but didn't look as if they had been touched in months. No sign of entry there, but as Piotrowski pointed out, there wouldn't necessarily be. There was no mark on the office lock, either, so the intruder probably had access to a passkey of some sort.

"So . . ." Piotrowski zipped up his winter jacket, a new one, I noticed, navy blue with gray collar and pocket flaps. ". . . If not there, where? That's what worries me: Where? And when? And, even more, who? Who'll be in his way this time?"

He pulled on gray wool gloves that matched the jacket trim. He actually looked put-together. I wondered if his wife had gotten him the jacket and gloves for Christmas. I wondered if he had a wife.

As we walked down the library steps, the campus carillon rang noon. Piotrowski invited me out for a sandwich. On the BCI, he said. And over a hamburger and thick fries at Rudolph's he made me a proposition. Well, yes, a proposition. Out of what seemed like the proverbial clear blue sky the lieutenant offered me a consulting fee for investigating Randy's research interests.

"You may not be an expert in Astin-Berger's particular subject, but you know the field and you know how to go about researching it professionally. Am I right? You know all this archive shi—er, stuff. Right? And you know the larger picture—what, the historical context, is that it? You'd know what to look for. You'd know how to recognize the significant detail, the incongruity. And you're not working right now. Am I right?"

"Well, I *am* working." I gave vent to my usual knee-jerk reaction to people who think academics have a soft life. "I'm just not *teaching*."

"Yeah, well . . ." He waved my objection away.

"You mentioned a per diem earlier. What do you get a day for consultation?"

"Piotrowski, I was just mouthing off. I wasn't serious. . . ."

"Well, I am, Doctor. There's a lot of pressure on us about this case. Ya know what I mean? High-level pressure. Enfield grads are everywhere—in the senate, in the governor's office. This investigation is being watched closer than a drag queen at a DAR ball."

I blinked at his simile.

He went on, "You may not realize it, but you've been real helpful, and I really do need a professional researcher. The BCI does not run to scholarly types. What do you get?"

"Well . . ." I foundered around in my brain for a figure, finding one that could only serve to get me off the hook. "Last month Amherst College paid me five hundred dollars for an evening lecture on working-class literature. Wined me and dined me, too."

"Five hundred, huh?" He nodded his head slowly and looked impressed. "I *might* be able to get you that. I definitely couldn't get you any more."

I choked on my hamburger, then croaked, "You could get me five hundred dollars a day? Are you serious?"

"And expenses. I'd have to clear it with the suits, you know. And it could only be for a limited time. But if that's your professional fee . . . Hey, we've been known to hire psychics to assist in investigations. Why not a scholar? I think they'll go for it. Like I said, my hunch is that the motivation for these murders lies somewhere in Astin-Berger's work, and with your professional expertise we could maybe get at it a little sooner."

"You're serious, aren't you?"

He nodded. "What do you think?"

I thought about my still-unpaid education loans. I thought about Amanda's tuition. I thought about my MasterCard balance. I thought about the leather jacket I'd been wanting to buy my daughter for her birthday. Maybe now I could get a really good one—one like Randy's. "I'll think about it." My voice came out with a bit of a squeak.

"Good." Piotrowski sat back and signaled for more coffee. I noticed he was drinking it black. "Good. And just one more thing, Doctor. Don't tell anyone you're looking into this, will you? And I do mean *anyone*."

Sixteen

SEVEN P.M. on New Year's Eve found me soaking in my big, claw-footed tub trying to get sufficiently relaxed to go to a party. It was difficult to reconcile such a frivolous pursuit with my day's activity. I'd spent a full eight hours in an evidence room at BCI headquarters sorting through cartons of papers the police had removed from Randy's office. When I protested to Piotrowski that I could just as easily do that at the college, even in Randy's office, he said, "No. No, I don't think so." When I pressed him he elaborated, "As far as people at Enfield College are concerned, you have nothing to do with this investigation. You're simply out of town for the day. Ya got that? I'm serious about this, Dr. Pelletier. Dead serious."

So after a mind-numbing day of separating index cards from call slips, photocopies from hand-written notes, and the Reverend Mr. Abbott from the Reverend Mr. Beecher from the Reverend Dr. Sprague, trying to recreate Randy's research patterns, I was up to my neck in hot water and Chanel No. 5 bath oil. Thinking about what I would wear. Thinking about who I would see. Wondering if Avery Mitchell would be there.

And feeling a little bit like Mata Hari.

At the last minute, Greg had decided to have a party. He had called the day before to invite us.

"I know this is in bad taste," he said. "What with two murders hanging over our heads."

"You could say that." I was ambivalent about getting together with a group of people I had last seen just before the corpse of a colleague fell at my feet. "And your metaphor is lousy."

"Yeah. Kind of chokes you up, doesn't it? You will come, though? Things are so grim around here, we need some festivity. And I've got a lot to celebrate: getting tenure, turning forty. . . ."

Getting back with Irena, I thought, but didn't say it.

"You're forty? Hey, that is something to celebrate. Let's set a precedent for wild fortieth-birthday bashes; mine's coming up in the not-too-distant future."

"Noooo, Pelletier. Can't be."

"Flattery will get you anywhere, Samoorian."

"I wish." His retort was properly lascivious, but the undercurrent of genuine possibility had vanished. We were back to the joking innuendo of buddies.

As I soaped my legs and ran the pink plastic razor over them, stroke after stroke, I wasn't feeling very festive. Piotrowski's insistence that the violent events were not finished had made them more real to me.

He'd asked me that morning if I was going out to celebrate the new year. I'd swallowed my resentment at the intrusion into my privacy; I was becoming very tractable.

"I've been invited to a party, but I don't think I'm going."

"Why not?"

"Well, Sophia doesn't want to go, which I can understand. She's too embarrassed. And Amanda won't leave her. And, Piotrowski, you've got me so spooked I don't think I should leave them alone out there in the boonies."

"You should go." After a moment's thought he added, "I want you to go. Don't worry about the girls, er—young women. I'll make sure they're all right."

"What do you mean?"

"Just that there'll be someone around to make sure they're not molested."

"You mean—surveillance?"

"Something like that. Go to the party. Have a good time. Everything is normal. Ya get my drift? Just . . ."

"Just what?"

"Just keep your eyes open. That's all."

"So, what, now I'm a paid informer?"

"*Doc*-tor Pelletier . . ." Very weary. And a supplicating gesture with the hands.

Well, if I was going to be Mata Hari I might as well play the part well. I rubbed Keri lotion on my legs, and dusted myself with Chanel No. 5 body powder. Then I put on the only set of fancy underwear I own, magenta lace. My wardrobe does not run to dressy clothes, and I still didn't know what I was going to wear to the party. The white dress was out. I'd worn it to the fatal Christmas reception, and I didn't think I'd ever put it on again. Otherwise all I had was a couple of silk blouses that would go with black silk pants or—the Suit.

I took the Suit out of the closet and eyed it assessingly. Tony had bought it for me at Bergdorf Goodman's last year. I'd never owned anything even half as expensive in my life. We had been invited to a formal dinner thrown by the commissioner, and I don't exactly know what image Tony had in mind for me, but it certainly wasn't professorial. Purple shot silk, with a long wide-shouldered jacket and a short straight skirt, the Suit was worn over a bright orange low-cut shell. It was designed to reveal a copious amount of leg and a discreet suggestion of cleavage.

"What the hell." I stepped into the skirt. Yes. Just as I remembered: lots of leg.

Amanda gave a wolf whistle as I walked into the living room in the purple suit, orange blouse, and matching purple suede high-heeled sandals. "Way to go, Mom!" Sophia just stared, eyes wide. Amanda took a second look, said "wait" and darted into her room. She came out dangling an outrageous emerald green drop earring between the thumb and forefinger of each hand. In the light from the Christmas tree they glittered like, well, glass.

I twisted my hair on top of my head in a dragon-lady coil and donned the earrings. Amanda applied eye shadow and bright red lipstick. The effect was quite—spectacular.

I wasn't able to see anyone watching the house when I left at eight P.M., but then I didn't expect to. Parked facing the house about a quarter mile down the road, however, was a Jeep very much like the one Piotrowski had driven to the state park the previous week. Just pulled over into the hedgerow as if it belonged to a hunter out illicitly jacking deer. As far as I could tell, the car was empty.

In front of Greg's house, automobiles, mostly Volvos and Hondas, were parked on both sides of the road. He and Irena lived in a sprawling contemporary on a wooded hillside just outside of town.

With two incomes and no kids they could afford to live quite well: handcrafted Scandinavian tables, Persian rugs, low-slung leather chairs and couches, hand-stitched Amish quilts decorating the walls.

I parked the Jetta behind Ned Hilton's battered Toyota. I was surprised Ned would attend a party with his colleagues so soon after he'd been denied tenure; he must be gutsier than I'd thought. Carrying a bottle of champagne in one hand and my dress shoes in the other, I trudged over the icy packed snow toward the brilliantly illuminated house in my heavy coat and boots. Greg met me in the foyer and gave me a quick hug.

"Thanks again for Christmas, Karen," he said. "You're a real pal." He checked out the bottle I'd handed him. "New York," he said. "Nice."

I smirked at him. "Snob!"

Greg directed me to a bedroom in use as a cloakroom. Magda Vegh's full-length mink was thrown carelessly on a pile of wool coats and down jackets. I knew it was Magda's, because in politically correct Enfield she was the only college-associated woman who had the nerve to flaunt a fur coat. She wore it, even to faculty meetings, with a raw sensuality, as if the coat were a natural manifestation of her own animal powers. For Magda, style was everything. She dressed as if she *lived* to dress. I threw my five-year-old black cloth coat on top of the mink, pulled off the clunky boots, and donned my purple suede sandals.

In the bathroom I brushed back a few tendrils of hair and touched up the bold red mouth. "Not bad," I informed my reflection in the full-length mirror, but I was nervous. The image that gets me through my daily life is intellectual, serious, maybe even a little prim. Blacks, browns, dark greens, denim. Now here

I was, cross-dressing as Madonna. I resisted a strong impulse to run home and change.

I paused for a moment in the French doors that opened into the Samoorians' large living room. The room was full of people. Irena, her blond curls up in a Lucille Ball curly do, wearing brown-and-gold leopard-skin leggings and a loose brown silk shirt, was circulating with a crystal bowl full of jumbo shrimp. Ned Hilton seemed to be deep in earnest conversation with Greg, who carried a tray. I hadn't had dinner, and my eyes fixated on the food. Thin-sliced whole-grain bread spread with salmon mousse? Yum.

Ned, in a sober brown tweed jacket, a cowlick of light brown hair flopping over his left eye, was listening intently as Greg spoke. I wondered if he'd heard the rumors suggesting he was Randy's killer. If so, it was doubly brave of him to be here tonight. As a fellow suspect, I decided to make a point of talking to him.

Avery Mitchell, with his back to me, was standing in a windowed alcove talking to Magda. As I stepped into the room, Avery turned around to survey the crowd. His eyes swept casually over me, and then swung back, as if in astonishment. For maybe five seconds—an eternity—he stared quite frankly, his mouth slightly agape. Then, abruptly, his expression became formal, his eyes hooded. He nodded at me stiffly, a polite recognition, and turned back to Magda.

I was thrilled. I mean that literally. That brief, unguarded erotic gaze sent an electric charge through my body. *Oh, woman,* I told myself, *you are swimming in dangerous waters here.* But, for that one brief heady moment, I didn't really care. *Send in the tidal waves,* I thought, *send in the sharks; I am riding the riptide.*

Fortunately, however, I have always been sane. Rationality came roaring back, and I reminded myself that Avery Mitchell was off bounds, out of my league and my *boss,* for chrissake. The reality check, a glass of champagne to sip at, and a plastered-on smile helped me through the next few minutes until my pulse rate slowed to almost normal.

I found Ned in the dining room pouring Glenfiddich at Greg's improvised bar. For the moment we had the room to ourselves.

"That looks good, Ned. Make one for me, will you?"

He handed me the glass in his hand. "Here, take mine. Then you'll know I haven't put cyanide in it." His tone was bitter. He didn't smile.

"People a little leery of you, are they?"

"Aside from Greg, you're the only person who's initiated a conversation with me this evening. I'm obviously a pariah." He finished pouring his drink and took a sip from the chunky glass.

"Presumed guilty until found innocent? Yeah, me, too." I sipped the golden liquid. Smooth. Those Scots really know their stuff.

"You? But Randy hadn't done anything to you." His expression of pure hatred took me aback; I hadn't suspected Ned of the capacity for such rage. For that brief moment I thought that if hate could kill, this fragile-looking academic was indeed capable of murder.

"Not yet, he hadn't," I babbled, uncomfortable in the face of this powerful feeling. "But he was working on it." I sipped again, not wanting to be any more specific about what "it" might be. "And, besides, I was the last one to admit to seeing him alive. My social life's suddenly become extraordinarily limited—Greg, Earlene, Jill Greenberg."

"Jill's okay. She coming tonight?" Ned had himself under control again. He seemed marginally more stable than the last time I had seen him, slumped in the doorway to Randy's office.

"You kidding? A party? Jill wouldn't miss it for the world."

Then there wasn't anything left to talk about. I was grateful when new arrivals invaded the room in search of refreshment.

The evening elicited a few surprises, but not much that I thought worth passing on to Piotrowski. Surprise number one was Randy's wife. With a glint of mischief in his eye, Greg steered me across the room saying, "There's someone here I'd like you to meet, Karen." We were heading in the direction of Miles Jewell, who sat in a capacious black leather chair deep in conversation with a young girl of about twelve. She perched on an ottoman at his feet, her small face turned up to him, rapt with attention. When we reached the pair, Miles reluctantly fell silent, and the girl arose gracefully, seemingly in deference to her elders.

Greg introduced me formally. "Karen, I'd like you to meet Eve Astin-Berger. Eve, Karen Pelletier."

"Randy's daughter?" I asked.

The girl tittered. "No." Her voice was high and breathless. "Randy didn't have a daughter." *Silly,* her breathy tone implied. "I'm his wife."

Greg's grin grew wider as I stared at this apparition. She was at best little more than five feet tall and only beginning to develop, dressed in a knee-length black velvet dress with a white lace collar and a gathered skirt tied in back with a big taffeta bow. Her straight auburn hair was cut chin-length with bangs across the forehead. On her feet she wore red patent leather Mary Janes and white socks with a ruffle of lace around the cuff. The idea of this *child* being married to the highly-sexed Randy Astin-Berger was appalling.

Yet there was something about her. . . .

In the dim party light, I looked closer, and it became apparent that Eve Astin-Berger's presentation of herself as *jeune fille* was an exceedingly artful illusion. Her face was actually that of a woman in her mid- to late-thirties, slightly weathered, with crinkles around the eyes and lines etched lightly from the outside of her nostrils to the corners of her mouth. Her little-girl socks were worn over sheer stockings. She had made herself up with pale foundation, rosy childlike cheeks, a bowlike pink mouth, and wide innocent eyes. This mask of naïveté, superimposed on the experienced face, created a disconcertingly eroticized image of girlhood. At second glance it was clear that her body was not undeveloped at all. Rather, it was carefully starved and exercised, in the fashionable mode, to approximate prepubescent femininity. At second glance it was clear that the second glance was what counted. Was it possible, I wondered, that Eve Astin-Berger had, with her body, self-consciously created a commentary on femininity?

Well, yes, as it turned out, it was more than possible. I must travel in the wrong intellectual circles; I didn't know until that moment that Eve Astin-Berger was an up-and-coming literary theorist in the French feminist mode, which equates female writing with the female body: *l'écriture feminine*. Somehow I had missed her recent controversial study, *T/Sex/Ts,* and the op-ed piece on "Bimbos, Divas, and Drag Queens" in the *New York Times*. Within five minutes of meeting Eve, however, I knew all this about her— and more—because she told me, in a high girlish voice. What I didn't know was how she felt about Randy's death, because she never mentioned it, but it was safe to assume from the widow's demeanor that she wasn't totally devastated.

Eve taught Literary Theory and Gender Studies at New York University. Now that her semester was over, she had come to Enfield to pack up Randy's "effects"—as she kept calling them—and "close this chapter of the book of my life." *Hah,* I thought, *I'd better let Piotrowski know about this.*

"Thanks for warning me, pal." I smacked Greg on the arm as we moved away from this *faux* ingenue.

"I just wanted you to get the full impact." Greg's wide-eyed innocence didn't mask his wicked grin. "Some piece of work, huh? But what else would you expect from a creep like Astin-Berger? She contacted Miles yesterday, and when he heard I was having a party he called and invited both himself and her. What could I do? Exclude widows and orphans?"

Remembering Piotrowski's injunction to behave normally, I left Greg and circulated among several groups of colleagues and spouses. I spotted Jill Greenberg. She was perched on the arm of an over-stuffed chair looking up at Ned attentively. Her short black sleeveless dress rode high up her thighs as she crossed her long slim legs. A tattoo of a daisy decorated her left ankle, which she swung back and forth provocatively. *No, Jill,* I thought. *Please, Jill, don't. He's married. He's got two little girls. He's depressed about being denied tenure. He can't handle it.*

Stifling the impulse to play sex cop, I turned away. A minute or two later, Jill materialized beside me. She lightly fingered the purple silk of my jacket. "Bergdorf's, right? I can always tell."

"How're you doing, Jill?" I smiled at her. She had the wacky innocence of an Irish setter pup. Rebuking her would have been as futile as chastising a force of nature.

"I thought I was doing okay. . . ." She pushed a

strand of curly red hair off her face. "But then Ned had to go call his wife. His kids both have chicken pox. He's really sweet, isn't he?" She sighed, wistfully.

Then, in a swift change of mood, she grinned at me. "Did you see what's going on over by the window seat?" She gestured with what she clearly thought was a discreet motion to where Avery stood with Magda, his head bowed slightly to catch the fluid murmur of her voice.

I glanced toward them, returned Jill's grin, and shrugged smugly. After all, I'd seen him look at me earlier. I knew what I knew.

As the hour approached midnight the party became increasingly uninhibited. On a trip to the bathroom I inadvertently interrupted what seemed to be a fervid French kiss between two colleagues, both married to other people, both male. The heavy, sweet odor of marijuana smoke wafted from underneath a closed bedroom door. In the kitchen, a low-toned but intense squabble was taking place between Jerry Bingham from Philosophy and his red-headed wife Trudy. As I blundered in, looking for a glass of water, I heard her hiss "Who are you to be so goddamn self-righteous?" before they saw me and we were all embarrassed.

The champagne was flowing fast, but the gossip was flowing faster. I picked up tidbits of information but nothing that seemed related to either of the murders. Miles Jewell was still being pressed by the college administration to retire from the English Department within the next year and free up the chair for someone more progressive. Margaret Smith actually had a publisher interested in reading her twenty-years-in-the-works manuscript on Emily Dickinson. Magda Vegh was returning to Budapest in the fall after five years at various elite American colleges, during which time she'd missed the entire revolution she had ostensibly been agitating for. That kind of stuff.

The only thing that seemed even slightly relevant to the two murders was the information that Magda had known Randy in Budapest a few years ago when he was a Fulbright Fellow. I'd tell Piotrowski, but to what end I didn't know. Could we postulate a murder of sexual revenge? Or Randy's involvement in some smoldering Balkan feud? Neither seemed likely. I'd keep an eye on Magda, but . . .

As I lined up at the buffet for my portion of beef *en croûte* and au gratin potatoes, Magda, in puffy peach taffeta, was still holding court in the window alcove. As always she was the center of a fascinated group of male colleagues. Avery Mitchell, I noted, was walking toward the alcove carrying two plates of food.

I waited in line to fill my own plate and wondered, not for the first time, what it is that attracts men in droves to a woman like Magda. Maybe it's simply animal instinct, I thought, a knowledge that she's available and that, more than anything else in her life, she wants *them*. On the other hand, you have women like me, I thought virtuously, who enjoy men, but who have other interests and desires to flesh out a well-rounded and fully realized existence. . . .

It was close to midnight and Greg had turned the television on to the Times Square mob scene. With the ball about to drop announcing the birth of the new year, I noticed Greg put his arm around Irena and smile at her in anticipation of the New Year's kiss. At other New Year's Eve parties, I thought, Tony had kissed me—and kissed me and kissed me. Now I was alone, because I'd chosen to be. No, I corrected myself. Not because I'd chosen to be alone.

Because I'd chosen to fulfill myself in the career for which I had prepared so long and arduously. Yes. That was it. I had not chosen to be alone; it was simply a consequence. Besides, there'd be other men, other New Year's Eves. And I smiled a little as I remembered Avery's brief but enthralled gaze. A rudimentary but vivid fantasy began to form.

Then, simultaneously, three things happened: Greg's big grandfather clock chimed midnight, the Times Square ball dropped, and Avery, holding a glass of champagne in his right hand, placed his left hand possessively on the small of Magda's peach taffeta back, bent over her, and kissed her on the lips, lingeringly and with evident passion.

I spilled beef gravy all down the front of my purple skirt.

Seventeen

EXCEPT FOR the front door light, the house was dark when I pulled into my driveway at one-thirty A.M. I turned off the motor and leaned back in the seat, my hand still on the ignition key. My head was buzzing, not so much with alcohol as with a totally irrational sense of betrayal. When he kissed Magda, Avery had shattered a fantasy, nothing more—or less—than that. But I'd flushed, hot with shame, as if my humiliation were a public one rather than merely—what?—a simple correction of a romantic misapprehension? Driving home had been difficult, and now I felt too exhausted to negotiate even the short distance from the car to my front door.

The night was clear and bitterly cold, with a scattering of intensely bright stars. Within a couple of minutes the windshield began to frost over. I knew I should make the effort to get out of the car, but pulling the key out of the ignition was about as far as I was able to go. I was lost to the world, adrift in misery and self-pity. When someone tapped on the driver's window I barely stifled a shriek.

"I'm sorry, Dr. Pelletier." Piotrowski opened the car door. "I didn't mean to scare you. But when you didn't get out of the car, I started to worry. You okay?"

"I guess so." Then the significance of his presence struck me. "You haven't been hanging around here all evening yourself, have you? I thought you'd send a trooper or someone." I felt a pang of guilt about how hard Piotrowski worked.

"No." In the bright moonlight I could see concern in his serious brown eyes. "I just got here a few minutes ago, after the trooper called in a suspicious vehicle."

"What?" I jumped out of the car so fast I would've collided with Piotrowski if he hadn't taken a couple of instinctive steps backward. "What suspicious vehicle? Where are the girls? Are they okay?"

"The young women are fine." The lieutenant stressed *young women* as opposed to my retrograde use of *girls*. He was a fast learner. "Or at least I assume they're fine. And sound asleep. But not for long if you keep making that racket."

I lowered my voice. "What suspicious vehicle?" Each word came visible out of my mouth, a white puff of articulate breath in the frigid air.

"About a half hour ago a car came by and slowed down as it passed the house. The officer didn't think anything of it. Ya know, maybe a rabbit ran in front of it, or something. But then, about five minutes later, it came back from the other direction and slowed to a crawl. You know anyone with a brown Plymouth Duster, rusty, with a bad muffler, maybe ten, twelve years old?"

I tried to visualize such a car, but with no success. "No. Can't you trace the license plate number?"

"The officer didn't get the number." Piotrowski's lips were thin with censure. "It seems he'd gone into the woods around the side of the house for—something. When the car came back he heard it—its muffler was really shot—but only got it in his sights as it picked up speed and roared off."

The chill I felt was only partially from the frigid air. In any case, I thought it was time to get in out of the cold. I stamped my feet. Even in the heavy boots my toes were beginning to feel numb.

"We've got to talk, Lieutenant. Can you come in?"

"What about the girls?" *Gotcha!,* I thought: "girls." But somehow I didn't feel like pointing out his linguistic lapse.

"We'll go in the kitchen and shut the door. They won't hear us."

I unlocked the front door and opened it as quietly as I could, which isn't easy in this old house with its creaky hinges and door frames and floors. As we tiptoed toward the kitchen Amanda called out sleepily, "Mom? Is that you?"

"Yeah. I'm okay. I'm just going to get some cocoa to warm me up. Go back to sleep."

"Okay. See ya in the morning. Happy New Year."

We made it into the kitchen and shut the door. Piotrowski took off his jacket, the new blue one, and sat at the refinished oak table. He was wearing jeans and a pewter gray cable-knit sweater. The sweater looked new, too.

"Do you want some cocoa?"

"Yeah, thanks. That'd be real nice."

I unbuttoned my coat, shrugged it off, and threw it over the other chair as I turned to open the refrigerator.

Piotrowski said, "Wow!"

"Wow what?" I swiveled around with the container of milk in my hand to see him staring at me wide-eyed, with open admiration. Shit! I was still wearing the man-killer suit. What a drag.

"You look gorgeous." He seemed a little stunned.

Gorgeous! It's been decades since I've heard that word. Nobody says *gorgeous* anymore. The word died out with Jayne Mansfield and Marilyn Monroe. This man was a dinosaur.

Piotrowski couldn't know it, but the last thing I wanted to hear in my exhaustion and humiliation was anything about how I looked. My brief foray into sex appeal had brought me nothing but pain. "I do not look *gorgeous,* Piotrowski! My hair is falling down, my makeup's all gone, I'm wearing huge, clunky boots, and I've spilled gravy all over me. Get real."

"Sorry if you don't like it, but I can't help what I think. If you don't want men to think you're gorgeous, you shouldn't dress gorgeous."

That did it. I launched a direct attack.

"Okay, Piotrowski. So you think I'm gorgeous and you suddenly seem to find me fairly distracting, as well. But we've got serious things to talk about here. Can't we just pretend I'm wearing jeans and a sweatshirt as usual? Can you function if we do that?"

My tone must have been even sharper than I intended, because Piotrowski's face immediately became stolid and official. "What serious things do we need to talk about, Doctor?"

I turned back to the stove to make the hot drink, getting down the Hershey's cocoa and the sugar, measuring them into the pan. This was the most personal Piotrowski had ever gotten with me. I noted that and tucked it away in a far corner of my mind to think about later. It hadn't been bad working with him this past couple of days. He was smart, an independent thinker, and totally free from pretension: qualities I often find lacking in my academic colleagues. I liked this man, felt at home with him, and didn't want to offend him. And now, like a klutz, I had hurt his feelings.

"Sorry." I was genuinely contrite as I moved back toward the table with the steaming cups. "I've had a really shitty evening, plus I ruined my good suit, and then you frightened me with the stuff about the car. But I shouldn't take it out on you. I'm a jerk, okay? Forgive me?"

"Yeah." He smiled, just a little. "You do look very nice, though, even with your hair falling down. *And* no makeup."

"Okay. Okay. Enough!" I sipped at the hot drink. Glamor can be very inconvenient, I decided. It can really get in the way.

"Piotrowski . . ." After a long sip I put the cup back on the table. "Something weird is going on here. I'd forgotten about it, but this thing about the car reminds me: I've been getting anonymous phone calls."

"You have?" he broke in. "Why didn't you mention it before?" He was looking at me intently.

"Well, as I said, I didn't make the connection. Besides, it's probably some student prankster—maybe someone to whom I gave a bad grade."

"Maybe so. But—maybe not. Your number's listed, right?"

"Right."

"Hmm. So it could be anyone. Is there any pattern to these calls? Do they come at any particular time of the day? Does the caller use obscene language?"

"They come at all different times, and the caller doesn't use any language. He just listens silently for a minute, and hangs up."

"Hmm. I don't like this."

"Neither do I. And now this car. Piotrowski, I'm scared. Not for myself, but for the girls." He grinned, just a little—"girls." Now I'd slipped. "You know, when I'm working at the research libraries I'm going to have to be gone overnight. And Amanda has no car right now. We're miles from anywhere. If someone wanted to get at them, they'd be sitting ducks."

"And if you *were* here?"

"I don't know. I'd think of something."

"Right!" His tone was sarcastic. "Did your Ph.D. work include training in self-defense?" He said *pee. aitch. dee.*, deliberately sounding like a rube.

"Well, yes, in a way it did." I grinned ruefully, thinking about my dissertation defense. "But only verbal. Not in the ways you're thinking about."

"I'm concerned about the girls, too." He got up to rinse his cup out at the sink. When he was done, he looked back at me. "And I'm also concerned about you. Is there someplace you can take them away from here until this is cleared up?"

I thought about it. My mother's house was out of the question, and had been for years. My sisters' too. We didn't really talk anymore. My friendships didn't run so deep that I knew anyone I could impose three people on for an indefinite length of time. Only Tony . . .

"Well . . ." I thought about the complications. "Amanda was going to spend a week with an—an old friend in Manhattan. There's no reason she couldn't go now and take Sophia with her. He'd understand and—they'd be safe there."

Piotrowski had found a dish towel and was drying his mug with elaborate care. "Would that—old friend—possibly be Captain Anthony Gorman of the New York State Police?"

My mouth fell open with astonishment—and

something akin to rage. "Goddammit, Piotrowski! You've been investigating me!"

"Of course I have." He placed the mug neatly on its proper shelf and sat back down at the table, comfortably in charge once again. "What do you think? I've been investigating everyone. That's my job."

"Damn you." I felt tears come to my eyes. Suddenly I'd had just about as much as I could handle. My life wasn't my own anymore, between the damn killer and the damn cops. I brushed the tears away with the heel of my hand.

Then there was a tentative knock on the kitchen door. "Mom?" Amanda queried. "Mom? Do you have a man in there?"

I looked at Piotrowski and grinned. He snorted with laughter. I tried not to smile as I wiped my eyes with a paper napkin and opened the door.

"Yes. Yes, I do, honey. But it's all right, dear; we're in the kitchen, not the bedroom."

She stood sleepily in the doorway, dressed in yellow sweatpants, an oversize faded purple sweatshirt, and mismatched wool socks, one red, one brown. She hadn't worn pajamas in years. Her hair spiked out in a number of directions. Sophia must still have been asleep; Amanda was alone.

"Mom." Her lips were tight with disapproval, my sarcasm having gone right past her. "It's almost two-thirty." As if I were some wayward adolescent sneaking a boyfriend into the house after hours.

"Amanda, this is Lieutenant Piotrowski of the Bureau of Criminal Investigation. He's here on business."

She looked at the plate of sour cream cake. *Yeah. Right.*

"I guess I'm going to have to tell her." I turned to Piotrowski. I couldn't quite believe it, but I was looking for permission.

He nodded.

I told Amanda about the suspicious car and its implications and suggested that she make her visit to Tony tomorrow, and take Sophia with her. "Try not to frighten Sophia, will you? Just tell her—oh, tell her something. . . ."

"I'll tell her I'm bored out of my gourd here in the sticks, and I need a massive infusion of carbon monoxide and hot pretzels," my daughter replied flippantly. Then her expression grew more serious. "How's that? It's not far from true, anyhow."

"I think that'll do it, kid. I'll call Tony in the morning." I quailed inwardly. I hadn't spoken to Tony in months. "Now why don't you go back to bed while the lieutenant and I finish up here. I'll be in soon."

"You're coming too?" She meant to New York, not to bed.

"We'll see." My reply was evasive. I didn't feel up to arguing with her.

But Piotrowski pounced on it when Amanda left. "So? Will you go to Manhattan?"

"No." I hoped my response wasn't too forceful. "No, not me." I noted him noting my vehemence. "And besides, I've got work to do here, remember? For you. Most of the archives I'm researching are in New England. I'm better off using this place as a base. Right?"

He nodded, not quite convinced. He didn't seem ready to leave. I made more cocoa and told him about Randy's wife. Piotrowski hadn't met Eve, but Sergeant Daniels had gone to New York to interview her. The woman was a nut case, according to Daniels, a real fruitcake. If this was who was educating our youth, Daniels had said, no wonder this country was in such deep—er, trouble.

We talked about possible motives for a "scholarly" murderer. "The seven deadlies . . ." I said, elaborating on my conversation with Avery: "Anger, envy, greed . . ." Piotrowski liked the idea. He ruled out only gluttony and sloth as possible motives.

"This perp," he said, "kills on the spur of the moment, and reactively. Nothing is planned; no weapons brought in. At least not so far. I think that he—"

"Or she—"

"She? Maybe. Now your Miss Warzek, she couldn'a done it: too slight. You? Maybe. But you'da had to been real mad. Outta control. I somehow can't picture that."

Gee, thanks. I tried to register nothing but control.

The lieutenant went on to speculate that our killer might feel his (or her, I thought, somewhat perversely) career to be threatened in some way, or, even more dangerous, that some cherished idea was somehow placed in jeopardy by Randy's research. *If* we were correct about the research being the motive. Which we might well not be.

We finished the rest of the sour cream cake. I ate most of it as I listened to Piotrowski. I hadn't much felt like eating my supper. Piotrowski limited himself to one thick slice.

When his wristwatch beeped three A.M., Piotrowski rose and put his jacket on. I was almost sorry to see him go. The warmth and coziness of the kitchen, the lateness of the hour, and our shared concerns had served to create an illusion of intimacy, as if we were brought together by more than official business.

At the door Piotrowski pulled out a card case, extracted a card, and wrote on the back. "This is my home number. Anything comes up that could be related to these homicides—and I mean *anything*—try me at the office first and then here. Night or day."

He reached out to shake hands. "Good night, Doctor."

"Why don't you cut out that 'Doctor' business, Piotrowski? It's really annoying. Just call me Karen."

His eyes glinted with something that to my exhausted brain momentarily resembled amusement.

"I think it'd be for the best if I just keep calling you Doctor. You don't mind, do ya."

"No, I don't mind." But I did.

It wasn't until he was gone and I was undressing for bed, dropping the purple silk suit in a wrinkled heap and donning my sweats, that I realized I didn't have a clue as to what *his* first name was. *He must have a first name,* I thought, as I brushed my teeth, *how come I don't know what it is?* I found the card he had given me; it said *Lieutenant C. Piotrowski.* "C.": Charles? Maybe. Christopher? He didn't look like a Christopher. I thought hard; I couldn't come up with any other "C" names for men except rather effete British ones. I was too tired to think any more; I just wanted to sleep.

Avery's face floated behind my closed eyes as I drifted off, but I didn't dream about him at all. At least not that night.

Eighteen

TONY WAS ASTONISHED when he heard my voice. "Karen?" he said, with a rising inflection, an unguarded response from this habitually unflappable man. Then, in an immediately controlled manner, "What's up?"

Like Piotrowski, Tony is a skilled listener—an unusual trait in a man. He listened intently while I gave him a full report. After asking a few questions he fell silent for a moment or two before he spoke. "Karen, I want you to come to the city, too."

"I can't do that. I've got work to do. And besides, what about—you know . . ."

"I'll explain to her. She'll understand."

"Sure she will. *Darling, my old lover is coming to town. Of course you'll understand if she stays with me. She just needs a little protection.* I assume you had in mind that I'd stay at your place; I don't know where else I'd go."

"It's a big apartment." His voice was curt. "You could have your own room."

"Not a good idea, Tony. You know that. Not a good idea at all."

"No, maybe not. I'll think of something, though. At least have lunch with me when you bring Amanda and this other girl. We can talk about it then."

I had planned to put Amanda and Sophia on the bus in Springfield. I really hadn't thought about driving into the city. Amanda knew her way around Manhattan. Even in as sleazy an environment as Port Authority, with the hustlers and homeless all around, they'd be fine. Amanda could handle anyone who tried to hassle them.

But the thought of sitting across the table from Tony again, just once more, of having him concerned again, if only for a little while, about what was happening to me, seemed irresistible. Self-destructive, but irresistible. Particularly now, when I felt so betrayed by my own desires. Impulsively I agreed to drive in with the girls the next day, and to have lunch with him. I knew immediately that I would regret it, but pride prevented me from changing my mind. I didn't want Tony to think I attached too much importance to seeing him again. And besides, I didn't. I was over him. I was fine.

I had called Tony fairly early, wanting to make sure I caught him before he went out. Also, I wanted to talk to him before Amanda and Sophia woke up. Neither of them needed to know just how worried I was. As I hung up the phone, Sophia came into the kitchen, gave me one of her wan, tentative smiles, got out the box of Müeslix, the container of two-percent milk and a bowl, and sat down at the table.

She'd been with us for over a week now and her manner was ever so slightly more animated. She was eating something at every meal. I no longer watched each spoonful carefully to make sure it went in her mouth. From skeletal she had advanced to merely emaciated. Skinny would be the next step up. When you looked at her now you saw the facial structure before you saw the face, the skin pulled tight over the fine bones. Then you noticed those pained eyes in their still-bruised sockets. Then her face became a face.

She poured about half a cup of cereal into the bowl and dampened it with milk. Without being asked I brought her a glass of orange juice, thinking she might drink it just to be polite. She sipped at the juice but didn't touch the cereal. Sitting there in a pair of Star Wars pajamas with Princess Leia on the top, she looked like the twelve-year-old Amanda had been when I'd bought them for her. She picked up her spoon and held it in her right hand, looking at it quizzically, as if it were an unfamiliar tool with whose function she was not acquainted. Then she put it in the bowl, released it, and dropped her hand back into her lap. I sighed.

"Karen . . ."

"Yes?" I felt heartened: At least she was initiating a conversation.

"Karen, my father called last night."

My stomach constricted. For a moment I wished I'd mentioned the encounters with Warzek to Piotrowski. Then I reminded myself I hadn't wanted to make a bad family situation any worse. That was still the case.

"I answered the phone because Amanda was in the shower." Sophia hesitated. It seemed to be important that I understand she hadn't been overstepping the line in answering the phone. I nodded, *Yes, go on*. Nonverbal communication often worked best with her, as it might with a half-tamed fawn.

"He wanted to come get me and take me home. He *ordered* me to come home. When I said no he got really angry. He's not used to anyone saying no to him." Her eyes were very still. "At least no one ever says no to him at home. Maybe everywhere else, but not at home. If he could have hit me he would have, I know. And . . ."

She paused again, staring down at the soggy cereal, stirring it a bit with the spoon. I waited. She looked up abruptly, and her voice was stronger. "I know you think I should hate him. . . ." I shrugged, shook my head. *No, not necessarily.* "But I don't—I can't. Can you understand that? I can't hate him." I nodded. *I can understand that.* "You know, he's just trying to make it. Ever since I can remember, he's worked two jobs. Just so we could get by. You know? Can you imagine? Two jobs? He's always so tired. Now he's lost his job at the cement plant. It shut down, just like that, no notice. Twenty-five years and he's got nothing to show for it. So now he's working nights at the college, cleaning bathrooms and mopping floors. And weekends at the Seven Eleven. He hates it, the Seven Eleven. He's so tired and people get so nasty to him. Can you understand that? He's not a bad man. He's just tired. All he wants is for his family to be together and to—to behave. That's all. He just wants my mother and me to *behave.*"

She picked up the cereal spoon, contemplated its dripping contents, then dropped it back in the bowl. She bit her lower lip, hard. When she began speaking again, I could see the impress of her teeth. "But I do hate him." Her eyes were bleak, for once more gray than blue. "I'm such a bad daughter. All he wants is the best for us—and I hate him." She whispered, "I think I'm crazy?" It was a question, not a statement. The gray eyes scanned mine, as if I had an answer.

"You're not crazy." I judged it safe now to speak. "You're not bad and you're definitely not crazy. It's the situation that's bad—that's crazy. Not you, sweetie."

I reached out to grasp her hand reassuringly but she pulled it away rather sharply.

"And—he's really mad at you." Here her words dried up again, like a stream that's run into an obstruction. She turned her head away from me and bit her upper lip. When she looked back at me, the dam broke and the words came rushing out. "He says you're a meddling bitch, sticking your nose in where it's none of your goddamned fucking business. He says you're an evil influence on me. He says you're a—a dyke, out to ruin me forever, to turn me into a pervert. He said you'd better watch your step because he'd see that you weren't going to get away with it for long."

Tears began to pour from her eyes, not individual tears, but a whole wash of them, as if a river had crested and overflown its banks. She hadn't cried like that before, at least not in front of me. I handed her the tissue box. She cried for a long time while I patted her on the arm. I wanted to hold her, but the word *dyke* hung in the air between us, preventing a natural act of compassion. That must be why she'd pulled her hand away. I sighed. *They were better off in the nineteenth century,* I thought, *when love between women was just* love, *no matter what form it took.*

When she had recovered sufficiently to speak, Sophia murmured, "I didn't tell Amanda, because I didn't want to frighten her, but I think I should tell you because now I think I should leave, because I don't want to be any trouble to you, only I don't know where I could go." All in one breath. Then, "He was drunk, of course."

"You're no trouble to me, Sophia. Don't worry about that. And don't worry about your father. I can handle him." I shrugged off the notion of any danger from Warzek. With what I seemed to be facing, an angry, drunken father was of little consequence. I had dealt with abusive fathers before. My own and Amanda's.

His call, however, provided a tailor-made opportunity to suggest that the girls leave Enfield. "Sophia, I've been thinking—Amanda was planning to spend a week in New York City with an old friend, and now might be a really good time for her to go, and take you. What do you say? I know you'd be welcome, and maybe by the time you get back your father will have cooled off."

"New York? Really?" It was wonderful to see how perfectly ordinary things, like a trip to a city she'd never seen, like a dozen roses, could bring the light back into those lusterless eyes. "But . . ." and she looked dubious, "do you really think it would be okay? If I went, I mean? I don't want to intrude. . . ."

"I've just been talking to our friend and I know it's fine. He'd love to have you."

"I'm going to tell Amanda." She jumped up from the table as if she were much younger than twenty-one.

"Eat your breakfast first," I replied, also as if she were much younger. And she did, sitting down obediently, eating the soggy Müeslix and finishing the orange juice before she ran off to the bedroom.

I washed out her bowl and glass and, as I dried them, wondered if it was possible to adopt someone who had already turned twenty-one.

The college pool was closed for the semester break, so I drove over to the Y in Greenfield to swim my laps. It had been days since I'd been in the water. I desperately needed both the exercise and the tension release. Especially after talking to Tony. Indeed, I was so preoccupied with the echoes his voice had raised in my heart I lost awareness of everything else during the drive to town. When I hit the blinking red traffic light in the center of Greenfield's business district, I came awake with a start. How had I gotten there? I didn't remember anything about the trip after backing out of the driveway. I had totally blanked out fifteen minutes of my life.

Then, to top it off, I didn't notice, even when I had pulled into the empty parking lot, that the Y was closed. Of course it was closed. After all, it was New Year's Day. But, distracted, I pulled my car up close to the building, exulting in the good parking spot, got my gym bag out of the backseat, and headed for the door, thinking all the while about seeing Tony again. It was only when the glass entrance door refused to yield to my push that I surfaced sufficiently to read the small print on the sign posted on it: *Closed Easter, Thanksgiving, Christmas, & New Year's Day.*

I stood there with my hand on the knob, trying to adjust to the fact that I wasn't going to get to swim, when I saw someone walking down the empty sidewalk toward me. The figure also carried a gym bag. As she got closer I realized it was Margaret Smith. If it had been a stranger approaching and not a colleague, I would simply have turned away and walked back to my car. Now, however, I waited politely until she got within speaking range and smiled ruefully at her. "I'm afraid we've both been a little forgetful. The Y's closed today."

"Why would it be closed?" Margaret glared at me accusingly, as if I were somehow responsible for this disruption to her plans. She wore a brown quilted jacket, baggy gray corduroy pants, and the duck boots I remembered from the college locker room. A navy-blue watch cap was pulled low over her forehead and ears, and her round face, chapped with cold, looked withered. She reminded me of a doll handcrafted from dried apples.

"It's New Year's Day."

"Oh, it's a holiday, is it?"

"Yes. . . ."

She turned to leave, the functional part of our conversation completed.

"Good-bye." I don't know why, but I was stubbornly determined to preserve the amenities. "Happy New Year."

At the sound of my voice, she turned around again. The look she gave me was fairly chilling—straight, sober, and unreadable. "So." Her voice was oddly uninflected. "So. Karen Pelletier. The rising young star of the English Department. You're one of the lucky ones, aren't you?"

I stared at her, for once flabbergasted into total silence. Her dark gaze was direct and opaque. "You've done a book on Dickinson, haven't you?" Her eyes slipped past me to scan the wide street, bare now of its usual tumult of pedestrians and traffic. The gray sky was heavy above the low buildings. The traffic light blinked red at the intersection, but no cars appeared to obey its command.

"Well, no. But I have a chapter on Dickinson in the book that's about to come out." As usual it was difficult for me to discuss my work with anyone I suspected wouldn't have sympathy with it.

"What's it about?"

"The book? It's a study of the ways in which many nineteenth-century American writers were hampered by class privilege in their perceptions and expression of American experience. I look at Emerson, Melville, Hawthorne, Thoreau, and Poe, as well as Dickinson. I call the book *The Constraints of Class: Six Classic American Authors.*"

"Oh." Margaret turned to walk away. She had received the information she wanted. She was not interested in continuing the conversation. Then, turning briefly back to me, she added impassively, "Very trendy."

I stood there, on the wide, empty sidewalk, with the cold wind whipping down the street. Then I shrugged. If I'd wanted to be trendy I would have called the book *Class(ic) American Authors.* As usual, it was too late for a cool rejoinder.

Margaret plodded away down the sidewalk, pausing only to remove a sheet of newspaper that the sharp wind had blown against her leg. Although a large wire wastebasket was close at hand, she dropped the paper back on the sidewalk. I resisted an impulse to run after her and pick it up.

At last night's party someone had mentioned that Margaret had been working on a book about Dickinson for over twenty years. It was apparently the joke of the campus. Nobody believed she would ever finish it, but just this month she had told her chairman that she was about to send the manuscript off to a publisher. I wondered what anyone could possibly have to say about Emily Dickinson that would take two decades to write.

My nose and ears were numb. I tugged my purple scarf up to cover my face. Walking back to the parking lot I checked out the money in my wallet. Four dollars and some change. It was midafternoon, and I hadn't had any lunch. Four dollars should get me a Fishamajig at Friendly's, and maybe a cup of coffee. If Friendly's was open. Then I'd stop at the BayBank and use the cash machine. If the cash machine was working.

Friendly's was open. The Fishamajig was flavorful

and juicy. The coffee was fresh and hot. And, even though it was a holiday, the ATM actually dispensed cash. And when I got home, my young housemates were just setting up a game of Trivial Pursuit. My mind is luxuriant with trivia. I absolutely love that game. Maybe Margaret was right: Maybe I was one of the lucky ones.

Nineteen

T HERE WERE FLOWERS in my salad, blue flowers and orange ones. The orange ones looked like nasturtiums. I picked up my fork and regarded them warily. I had never eaten a flower before, at least not since I was two years old and would eat anything. Maybe they were garnish, not meant to be eaten. Out of the corners of my eyes I peeked around at the other diners. It had been six months since I'd been in a Manhattan restaurant, and I was obviously out of touch. Hearty homestyle American fare had been the last thing I knew, and I'd never been offered pansies with my pot roast. No one around me seemed to be at the salad course, however, and Tony had chosen to begin with split pea soup. Well, there were hospitals close by if I had a problem. I chomped down on a blue flower. It had no flavor. Paralysis did not set in. I ate an orange one.

Seeing Tony had been more difficult even than I had anticipated. The sight of his square, somewhat battered, face across the table, the total familiarity of it, brought an intensified sense of just how alone I now was without this man with whom I had once shared everything. He was fresh-shaven, and his curly black hair looked moussed; he had obviously prepared carefully for this meeting. His soft off-white Irish fisherman's sweater looked new. I wondered if what's-her-name—I never could remember her name—Jennifer or something—had given it to him for Christmas. Maybe even knitted it.

I glanced around the room. It was intriguing to be back in New York again. Enfield tried hard, but it offered nothing that could begin to approximate a Columbus Avenue restaurant. This one featured functionalist decor, its brick walls sandblasted bare, its utility pipes bared and painted a shiny black against a high white ceiling. Sections of the former pressed-tin ceiling, alternating white and black, were framed in shiny chrome plumber's pipe, elbow joints and all, and hung by steel chains from the overhead pipes. The pure white damask tablecloths and crystal bud vases on the jammed-together tables provided an incongruous elegance.

The lunchtime crowd seemed well-dressed and harried. At nearby tables at least five people were conducting business conversations on cellular phones while they wolfed down exquisitely prepared thirty-five-dollar lunches, seemingly without tasting the food. While they wheeled and dealed on the phones, their lunch companions carried on conversations around them. I had never seen a cell phone in a restaurant in Enfield, I realized. It would have seemed the height of rudeness. And I'd never been offered blossoms in my salad. Six months away, and I was already becoming a hick.

I tore my bemused gaze away from my surroundings and turned my attention back to Tony. From his close concentration on the wine list and his finicking with the water glass, I could tell he was nervous. His left hand played up and down the stem of the glass as if it were the neck of a stringed instrument. With his right forefinger he was tracing a pattern around its base. To tell the truth, I was surprised he wanted to see me at all after the pain I had caused him.

By most people's standards I had been the guilty party, walking out on a six-year relationship with a stable, loving man who was devoted to home and family. We could work it out, I had argued when the job offer had come from Enfield College. We could commute the hundred and seventy-five miles between Enfield and Manhattan on alternate weekends. I knew lots of academic couples who lived that way. It would be fun, I said. It would give us two homes, his upper West Side apartment and a small place in the country. It would give us two very different life-styles—the vitality of the world's most exciting city and the peace of the New England countryside. It would be an enviable life, I proffered.

What about his unpredictable schedule? he countered. Given the realities of narcotics investigation he never knew in advance if he would be able to take the weekend off. And he couldn't be so far away on a regular basis, because he never knew when something unexpected would break. And what about marriage? And what about children? Amanda was great, but hadn't we planned on having at least one child together? And, anyhow, didn't I have a perfectly acceptable job right here in the city?

With the current budget cutbacks, my job was uncertain, I replied. And it was oppressive. I was overworked, underpaid, and unappreciated. Enfield was a prestige job, a dream come true.

Was I going to let ambition rule my life? he asked. Wasn't it ruling his life? I asked. Why didn't he take early retirement now that he was eligible for it? He could go back to school, get another degree, change his life.

He loved his work, he said.

I love mine, I said.

But what about me? he said.

I love you, I said. But I'm going to Enfield.

"Listen, I talked to Piotrowski." Tony had torn his roll into crumbly fragments on his bread plate and arranged those pieces with his soup spoon into a neat concentric pattern. We had been talking about the weather.

"You *what?*"

"I called Piotrowski. I figured if he wants you to send Amanda and that girl away from home, some fairly sinister possibilities must be playing around in his mind, so I called him. He said he's had protection on you for the last few nights."

"He's *what?* Last *few* nights? I knew about New Year's Eve, but not about any others. Why didn't he tell me?"

"Hey, don't snap at me. I wasn't there. I'm just telling you what he told me." He stopped fidgeting with his water glass, and leaned toward me, into the argument now, comfortable again, bickering with me just like the old days.

"I'm not snapping," I snapped. "And why did you call him? I didn't ask you to get involved. Amanda was coming to visit anyhow." If that wasn't just like men. One minor request for help from a woman and they circle the wagons.

Tony's beeper went off. He reached down and pressed a button, and then seemed to forget about it. This was new. He used to head for the nearest phone at the first beep. "I called him"—he pursed his lips in a manner I had always found particularly self-righteous and annoying—"because . . ." And then he was off on some long, jargon-ridden, technical explication of crime analysis, methodologies of investigation, psychological profiles. . . . My temper flared.

"Face it, Tony, you didn't call him for any of those reasons. You called him because you didn't think I could handle myself. You called him because you were worried about me."

Interrupted in midsentence, he shut his mouth, reached across the table and took both of my hands in his. His blue Irish gaze was so full of our life together I could have walked into it as into an old familiar room. I could have walked into it and mislaid my life forever. "I called him," Tony told me, "because I am worried sick about you." I pulled my hands back a little, but he didn't let them go.

"Piotrowski says you're living way out in the woods, and you're too damn stubborn to even talk about going somewhere safer for a few days."

Stubborn? Piotrowski had said I was *stubborn?*

"Now listen to me, Karen. I want you to stay here, in the city, until this is cleared up. You can stay with me. You know how much room there is. Karen, stay here with Amanda and Sophia. It's for the best. You know I'm right."

If he had said *please,* instead of issuing commands, I might have stayed. But I never could stand anyone telling me what to do. He should have known that by now.

I finished about half of my angel-hair pasta with sun-dried tomatoes and porcini mushrooms, had the rest doggie-bagged, and, on an impulse, gave the bag to a homeless man on the corner of Columbus and Seventy-seventh. Tony and I argued all the way up Broadway to his apartment house. By the time we got there and he opened the massive front door with his key, we had stopped speaking, and we rode the elevator to the eighth floor in silence. The girls weren't home. The note Amanda left us said she had taken Sophia window-shopping and to see the tree at Rockefeller Center.

The apartment made me nostalgic. It was great in a particularly New York City way—a little shabby but spacious, with ten-foot ceilings, high, wide doorways, and tall rectangular windows looking out toward the river. I wandered around for a few minutes, just looking at things: the *torchère* floor lamp we had bought at the Bombay Company; the Indian rug from Ikea; the huge, extravagant arrangement of dried roses and eucalyptus leaves from a place on Madison Avenue. I wondered if Tony could ever forget me with all these things around. We had planned a life together, and I had put my mark on this place. The apartment made my little country house seem cramped and styleless. It *was* cramped and styleless, but until Amanda finished college and I paid off my own education loans, it was all I could manage. But this place—this place looked like home.

As he helped me back on with my black coat, the only thing I had with enough style to wear in Manhattan, Tony asked, "Are you sure you won't change your mind?"

"Tony, I'm hardly going to be there. I'll be in Boston and New Haven and God knows where until school starts again. I've told you that. I may even come back here. Wherever the research takes me. I haven't mapped it out yet. I'll let you know."

"Piotrowski had no right to drag you into this." Tony's lips set in a straight, hard line. "You're not a professional. And you're right—what you said before: I do think you *don't* know how to handle it, Karen. How could you? You're an *academic,* for God's sake. He had no right—"

"Piotrowski didn't 'drag' me into this. Whoever the killer is did that. I had just been talking to Randy, and he was trying to tell me something, but I wasn't listening. I wasn't listening! His body fell right out at me, for chrissake. And then my student . . . My God, Tony, I saw her corpse. Her face . . ."

"There's plenty of dead bodies. That doesn't mean you have to become one of them."

"Jesus, Tony, what do you think I'm planning to do—get involved in a shoot-out? I'm simply going to a few research libraries—noted for being secure places, by the way—and read through a few old papers. My God, some places you have to be interviewed before they let you in, and then you have to show your bona fides at the desk every day. And you're not allowed to take anything into the reading room but a pad and a couple of pencils. The first time I went to Harvard, I honest-to-God thought they were going to frisk me. And once you're in there, with your hands actually on the precious papers, you're under constant surveillance. What could happen?"

"Who knows what could happen? There's no good reason for you—"

"And you forget something, Tony. I may not be a professional when it comes to criminal investigation, but you could say I *am* a trained investigator. I know you don't think much of academics, but I have picked up a few skills along the way. I know how to do intensive research and close analysis. And, if I say so myself, I am a little more knowledgeable about nineteenth-century America than, say, your average street cop. I know how to look at evidence and wrest meaning from it. If Piotrowski is right, and there's something unsettling to be found in Randy's research material, I'll find it."

"I know you will. That's just what I'm afraid of."

By this point in the conversation we had moved from the living room to the apartment foyer. We were facing each other in our classic antagonist stance, feet apart, hands on hips, jaws set in righteous anger. Clearly neither of us was going to convince the other. It was time for me to leave.

As I fished through my tote bag for keys, Tony startled me by asking, "Do you still have your gun?" A few years earlier there had been a series of brutal rapes in the neighborhood, and Tony had somehow procured a handgun for me, a lethal little semiautomatic. Its provenance was shady, I'm afraid, having something to do with one of his drug busts. Then he had insisted on dragging Amanda and me up to a friend's weekend house in Columbia County every Sunday for shooting lessons in the back field. I was okay at it—adequately trained to hit a target cooperative enough to allow me time to steady my aim. Amanda, however, had become a crackerjack shot. She could hit anything. Tony had laughed and called her "Calamity Jane." I'd just stared at her in wonder. My secret fear was that she was passionate enough about this stuff to go into police work.

"Yes." My reply was impatient. "I still have the gun. It's right where you told me to keep it, in the bedside stand. And the clip is there, ready to hand, if I should need it."

"You remember everything I told you about using it?"

"Yes, for God's sake, Tony, I remember. But I'm not going to need your fucking gun." I was furious by now, glaring at him. "Why the hell are you smothering me like this? I'm a fully grown adult, and I can damn well take care of myself."

When I realized that I had just stamped my foot like a spoiled adolescent, I closed my eyes for a moment to calm myself and then smiled ruefully at Tony.

"Sorry. I know you're genuinely concerned; I shouldn't react like that. But really, I'll be fine."

We stood there in the foyer, silent and awkward, cooling off, and not quite knowing how to say good-bye. Like an idiot, I stuck my hand out to shake his. But Tony took me in his arms and kissed me so long and hard he left me breathless. Then he opened the front door, gently guided me outside, and shut the door. I stood there stone still until I heard the bolt slide shut, then I turned and headed slowly down the long hall toward the elevator.

By three o'clock I had turned the Jetta north on the West Side Drive. As if I needed more grief, the pale January sun that had shone on us during our morning's drive down gave up the struggle by the time I hit I-684 at White Plains. By Brewster and I-84, the clouds were pulled tighter across the sky than a hospital bedsheet. From Waterbury on, it sleeted all the way home.

Twenty

I HAD WRITTEN a dozen names on the yellow lined pad, names familiar to me such as the Reverend William Ellery Channing and the Reverend Henry Ward Beecher, and names I'd never seen before I began my research into nineteenth-century ministers. Randy, it seemed, had intended to run the entire gamut of midcentury American divines, from the most liberal to the most conservative. There were call slips for manuscripts from Unitarians, such as Channing, and evangelicals, such as the Reverend Thomas Skinner. How deeply he had intended to look into their work I had no idea. Simply thinking about reading all those sermons made my eyes glaze. To date, however, it would appear that he had dipped into their archives only randomly, testing the waters, I imagine. Perhaps testing his tolerance for crabbed handwriting, crabbed prose, and crabbed thinking. I hadn't read any nineteenth-century sermons yet, but I was already biased against them.

Next to each name on my list I wrote down the libraries where Randy had requested papers and the number of files he'd asked for. The evidence of the call slips in his office showed that the only preacher whose work he had looked at with more than perfunctory attention was Beecher, whose papers were deposited mostly at Harvard, Yale, and the New York Public Library. Good, none of these libraries was more than a few hours' drive from Enfield.

I leaned back in my desk chair, chewing on the top of my pen. Then I sat forward and drew an arrow next to Beecher's name. Then another. Then a third. This was where I would start.

Ignoring Piotrowski's warnings, I was working in my office at the college. It was quiet on campus, but not as quiet as it was at my all-too-quiet house now that Amanda and Sophia were gone. I missed them—the ceaseless beat of R.E.M., the bathroom cluttered with hairbrushes and apricot scrub, the burnt popcorn pans. The racket. The energy.

Sunlight shone in squares through the high window behind my desk, illuminating the work I had planned to do on my semester break—the essay I needed to revise for publication, the book I'd agreed to review. This was the work that would advance my career, but it paled beside more immediate concerns. I had begun this investigation with Piotrowski's per diem as incentive, but in the past few days the search itself had somehow taken on momentum. If Piotrowski and I were right—and there was always the possibility that we might both be off the wall here—someone, for some reason, found Randy's research sufficiently threatening to kill for. And not once, but twice.

I thought about the lieutenant's analysis of the killings as reactive rather than planned. With chin in hand I sat at my desk and stared at the name to which the arrows pointed. Was there any possibility that anyone alive in the final decade of the twentieth century could care passionately enough about the nineteenth-century Henry Ward Beecher to kill for him—impulsively or otherwise? *No,* I thought. *No. No. This is ludicrous. I must be on the wrong track here.*

I went back over the other names on my list: Horace Bushnell, W. B. Sprague, John Abbott—even less likely. Suddenly a sense of the futility of this endeavor overwhelmed me. If I'd thought it up on my own, I would have abandoned the investigation right then and there. But Piotrowski was a seasoned police investigator, wasn't he? He knew what he was doing, didn't he? Unless we were involved in some kind of delusional *folie à deux,* he did. Well, if he wanted to continue to shell out taxpayers' hard-earned money for this academic wild-goose chase, it might as well go to me rather than to some La-La Land psychic. At this point, however, I didn't have much more faith in any results I might produce than I would in those of a clairvoyant.

Let's see—what did I know about Beecher? I remembered telling Piotrowski about the affair with Libby Tilton that had rocked the nation in the 1870's. Did I tell him, I tried to recall, that it had actually gone to trial in 1875, with Theodore Tilton suing Beecher for alienation of affection? That the trial had lasted for six months and received international media attention? I knew I hadn't told him that, at one point, the reverend's sister, Isabella Beecher Hooker, outraged at his behavior, threatened to march into Plymouth Church in Brooklyn Heights when the renowned Henry was preaching from his illustrious pulpit and denounce him. Or that another sister, Harriet Beecher Stowe, even more famous than Henry, attended services with the express intent of stopping her. This stuff was worse—or better—than soap opera.

But that was such an old scandal and very well documented. It might emphasize the human frailty of even our most celebrated public figures—the uproar over Bill Clinton and Gennifer Flowers sprang to mind here, a blip on the screen compared to the Beecher brouhaha—but it certainly wouldn't cause anyone today to flip out to the point of unpremeditated murder.

I was deep in thought when someone knocked on my office door. I jumped, and the pen in my hand drew a crazed squiggle through Beecher's name. I shrugged; the squiggle seemed just as comprehensible an addition to my notes as anything else there. I scooped up the papers I'd been working on, dropped them into the center drawer, and shut it. "Who is it?" I called as I rose and walked to the locked door. Both the lock and the question were recent, due to Piotrowski's enjoinders of prudence.

"It's me." It was Greg's familiar, cheery voice. When I opened the door he continued, "Awful cautious all of a sudden, aren't you?"

"You never know. How'd you know I was here?"

"Easy—no one answered the phone at your house, and when I walked by the light was on in your office. How's that for brilliant deduction?"

"Awesome." I was in no mood for banter. "Did you want me for something in particular?"

"Well, I was going to invite you to dinner, but with a welcome like that maybe I'll invite someone friendlier—Attila the Hun, perhaps, or maybe even . . . Margaret Smith."

"That bad? I'm sorry. I'm just preoccupied. I'd love to come to dinner. If I can come as I am, that is." I looked down at my jeans and baggy red Gap sweater—not too bad, considering. And I didn't feel up to driving all the way home to change.

"You're fine. It'll just be you, me, and Irena, and God knows you don't have to look good for us. . . ."

"Thanks a lot, pal." I punched him on the arm.

"And," Greg continued with a flourish, "I'm making your favorite: angel-hair pasta with sun-dried tomatoes and porcini mushrooms."

"Yum." He didn't have to know I'd given half my last helping of this dish to a derelict on a Manhattan street corner just two days ago.

"Well, you look busy. See you around six for a drink?"

"Hang on, Greg. Are you in a rush? Or can I pick your brains for a few minutes?" In spite of Piotrowski's admonitions, I wanted to talk to Greg about Beecher. Without saying why, of course. Greg had an absolutely amazing mind. Facts, significant and trivial, adhered to it as if it were composed of Velcro. When I needed some obscure, recondite information I went to Greg first, then to the standard reference works.

"No, I can talk." He loped over to the green armchair and settled himself down willingly enough. Always ready for a good schmooze.

"What do you know about Henry Ward Beecher?" I pulled up the black Enfield captain's chair.

"Beecher? That sanctified lech?" He grimaced. "Why do you want to know?"

I waved my hand in a generally dismissive way—just curious. "I know you've done work on ethnicity in nineteenth-century America. I wondered if you'd run across him at all."

"Well, he didn't like the Irish, that's for sure. But then nobody did. I don't think they liked themselves much, either, from what I can tell. But other than that, I just know the general stuff—that he had an income of over forty thousand a year when the average working man's family was starving on less than a dollar a day; that he walked around with uncut gems in his pocket because he liked to run them through his fingers. That kind of stuff."

"That's the general stuff, huh?" It always amazes me what scholars think is common knowledge.

"Why do you want to know?"

"Oh, it's this article I've been thinking about—the one on the women writers. I've been reading about Stowe, and her brother keeps popping up. I couldn't believe that what I was reading was correct. Did he really hold slave auctions at Plymouth Church?"

"Better believe it, honey. Beecher's so-called 'auctions' were to raise money to buy the freedom of fugitive slaves, an admirable cause, of course. But for some reason most of the slaves 'auctioned' were female, light-complected, and young. He could whip a congregation into a frenzy by asking them to picture their sisters—their very own sisters—in the hands of just such lecherous masters as these young women had to deal with every day."

"Jesus."

We went on to talk about Beecher for a while longer. I didn't learn much that I hadn't already known. I did, however, confirm that Greg cared nothing about Beecher and didn't have the slightest suspicion that I was endeavoring to associate the reverend gentleman with our current violent happenings. We drifted off into other topics.

"So'd ya have a good time at our party?"

"It was great, Greg. I was just a little wiped out, especially by the end. I couldn't get into it as much as I wanted to."

"Yeah, I saw you just before you left. You looked

like you'd been hit by a snowplow. But it was a
swinging evening by Enfield standards, wasn't it?
People were really getting loose. Even Avery, for
God's sake. Did you see him with Magda?"

Here my renowned control came into play. "Oh,
yeah, I guess I did." Very cool. "I didn't know they
were an item."

"Well, I don't know for certain, but it sure looks
like they are. I'm surprised at his choice, but happy
he's found someone who, ah—interests him. He's
had a pretty rough time since—well . . ."

"His wife left him, right? And somebody said
something about Randy."

"Yeah, Avery's wife left him, all right." Greg's
mouth twisted, as if he had tasted something un-
pleasant. "Happened the first year I was here. She
was a real looker, Liz, a knockout, in a refined and
quiet manner. Looked a little like the young Kather-
ine Hepburn. From what I could tell they were fairly
happy together, at least until Astin-Berger started
making his moves."

"I thought she ran off with a musician."

"That's who Liz left with, but the whole thing
started with Randy. From what I heard, as soon as
he got tenured he started hitting on her. She must
have been a hell of a challenge to him—the president's wife. Think of the arrogance of that prick!"
Greg's tone was suddenly so bitter I wondered if he
had a *personal* reason for despising Randy. Certainly
Irena, who made a living by her looks, wouldn't have
escaped the notice of the campus Lothario. Hmm.

But Greg continued his story without personal disclosure. And I wasn't about to pry. "Everywhere Liz
went, there was Randy, admiring her clothes, the
way she walked, the books she read, playing tennis
with her, inviting her for walks through old grave-
yards and long afternoons in antiquarian bookstores.

All the things a busy college president wouldn't have time to do. Especially since he was cleaning up the mess ol' Bucky left behind.

"Well, as the quintessential Don Juan, Randy knew how to get what he wanted. It took a while, but he hooked her. Then she began to weary him, and he brushed her off, not very gently. Word got around, and Avery heard. I guess things were never the same between Avery and Liz after that. Months later she took up with this young composer from the Music Department. Ran off with him in the late spring, just after graduation."

"Wow."

"Avery was devastated. He took a leave of absence for the fall semester, and rumor had it he wasn't coming back. Pulled himself together, though, and he's been doing a great job ever since. Never saw him cozy up to a woman like he did the other night, though."

"Hmm. How interesting." And it was. Oh, it was.

"Speaking of Magda," Greg said, "she and *Randy* went way back. She's hinted to me that they were acquainted—*well* acquainted, if you get my drift—during Randy's Fulbright year in Budapest. But, oddly enough, I always thought they avoided each other while she was here."

"Did they? Well, I think now she's angling for another year at Enfield, Greg, or maybe something even more permanent. She certainly is giving Miles Jewell the full treatment—cleavage and all."

"Lucky Miles."

"Greg!"

"Hey—I'm only human! But you may be on to something. Could be Magda's got a better future here with Miles in charge of the department than if Randy had taken over."

I let Greg talk on about the latest complex maneuvers in the attempt to remove Miles from his stranglehold on the English Department. We all knew the Dean of Faculty had had Randy in mind for the position of department chair, and I'd offered up several little prayers of thanksgiving that now he would never be my boss. Sometimes I can be such a coldhearted bitch.

My mind wasn't really on the English Department, however. I was thinking about Greg's account of Avery's marriage. That explained Avery's reaction the night of Randy's death. I was pretty hazy about the ride home in his car, but even in my tranquilized stupor I'd noted that Avery was brooding. And hadn't he told me he detested Randy? Now I understood why. *Detest* would surely be too cool a word to describe the feelings of betrayal and loss Avery must have harbored for years. My God, the man screwed Avery's wife and then dumped her. *Hate* would certainly be a more precise term for Avery's feelings. If it were me, anyhow, *hate* would be the right word, but Avery was such a civilized human being. . . .

I began to speculate about the day he had called me into his office. What was that all about? He had asked a number of pointed questions. Was it possible that the real purpose of his summons was to see if I knew anything that would incriminate him? I couldn't believe I was thinking that. The implications . . . No! Avery couldn't possibly be the killer. I couldn't have been so naive as to trust a murderer. Could I? I knew there was something seriously wrong with that reasoning.

Greg was going on about Miles's tenacious grip on the English Department chairmanship. It was not solely an Enfield College eccentricity that people identified themselves so intensely with their role in the hierarchy, but—

"Greg," I interrupted, "speaking about Enfield eccentrics, you mentioned Margaret Smith before. What do you know about her? I had a very unsettling experience with her the other day." I told him about our encounter in front of the Y.

"Sounds just like Margaret. I wouldn't worry, Karen. Don't be afraid you've done something to offend her. She treats everyone like that, even her students. She's got the lowest course enrollments of anyone at Enfield. The Religion Department keeps assigning her the required courses—then the poor saps don't have any choice but to take her. Can't get rid of her, of course; she's been tenured since, oh, the New Deal." He grinned in conscious exaggeration.

"Did I hear she has a publisher interested in reading her book manuscript?"

"So she says. She's been working on that thing for generations, but nobody's actually seen it. She doesn't even give talks from it at professional conferences. Word is that it's a study of Emily Dickinson and God."

I groaned. Just what we needed, another attempt to skewer, categorize, and embalm Dickinson's multifaceted, ever-shifting—even comic—metaphysical inquiries.

"From what her students say," Greg went on, "it seems that she's prefeminist in her theology, so God knows what retrograde readings she gives to poor Emily's poems. And what she must do to Dickinson biography . . . It doesn't bear thinking about.

"Well," he added, as he rose and stretched. "I always love our little natters; I never know where they'll take us. But I'd better get on over to Giovanni's and get my shopping done if we're going to eat tonight. See ya later, kid. You really look washed out. You could use a good feed." He kissed me on the cheek, squeezed my arm and left.

I locked the door behind Greg, walked slowly back to the desk, sat down, and pulled my list of names out of the center drawer. It made no more sense to me now than it had an hour ago.

Later that afternoon I had an appointment with Miles to discuss my courses for the next fall semester. He was in his lair when I entered the English Department office; although I couldn't make out any words, I could hear his ponderous tones through the closed door. Magda's accents, too, emanated from the room, lilting coquettishly in the heavy academic air. Although the students wouldn't return for two and a half weeks, the department office was bustling this first day back from the Christmas holidays. I poured a cup of coffee and gossiped with the secretaries while I waited for Miles.

It was painful to have to think about next September's courses when I hadn't even begun to teach January's yet, but everything had been complicated by Randy's death. He and I together had covered the teaching of American literature to 1900, and now the English Department was short a crucial member of the team. Miles would know better than I what courses should be offered next fall, but I was also concerned about this upcoming semester's courses—and for purely selfish reasons. The students registered for Randy's Transgressive American Texts and American Sexualities courses would now be flooding my Survey of American Literature class and my course in Literary Realism in order to fulfill their Amlit requirements. I was about to be swamped.

After fifteen minutes, I'd exhausted department gossip and the current issue of *PMLA*. I'd begun to think about walking out when Miles's door opened, and Magda emerged. Today she was disguised as an American—form-fitting jeans, an unbuttoned-to-where-it-mattered white silk shirt, and gunmetal gray snakeskin cowboy boots.

"Darlink," she said, on seeing me, "zuch good news. Dearest Miles hass given me Randy's American literature courses; ve vill be colleagues, you and I." Her dangling silver-and-turquoise earrings jingled as she threw back her head and laughed with delight.

"What?" I was astonished. Magda's specialization was poetry writing, not American literature. "What about your writing courses?"

"Ach. Zo few students zigned up, I vas hafing to cancel. I vas afraid . . . But, nefermind—now I teach zis delicious Zexualities course. Und American Dransgression."

"But you don't have a degree in American lit—"

She shrugged, her hands spread wide. "Ze vicked little zgarlet letter. Ze naughty little Huck und Chim. How hard can it pe?"

Miles knew he should be ashamed of himself. His gaze was slippery as I perched on the edge of the straight chair next to his desk; rather than look directly at me, he fixed his eyes on a large metal clip holding together the sheaf of papers he kept fiddling with nervously.

Our discussion of the fall courses was brief and guarded. He didn't tell me if Magda would be staying over until September, and I didn't ask. His fixation on the manuscript—or whatever it was—in front of him drew my attention to the cluster of yellow, lined pages. Covered with a bold, left-slanting handwriting, they looked familiar. When Miles saw me scrutinizing the fascicle of pages, he dropped it on the desk, as if it suddenly had become thermonuclear. Then, somehow, it went missing under a pile of colorful English Department course-offering booklets. Miles was too late, though; I had already recognized the distinctive penmanship on the sheaf of papers I'd last seen on the floor of Randy Astin-Berger's office.

I was puzzled. Randy's radical politics had threatened everything Miles held dear about literary study. Miles had despised him. What use would any of Randy's unintelligible jottings be to him? One thing was certain, though: I had learned my lesson; I wasn't about to break into any offices to find out.

Twenty-one

I DO NOT LIKE the Enfield College library at the best of times. Even when sunlight streams through the narrow medieval arches of the leaded windows, gloom prevails. The library's dark corners, oddly sequestered oak benches, desks and carrels in out-of-the-way nooks, and eccentric circular staircases seem straight out of some deranged gothic imagination.

At four P.M. on a midwinter afternoon, sinister shadows abounded in the vaultlike chamber that housed the American religion stacks. I half expected to see Poe's raven leering at me from one of the dozen or so marble busts of American clergymen the college fathers had seen fit to commission for this room.

The religion stacks were lit only by fluorescent strip lights on the two side walls and the red Exit signs at either end of the room. This eerie combination cast a feeble and bloody glow over the high shelves and the marble busts in their secluded niches.

So few people visited the library during the semester break that individual stacks were lighted only as people used them. Each row of books had its own switch. Cost-efficient, perhaps, but a nuisance. I fumbled along the end of the shelving for the first light switch, then walked down the stacks, searching for the BX section, switching on lights here and there as I went.

The last time I'd been in this section of the library was when I'd visited Randy's carrel a week earlier with Piotrowski and a security guard, so my dead colleague was doubly on my mind as I made my way through the stacks. When the door to one of the carrels at the far end of the hall opened, I couldn't tell in the dim light who it was that emerged. My mind had only enough time to register *tall, male,* and *not Randy* before the figure vanished through the door at the top of the library's west staircase. Was it Randy's carrel this shadowy library patron had exited? And why hadn't he bothered to turn on any lights?

After I'd left Miles's office, I'd gone back to my own and had taken another look at my investigative notes. Then I'd put them away with a sigh. There was nothing more I could do with the sermon stuff until I actually got my hands on some manuscripts. Also, I needed to read the book, a history of nineteenth-century women's magazines, I'd agreed to review for *American Quarterly.* In a couple of days I would head for Cambridge, the closest research library being the Houghton at Harvard, but now I would do my own work. I picked up the history and began to read, but the words made no sense, were merely black ciphers on a white field. I couldn't keep my mind off the Reverend Mr. Beecher.

Other women had evidently had the same problem, but they'd all been dead for a long, long time.

I'd closed the book and stared at the cover. The jacket featured a *Godey's Lady's Book* fashion plate from the 1860s—a fragile blonde with a rosebud mouth wearing a full-skirted, multitiered magenta silk evening dress, her hair caught back in a black snood. She drooped fetchingly against a grand piano. Was this the type of woman whom dear Henry Beecher would have found attractive?

Goddammit. I might as well forget about doing anything else and see what I could find out about Beecher right here at Enfield. Surely the college library would have a study of this illustrious American.

BR, BS, BT—BX: Here it was. I flipped the switch and searched the shelves. Ah, yes, *The Meaning of Henry Ward Beecher*. Hmm. I pulled the volume off the shelf, blew a twenty-year accretion of dust from it, and settled down at a desk that had not been designed for a twentieth-century female anatomy. I tried hard to concentrate. Really, I did. But once again my attention wandered. Nothing I was reading here was of any possible relevance. My uninspired hands let the book fall shut of its own weight. My uninspired mind began a series of speculations, mostly involving the erotic misadventures of men in high places. My uninspired eyes roved aimlessly around the room, hesitating at one particular marble bust, and then moving on. When I found myself ruminating about Avery Mitchell and his love life, I pulled my imagination up short and gave it a rap on the knuckles. This day was undeniably shot. I might as well abandon all pretense of work.

I replaced the Beecher book where I'd found it, on a lower shelf that required awkward bending. As I rose from my crouch and turned to leave the room I suddenly, incomprehensibly, came face to face with

Henry Ward Beecher. Nose to nose we came, eyeball to eyeball. His countenance was ashen, his eyes stony and unseeing. A lurid red glow from the Exit sign above his head bathed the white shoulder-length hair in a wash of pink. I gasped.

The marble bust did not respond.

When I recovered from my shock, I took a closer look at the statue. Squinty, hooded eyes, prominent nose, girlish mouth, heavy cheeks, long straight hair—surely this was not a face that could possibly have launched a thousand amorous fantasies?

This place was really starting to get to me. Here I was, a rational, highly-educated, late-twentieth-century scholar speculating on the erotic attractiveness of a marble bust. It was time to get out. I headed toward the door and down the stone steps, worn concave by generations of book-laden students. The lighting in the stairwell was dim and the stone walls rough and pockmarked. I knew they weren't damp, cobwebbed, and menacing, but I was in the mood to see them that way. Picking up speed as I rounded the half-landing from the third floor to the second, I sprinted down the steps, rounded the landing from the second floor to the first—and collided full-length with Avery Mitchell.

Avery staggered and grabbed the banister to prevent himself from falling backward down the stairs. His armload of books went flying. I plopped down unceremoniously on the steps. He loomed above me, his face shadowed in the dim light. Unable to catch my breath, I fluttered a hand to my throat in a particularly feeble manner. We must have looked like heroine and villain in a 1930's horror film.

Avery reached out a hand to grab mine. "Are you okay, Karen?" His grip was strong, even for such a slender hand, and before I could protest that I'd rather get up by myself—thank you kindly, sir—he'd pulled me to my feet. A lock of sandy hair had flopped forward on his forehead, perhaps with the impact of our collision. As I resisted an impulse to reach out and push it back in place, he did so himself.

"You're very pale, Karen. Is everything all right? You know, you really are *white*. You look as if you've just seen a ghost."

"Maybe I have." I put some feeling into my reply. "Maybe I have." Then, in an attempt to regain some semblance of dignity, I began to apologize. "I'm so sorry, Avery. I don't usually go crashing into people. You must think . . ."

"Well, Karen, to tell you the truth, if I had to choose someone to collide with— Listen, I never know anymore when I'm in danger of making a sexist remark, so just forget I said that."

I smiled, wanly, I imagine. I have trouble myself with the fine line between the sexy and the sexist. To smooth over the awkwardness I bent to retrieve his books. Of course, this was the moment he chose to do the same, and our fingers clasped on a large red volume. I yanked my hand back immediately.

"Avery." I stood up bookless. "This has simply not been a good day for me. I think I'd just better go before I make things any worse."

"Don't worry about it. My day hasn't been terrific, either. You know what? How would you like a drink?"

Astonishment is not good for the brain. I looked around, stupidly, for a drink. Was he offering me a glass of water? A soda from a machine? What?

"I don't know about you," he continued, "but I could really use a stiff scotch."

"Oh, a *drink*."

"Yes. We could go to Rudolph's."

"Well, I'd like that. But—I have a dinner date."

He glanced at his watch. "It's only five. Surely you have time before dinner." Was it possible he was a little hurt? "But don't worry about it if you don't have time. I'll survive sober."

"Oh, it's only five?" What had I gotten into here? This was a no-win situation. I shouldn't spend any more time than I had to with a man I couldn't be rational about, but I certainly couldn't turn down a casual drink with my boss. "Five? I thought it was later. Sure, I'd love to go for a drink."

"Good. Let me put these books in my carrel and I'll meet you by the desk." He smiled, his blue eyes crinkling at the corners in a way I'd never noticed before, and bounded up the stairs, lean, athletic, and—dammit—fascinating.

Rudolph's, with its tropical murals, thatched roof over the bar, and bar stools with high chrome risers and caned seats, was crowded with the usual happy-hour denizens. As in any other upscale Northeast watering hole, the younger group was now health-conscious, sipping Perrier or wine spritzers. The older drinkers remained faithful to their martinis and manhattans. No one was smoking.

College types filled the bar. Miles Jewell and a couple of his henchmen conspired over tall glasses of dark beer. Magda Vegh was just leaving them. She had a senior member of the religion faculty in tow. Her soft hair dipped beguilingly over one eye, and she had added an oversized brown leather jacket to her jeans and cowboy boots. The theologian couldn't take his eyes off her. Her own eyes flickered in our direction when Avery and I entered the room, then swiftly slid back to her latest conquest. I watched her glide out of the bar with a sense that I was missing something significant, that some odd detail had just glanced off my consciousness. Then my attention was caught by Ned Hilton, who sat at a small table by the window talking to Jill Greenberg. Shoulders slumped, face drawn, he was waving his hands distractedly and monopolizing the conversation. Jill's fiery hair was pulled back in a tight bun at the nape of her neck. Any errant strands had been severely disciplined with mousse and barrettes. She wore no makeup. In a white turtleneck and black sweater, she looked demure and innocent, like a little Jewish nun. The total effect was delicious. I doubt Ned even noticed.

Avery's trip to his carrel to dispose of his books had allowed me time to recover my self-control, and as we elbowed our way up to the bar, standing for our first drink, sitting for the second, we had a genuinely enjoyable conversation—light, witty campus gossip; light, erudite book talk; light, circumspect personal disclosure. I completely forgot the possibility that I might be drinking with a murderer.

Avery orchestrated the conversation, in the way that only the truly sophisticated can, to touch exclusively on unproblematic issues. As a conversationalist, he was a virtuoso, banishing my embarrassment and confusion with humor and self-deprecation, causing the spotlight of his attention to shine only on my very best verbal pliés and pirouettes. Then, concluding a witty commentary about fellow party-goers at Greg's New Year's Eve party, he startled me. "And you . . ." he reached out and squeezed my hand gently before relinquishing it almost immediately, "you looked absolutely stunning."

Never one to accept compliments gracefully, even when unruffled, I replied with abject stupidity. "So did Magda," I said. And then I wanted to die.

Avery seemed taken aback. Then he spoke carefully and in lowered tones. "Well, yes. But, then, one expects that from Magda. The central purpose of Magda's life is to look sensational. But with you it's—well—an occasional by-product of a life lived for varied purposes. And a delightful by-product, if I may say so."

I was stunned speechless. But Avery went on smoothly, seemingly not noticing my discomfiture, to discuss Hungarian politics, and the differing political responses of Hungary and Yugoslavia to the breakup of monolithic Communism. Cool. Very cool.

When I regained my composure, I sat back in the low-backed bar stool and regarded Avery as dispassionately as I could. He was dressed casually in gray cords, a charcoal gray mock-turtleneck jersey, and a heavy black zip-up sweater. The dark colors emphasized the long line of his jaw and shadowed his eyes, which were now the murky blue-green of a choppy northern sea. As he spoke, he moved his slender hands with instinctive grace.

The charisma of this man was so natural and persuasive that I just about gave up and succumbed. But some small, remote, annoyingly rational node of consciousness wouldn't quit. Kept suggesting that, for some reason, incomprehensible to me, I was being deliberately charmed. The funny thing was that I didn't give a damn. *Charm away,* I thought. *Beguile me. Captivate me. I like it.*

And then, about halfway through our second drink, Avery's mood changed rather abruptly. He fell silent. As the cocktail chatter swirled around us, he met my attempts at picking up the small talk with abstracted smiles. Then, eyes focused on his glass, he spoke quietly. "I don't know why I do this." With long, slender fingers he smoothed out the lock of sandy hair that had fallen again across his forehead. That was it. Just "I don't know why I do this." And silence.

After waiting in vain for elaboration, I asked, hesitantly, "Do what?"

"This performance I'm putting on." He looked over his shoulder, away from me, as if suddenly taking an intense interest in our fellow drinkers. Following his gaze I saw Ned smile wanly and wave his arm to attract his petite blond wife Sara, who was ushering their two little girls through the restaurant's front door. As Ned introduced her to Jill, I brought my attention back to Avery.

"I don't . . . know what you mean."

"Oh, I spin this web of—what?" He looked up at the ceiling fan and rubbed the fingertips of his right hand together as if trying to conjure up an elusive word.

"Charm?" I couldn't help it. It just popped out.

"Charm. Yes. Charm. . . . You noticed." He smiled briefly, a flash of fine patrician teeth. Then he took another sip of his scotch and looked directly at me for the first time in five minutes. "I'm very good at charm, you know." I nodded. "It's a form of insulation. It protects me from human contact, or so my ex-wife informed me on any number of occasions. And when a situation threatens to get out of hand, it allows me total control. Liz never liked that about me, my need for total control." His voice tightened when he mentioned his wife. He looked down into his drink again. When he spoke his words were so quiet I almost didn't hear them. "But I don't know how else to handle you."

I felt as if my breath had been sliced in half by a very thin, exceedingly sharp knife.

"Really?" It was more a sigh than a word.

"You intrigue me." He glanced cautiously around the bar, and then looked directly at me again. His blue eyes held a wistful curiosity. "But it wouldn't work, you know." He shook his head, with slow, determined emphasis. "I won't put you in that position." His eyes focused intently on the South Seas mural over the bar.

"Avery." I reached over to touch his hand. He pulled it away and stood up immediately.

"Let's get out of here." He grabbed my jacket and held it for me to put on.

The crowd at the bar was dense and our seats were commandeered almost before we relinquished them. Avery took my arm to guide me through the crush. Pushed against me by the crowd, he spoke directly into my ear. "I'm tired and I don't usually drink this much anymore, and the booze is talking, and I'm making a fool of myself. Forget I said anything."

I didn't reply until we had left the restaurant. In Enfield, even the doorknobs have ears.

"Avery," I said, as we began the short walk to the college parking lot. "You can't really expect me to forget you said anything—"

"God," he interrupted. "I've put you in an awful position, haven't I?" He stopped in the shadow of the library wall. He had, I noticed, let go of my arm. "Karen, I'm sorry. Listen. I want to get something clear. Don't exaggerate what I'm saying to you. All I'm saying is that I'm attracted to you, nothing more. I'm attracted to you, but it won't work. Given our relative positions here at the college, it would be extremely—shortsighted—for me to get involved with you. And it wouldn't be ethical. I feel very strongly about that. All the issues it raises . . ."

I knew he was thinking about the fierce faculty-meeting battles about sexual harassment and abuse of power. I opened my mouth to protest, but he kept right on.

"I should have kept quiet about it but I was making such an ass of myself. . . . Well, I wanted you to know there was a reason."

"Avery, you weren't making an ass of yourself. And I find you—well—enormously attractive."

"But?" he broke in.

"No *but,* just enormously attractive. It's only that you've caught me off guard. I—"

He reached up, as if to stroke my cheek, but let his hand drop without touching me. "Karen, listen to what I'm going to say, and then I'd better go. I will not call you. Don't expect to hear from me other than in the normal course of things. I mean that. I know you've worked hard to get where you are. I will not complicate it for you."

All I wanted at that moment was his arms around me. The hell with sexual ethics. The hell with my career. That bothersome little core of rationality was sinking fast. I reached out my gloved hand. Maybe I could just touch his arm.

But then he said, "And—I know this makes me an SOB—but it would be disastrous for me, too. I just can't take the heat right now. You know how the shit would hit the fan if I started fraternizing with an untenured woman." He said "fraternizing" ironically, to stress its absurd inadequacy to the whole extraordinarily complicated business of erotic life.

His words arrested my caress. I put my hand in my pocket. He was right. He *was* an SOB. A cold, calculating son of a bitch, and I would never forgive him. But he was also right on the mark. Any relationship between us, in this place and at this time, would be disastrous, for both of us.

I wanted him to kiss me anyhow. Just one little

kiss, I thought, what could it hurt? But he didn't. He squeezed my arm gently, gazed at me soberly for a heartbeat, then turned and strode away toward Emerson Hall. I watched him go. In the deep winter shadow of the library, my lips were cold.

Twenty-two

I SAT ON THE EDGE of my bed with the phone to my ear and listened as its ring shattered Piotrowski's sleep. At least I assumed he was asleep—it was 3:17 A.M. It was two nights after my encounter with Avery and record cold, even by New England January standards.

"Piotrowski." He picked up on the second ring, speaking in an uninflected tone, fully alert, revealing nothing. He sounded just like Tony. They must learn it at cop school.

"Piotrowski, we're on the wrong track." My voice, in contrast, was high and rushed. "These killings have nothing to do with Randy's research. I just woke up from a dream about corpses and it all fell together. The killer is—"

"Karen Pelletier? Is that you?"

"Yes, Piotrowski. Of course it's me. Now, you see—"

"Do you know what time it is?"

"Yeah, I know. It's an ungodly hour, but—"

"Has something happened?"

"No." I was losing patience. "No. But I've solved the murders!"

"In your sleep? You've solved the murders in your sleep? An entire team of highly trained homicide investigators has been working on this thing day and night, and you've solved it *in your sleep?*" It sounded like the unflappable Piotrowski was annoyed.

"Are you angry or something, Piotrowski?"

"Oh, no. I get far too much sleep. I always appreciate being woken at—what?—three-nineteen—by someone wanting to talk about her dreams. Keeps me from dreaming too much myself."

"Well, I didn't want to talk about my dreams, exactly. . . ." The lieutenant's uncharacteristic sarcasm was beginning to cool me down. Perhaps my middle-of-the-night epiphany wasn't so brilliant after all. Perhaps this phone call in itself was part of a lunatic nightmare. I pinched the back of my hand to see if I was dreaming. I wasn't.

At about a quarter after three I had awakened suddenly from a dream about bloodless corpses sprawled across a freshly mopped library floor. One of them seemed to be crying. I woke with the image of tears on an alabaster face only to hear a car slow on the road outside my bedroom window. As the desolate sobbing of the corpse blended into the sound of the car's motor, it struck me, with sudden heart-stopping clarity, that Piotrowski and I had been totally wrong in our assumptions about the motivation for the two murders. Randy's scholarship had nothing to do with them. With the cold, clear, rational certainty of dead-of-the-night insights, I came to the conclusion that the killer must be Stan Warzek, Sophia's father. My next thought was that Piotrowski had to know. And right away. But now, in light of the detective's reaction . . .

"Piotrowski, I'm sorry. I guess I should've waited till morning. I must be cracking from the stress. But it just seemed so clear all of a sudden."

"Well, Doctor, you might as well go on." He spoke grudgingly. "Now that you've got me awake anyhow." A vague image of Piotrowski in bed flashed into my mind. I tried to clarify it. Would he be sitting on the edge of the mattress as I was? Or would he be lying down? These were not questions I could ask him without sounding like a heavy breather. *Are you alone? Are you wearing pajamas?* God, woman, I thought, what's the matter with you?

The room was freezing and the telephone cord wasn't long enough to let me reach the thermostat in the hall. I burrowed back under the blankets. Even thermal socks couldn't keep my feet warm.

"Well, a few minutes ago I was awakened by a car going past the house very slowly. It was loud and seemed to take forever to get past. Or maybe that was part of the dream—"

"What time did this car go by?" The question slashed through my explanation.

"About—well, exactly—three-fifteen. I looked at the clock right away."

"And it was loud? You mean like it had a bad muffler?"

"Well, yes. But—"

"Then it wasn't the patrol car."

"*What* patrol car?"

"The one that's been keeping an eye on your house."

I sat up in bed again, letting the covers fall back. "Jesus Christ, Piotrowski! Why don't you tell me these things so I don't make a fool of myself calling in the middle of the night?"

"You're not listening to me, Dr. Pelletier. I just said it *wasn't* the patrol car. Listen, I'm sorry I snapped at you. I know you wouldn't call without a reason. It's just that I figured I might actually get to sleep all the way through the night tonight. But I guess not. So, go ahead. Tell me what you've been thinking."

Some retrograde part of my brain decided the man must be sleeping alone. Otherwise he surely would have switched to another phone before he settled in for a long conversation. I filed that fact away for future reference.

I told him my revelation, although I was nowhere near as certain about it as I had been when it first flashed into my mind. I phrased it more tentatively than I had planned. "Piotrowski, why couldn't Sophia's father have been the killer?"

"What makes you say that?" His voice on the other end of the line was very still.

"Well, it's obvious, Lieutenant. Think about it. He comes to work at the college because his plant closes down. Some busybody tells him about Randy and Sophia. He gets furious—he's got a savage temper—and strangles Randy. Then—maybe that busybody was Bonnie Weimer, you know—he kills Bonnie so there won't be any witnesses. It all fits together, don't you see?"

"Oh, yes, it does. Very neatly. And, of course, it isn't as if we haven't seriously considered that possibility. . . ."

"Oh." I felt deflated. Of course he had; that was his job.

"But that leaves some leftover pieces. Like why would Warzek search Astin-Berger's office?"

"Ah—maybe looking for incriminating letters, so the police—you—wouldn't get them? And—he would have had a passkey. For cleaning, you know."

"I dunno, Doctor, as far as we can tell, he wasn't at the president's house the night of the Christmas party. There were a couple of maintenance people there, but not Warzek. Unless—"

"Unless he came in wearing his uniform and nobody noticed him. They wouldn't, you know. I hate to say this, but any one college worker would look to the faculty like any other. Especially after a few glasses of champagne."

"Right. But his wife says he was home with her. Didn't feel well that night and called in sick."

"Well, she would, wouldn't she? She'd say anything he told her to."

"Yeah, but . . . And would he have computer expertise? Unless it was someone other than the killer who trashed Astin-Berger's office. . . . I don't know, Dr. Pelletier. We'll keep looking into it, of course. But it doesn't really fit my theory."

His *theory?* I longed to say something snide about people who force facts to fit theories, but I glanced at the clock and saw that it was almost a quarter to four. I was seized by a fit of contrition. "I'm sorry, Piotrowski, I should have known you would have considered that. I'm sorry I woke you up. I'm sorry. I'm sorry. I hope you can get back to sleep now."

"I'll have to make a coupla calls first. One thing is, I want to send officers over to look around your place. So don't be alarmed if you hear someone outside."

"Why on earth—?"

"Don't you remember the car, the noisy one that woke you up? I'm just a little concerned about what someone was doing, slowing down in front of your house in the dead of the night."

"Oh. . . ."

"Again. Remember New Year's Eve? Oh, and Dr. Pelletier . . ."

"Yes?"

"How do you know Warzek has a—I think you said 'savage'—temper?"

I told him about Warzek's visit to my office and the nasty scene at my house on Christmas Eve. And the call to Sophia in which he'd said I "wasn't going to get away with it."

Piotrowski's response was low and controlled. "And you didn't think to tell me about this harassment?"

"Well, it wasn't harassment, exactly. . . ."

"Sounds like harassment to me. You hear from this creep again, Dr. Pelletier, you get on the phone to me immediately. Ya got that?" He was really pissed.

"But I didn't—"

"You didn't *what*?"

"I didn't want to make him any madder than he already was. I figured it would only make a bad situation worse for Sophia if he found out I'd been talking to the police about him—"

"That is really *stupid!*" He was angry now and no longer holding it back. "Dr. Pelletier, I hope you don't mind my saying this, but did you ever think that for a very, very smart woman there's sometimes something a little *off* in your thinking processes? You *didn't want to make a bad situation worse!* Jesus Christ!" He paused. The line was dead quiet. "Just think about what you're doing, will you? Just fucking *think!*" The silence between us crackled. He said, "I'm not going to say another word. Good night, Doctor." He slammed down the receiver.

Fifteen minutes later, a state police patrol car pulled unobtrusively into my driveway, its motor silenced immediately. Two troopers got out and stood quietly, listening, I assumed. Another car pulled in a minute or two later. The officers surveyed the road, the yard, and the surrounding woods, their powerful flashlights slicing through the dark.

Finally a female trooper, the tall athletic blonde I remembered from the site where Bonnie's body was found, came to the house to ask if I was okay. Next to her bulky blue uniform jacket and pants, her heavy black boots, I felt frivolous in the hot-pink chenille robe Tony had given me. "We'll be around again." She was formal and polite, the strong Nordic planes of her handsome face stern under the wide brim of the trooper's hat. "We'll keep an eye on things." I could see her breath freezing in the frigid night air.

She turned to go, then turned back again. "The lieutenant says for you to go back to bed now." She flashed me a wicked grin and left.

Twenty-three

THE SUN was warm enough the morning I left for Cambridge to melt snow from the roof. Outside the kitchen window a four-foot icicle relinquished its frigid heart drip by reluctant drip. Rinsing out my coffee mug in the sink, I watched the icicle's demise until the sunshine glaring off its tip dazzled me.

It had been two days since my lunatic predawn phone call to Piotrowski, and in a couple of subsequent calls we had smoothed over the embarrassment caused by my impulsiveness and his harsh words. Even so, I was just a little nervous about seeing him again.

I toted my overnight bag and briefcase out of the house and threw them into the backseat of the Jetta. Piotrowski and I were having breakfast in Enfield. After that I planned to drive to Cambridge to research Henry Ward Beecher's papers at Harvard's Houghton Library. I glanced back at the house before I got in my car. It looked so safe and peaceful, nestled in the woods, with its peeling white paint and the water dripping hypnotically from its eaves. I was puzzled by my sense of relief at getting away from it for a while.

Piotrowski was at the counter of the Blue Dolphin, but he was not alone. Dressed in his truly ill-fitting gray suit, he was deep in conversation with a uniformed trooper. A miniature trooper, I thought, until she turned and I saw that she was an average-size young woman—not what my conditioning had led me to expect a state police officer to be.

"Oh, hello, Dr. Pelletier." The lieutenant was conspicuously nonchalant about my arrival, but didn't seem to be harboring any grudges. I relaxed a little. "I'll be with you in a minute. I have to finish up something with Trooper Schultz here. Do you mind waiting in one of the booths?"

Trooper Schultz looked at me, speculatively it seemed, and then turned back to Piotrowski. The sun through the window highlighted her roundish cheeks and very plain, unmade-up face, lent red highlights to her severely cut short brown hair. Surely no officer of the law should have such long eyelashes, I thought fleetingly, then chided myself for residual sexism. *I'm sure she's extremely competent,* I told myself, righteously. Then I turned my attention to the waitress and her offer of a menu and coffee.

I waited for Piotrowski to join me before placing my order of toast, sausages, and home fries. He ordered two poached eggs and an order of butterless whole wheat toast, coffee, and two large glasses of ice water. Hold the fries. I studied him more closely as he folded his menu and handed it to the waitress. His gray jacket was bagging under his arms and overlapping at his waist, overly large even for the good-size man sitting across from me. The planes of his countenance seemed more positively defined, as if a lens had suddenly come into clear focus, the flat cheekbones more prominent, a rugged jawline beginning to emerge, the full lips more sensuous now in the indubitably thinner face. Had something in my vision shifted, or . . . ?

"Piotrowski, are you on a diet?"

"Under orders." His voice was gruff and he flushed slightly, whether with embarrassment or with gratification that I had noticed I couldn't tell. "Captain's on a health kick." Then he shut those nice lips—very nice lips—firmly. Not going to say another word about it.

"Well . . ." Perversely, I wanted to tease him, to even the score just a little. "It's very becoming to you, anyhow." And I raised my eyebrows. His flush turned into a full-fledged, red-faced blush and I was immediately sorry. After all, I certainly knew how it felt to be sensitive about your appearance.

"Hurrumpph." He lifted the big white coffee mug to his lips, effectively hiding them, and his eyes, from view.

When he finally emerged from behind the mug, I told him about my plans for the next few days. I would go to the Houghton, which had about thirty folders of Beecher material, and read through the files until I was done. God only knew how long that would take. Until my eyes gave out from the strain of reading, probably, and my butt from the strain of sitting. If I didn't find anything there, I'd go on to Yale, and then to New York. I'd concentrate on Beecher, but I'd look at the other stuff as well— whatever Randy had requested. But I couldn't guarantee anything. This was all a wild shot in the dark.

"I know that," he said when I had finished my agenda. "And I appreciate that we may be on the wrong track here. But I want you to keep in close touch with me, anyhow. Call me a coupla times a

day and just talk. Talk about anything and everything—what you looked at, what it suggests, who
you talked to, what you had for lunch, where you ate
it. Doesn't matter if it's important or not—I want
everything. Ya got that?"

"Yeah, but—"

"No *but* about it. Just do it. You may be investigating the research, but I'm investigating the homicides. I need to know everything. Ya never know
when the most trivial detail is gonna knock everything else into place. If I could go with you I would.
But"—and he grinned ruefully—"I'd be pretty con-
spicuous in a library."

Not if you got a new suit, you wouldn't, I
thought. And indeed, there was something scholarly
about that high, wide forehead, something serious
and thoughtful about those brown eyes.

"You know how to get ahold of me at home
now?" His expression was bland, but I could detect a
gleam in his eye. I nodded, warily. "I mean what I
said—if you stumble across anything, call me. Don't
worry about it. I'm sorry I was testy with you the
other night."

I nodded again, slightly shamefaced. The wee-
hours phone call was still a sore spot. What embarrassed me the most, I guess, was my arrogance in
thinking that I could solve the murders in a brilliant
flash of intuition when the professionals had already
considered Warzek as a suspect and discarded him.
What for me had seemed like ingenious deduction,
for Piotrowski had simply been part of the ABC's.

Piotrowski sat back in the booth and carefully
eased his empty breakfast platter over to the edge of
the table, wiping the space in front of him with his
paper napkin. Then he crumbled up the napkin and
placed it on the platter, on top of the yellow egg
smears and toast crumbs. He brushed his hands to-

gether, as if to remove any recalcitrant crumbs. He finished his first glass of water and began on the second. I messed around with my fork and my second sausage. A small silence had fallen between us, and I was no longer very hungry.

Then he spoke, somewhat brusquely, as if he had been undecided about telling me something and had just this moment made up his mind to do it. "You're gonna have to be extra careful about what you do and where you go. Who you talk to. This isn't a game of Trivial Pursuit we're playing here, and I'm taking a lot of heat about getting you involved. High-level heat."

"Oh, yeah?" I was beginning to have my suspicions. "From whom are you taking heat?"

He winced, probably at my grammatical prissiness. "Just the brass, you know. They're a little antsy about getting untrained personnel involved."

"What do you mean 'untrained'? I know what I'm doing."

"That's not what I mean, and you know it. I mean untrained in criminal investigation."

"Why should it matter to them? I know it's not unusual to hire outside consultants. You told me so. Who's leaning on you, Piotrowski? Is it Tony?"

"Captain Gorman has made a few calls." Piotrowski's nice lips were now set in a tight line.

"Goddammit." I slammed my fist down on the table so hard my fork and knife leapt up off my plate and came down again with a loud clatter. Two elderly faculty wives in the booth across from us looked at me askance. I'd be fodder for the gossip mills at this week's bridge game. Losing my temper in public. Associating with poorly dressed men. Enfield just hasn't been the same since women were allowed on the faculty.

I lowered my voice in deference to the great god

Rumor. Enfield offers very little privacy. One has to resort to all sorts of wiles and stratagems simply to ensure oneself the basic American freedom of a private personal life. I leaned over the table so Piotrowski could hear my lowered tones. He had noticed our neighbors' interest as well, and leaned toward me. Whatever my colleagues' wives had thought before was assuredly intensified now by the secrecy of our manner.

"Piotrowski," I was almost whispering, "I can't tell you how furious I am that Tony Gorman has involved himself in this. Not only has he no right to mess in my life, he also has no business interfering in your jurisdiction. I simply can't believe he's done this, and when I get in touch with him I'll make it quite clear to him how I feel." The abstraction of my language didn't begin to convey the bloody hell I was going to give Tony as soon as I could get my hands on him. "I really am sorry, Lieutenant. If he's caused you any trouble, I apologize."

He shrugged his burly shoulders. No problem. He could take the heat.

"And, further, even if you pulled me off this investigation right this minute, I'd go to Cambridge on my own time and do what I'd planned to do anyhow, simply because when I start something I finish it."

He looked at me, expressionless.

"Yeah, you're right. Also out of sheer hardheaded orneriness. Goddammit! Nobody tells me what to do. And, especially, what *not* to do!"

He sat back and folded his hands on the table in front of him. He nodded. Then he spoke, slowly and with some pauses for thought. "Also, you're curious. Right? Am I right about that? This whole thing is so—mystifying. Right? It seems to be a mystery from two centuries, and that's got you hooked. It's like one of those anatomy overlays in a biology textbook.

You got Astin-Berger dead. You got the Weimer girl dead. You got his office tossed. That's one sheet—the one from the 1990s. But that page isn't quite transparent, is it? Underneath you see another picture. That's from the 1800s. But it's not clear to you yet. It'll never be clear to me because I've only got modern eyes. But you, you've got nineteenth-century eyes, like you can put on a pair of magic glasses and read the past, see right through the overlay. You're just itching to see through to that bottom page. Am I right?"

I sat there, openmouthed with astonishment at his metaphor, and at how precise it was. "Whatever made you think of a biology textbook?"

"What? You think I never went to college?"

I guess I had, but that wasn't the point. And besides, it didn't really matter.

"What I mean is you're absolutely right." I spoke with a kind of self-pitying melancholy. "I do have nineteenth-century eyes. Everywhere I go I see the past. It's lurking there, just beneath the present. New towns built on old foundations. New scandals spun from old desires. New storytellers telling old tales. Sometimes as far as I'm concerned the present isn't real at all. It's all merely overlay."

I fell silent, remembering an uncanny experience I'd had once while researching at the American Antiquarian Society. I'd spent the entire day reading through the *New York Tribune* for the year 1848. I was looking for anonymously published poems by a popular woman poet, but could I restrict myself to the poetry section? No, I damn well couldn't. I read everything: poems, politics, financial news, gossip columns, advertisements—even the shipping news. At the end of the day, when I lifted my eyes from the leatherbound volume of the crumbling newspaper, for one microsecond I was *in* the nineteenth century.

And it was alive—swarming with life. Then I shook my head to clear it and the modern world, with its too-bright colors and its too-loud noises and its too-intrusive realities, came roaring back into my consciousness.

I didn't think I'd tell Piotrowski that story.

"Well, it isn't," he said.

"What? What isn't what?"

"The present. It's real. It isn't all overlay."

"I know that." His admonishment annoyed me.

"I thought you knew it. But what you said was so beautiful, it convinced me you meant it." He grinned at me, as if we were amused together at my poetic self-indulgences.

"You love it when I talk pretty, huh?" I grinned back. God, this man knew more about me than he needed to.

He paid for our breakfasts, noted the expense in his little book, and took off in the red Jeep. I picked up a *New York Times* from a rack by the door and carried it over to the register. Then I waded out through the slushy mud to my car.

When I pulled out of the Blue Dolphin's parking lot, a noisy brown car followed close behind me. Around here there are a lot of old cars, but they're usually Volvos. This one wasn't. I didn't know *what* it was; I'm not exactly good with cars. So I didn't pay much attention until I turned off the winding country road onto Route 2, and the old sedan turned, too. Then I began to watch it in my rearview mirror. I was thinking, of course, about the noisy car outside my bedroom window a few nights back. *This* clunker stayed one car behind me for about ten miles. One car-length away, whether I sped up or slowed down. Just when I began to think about finding a phone, the driver turned off at a sign pointing south toward Amherst and Northampton. It was then I remembered Piotrowski had told me the car checking out my house on New Year's Eve was a rusty brown Plymouth Duster.

Was this car a Duster? I didn't have a clue. But I was grateful it was daylight and the roads were busy. And I tucked the little happening away to tell Piotrowski. At least this time he wouldn't be able to scold me for withholding information.

Twenty-four

CAMBRIDGE was its usual wintertime self—cold, crowded, icy underfoot. Walking down Massachusetts Avenue toward Harvard Square, I navigated piles of filthy, ossified snow and picked my way around the homeless people who increasingly populate the center of town. In front of the Harvard Square T entrance, next to the Out-of-Town-Newspapers kiosk, a short, plump woman wearing a full-length navy blue quilted coat stood, sobbing loudly and hopelessly. In one hand she clutched an Au Bon Pain paper coffee cup, in the other a sandwich bag. A longtime urbanite, I've become passive in the face of human tragedies that a decade ago would have caused me to spring into action, but this woman got to me. Never before have I heard anyone actually cry out "boo," "hoo," "boo," "hoo," as if they were actual words in the English lexicon. But I suppose the real reason I paused was that she looked enough like my mother to be her clone.

I stood there, not knowing what I should do, what I *could* do. Just then a young Cambridge cop walked over, bent down, and put his arm around the woman's shoulder, as if he had spoken to her before and knew what would comfort her. He led her to one of the stone benches by the T entrance, sat down with her, and helped her pry open the lid of her coffee cup. I watched as the woman chatted happily with him and sipped her coffee. He opened her paper bag for her and spread her sandwich out on a large paper napkin. I turned away and walked on toward the Houghton. She wasn't my mother, and there was nothing I could do for her.

I had arrived in Cambridge at about one o'clock and parked my car in the driveway of my friend Charlotte's house. Charlotte's place on Huron Avenue is my base whenever I come to the Boston area. It was semester break, and Charlotte was out of town. She professes to love Cambridge, but leaves it whenever she can. I brought my bag in and plunked it down on the red-and-black dhurrie rug in the tiny guest room on the third floor. Then I made myself a cup of tea and sat for a while in the book-lined living room while I drank it. Charlotte collected old books, and her living room—with cloth-bound and leather-bound volumes catalog on three walls of shelves, displayed proudly on small tables, and piled in corners waiting to be shelved—was comfortable, like a shabby English library. I leafed reverently through the three-volume first edition of *Jane Eyre* she kept displayed on a Chippendale table by the couch, and browsed through the books in a stack awaiting shelving.

Then, fortified by the tea, I set out for the long trek to Harvard, an ambitious and gritty walk. By the time I arrived at Harvard Square, succumbed to the lure of the Harvard Bookstore, ate a bowl of chili at Mr. Bartley's Gourmet Hamburgers, and was ready to attack the Houghton, it was half past three, an hour and a half before the library closed. That would give me enough time to go through the card catalog and fill out call slips for the items I wanted to see—which, since I had no idea what I was looking for, was everything in the Beecher archives. I got writer's cramp just thinking about filling out all those little spaces on all those little cards.

As I was crossing Massachusetts Avenue toward the high brick wall that surrounds the Harvard campus, I was startled to hear someone call out, "Karen. Karen Pelletier!" Looking up, I saw the tall, dispirited figure of Ned Hilton shuffling toward me through one of the lofty brick archways. His face was drawn, his angular features tight with anxiety. He wore a red hooded jacket and black hand-knitted mittens. His black scarf was wrapped tight around his neck and chin as protection against the increasingly blustery wind. In this getup he looked frail and vulnerable, like a boy, dressed by his mother, who had unexpectedly found himself stretched into a weedy, underdeveloped adulthood.

"Well," I said, after we'd exchanged greetings, "you can't get away from Enfield, can you, no matter where you go." I was only half joking.

"Half of Enfield heads directly for Cambridge as soon as school is out." Ned's diction, as usual, was precise, almost pedantic. "It's a primal herd instinct for academics, I think. Like lemmings heading off cliffs into the sea." Although his tone was wry, his metaphor reinforced my sense that he was teetering on the verge of desperation.

The wind had picked up, and the sun was hanging low in the sky, no longer lending warmth to bleak city streets. Awkward together, acquaintances rather than friends, neither of us knew the proper decorum for this unexpected encounter. Shifting from foot to foot, we tried to keep our toes from freezing while we continued to make small talk. Ned started to tell me what he was doing at Harvard, but I interrupted him. "Listen, how about we go back to Au Bon Pain for *caffè latte?* It'll warm us up." I was eager to begin my research, but Ned's gray eyes were opaque with despair, and I felt concerned about his well-being.

We walked briskly back to the restaurant, which, in spite of the fact that it's part of a chain, seems to have become the beating heart of Harvard Square. At any time of day or night you can see full professors in traditional British tweed jackets and homeless ex-graduate students in taped-up granny glasses and long matted ponytails hunkered over the tiny tables with coffee, croissants, and the omnipresent paperback tomes.

Ordering two double *latte*s, we carried them to a table in the far corner. I began sipping at mine immediately, but Ned stirred his distractedly and stared out the window at a tall gaunt-faced woman wearing a sidewalk-length army surplus overcoat. Her abundant gray hair swirled in a maelstrom of curls about shoulders hunched against the bitter cold. As pedestrians hurried by, she lectured them with the authoritative gestures of an accomplished public speaker and the fervor of an evangelist. I couldn't make out the words of her harangue through the window. A knitted wool cap sat by her feet, carefully cupped to catch the few stray coins flung in her direction.

"I'm not quite certain"—Ned finally turned away from the large glass panes—"but I think she was in graduate school with me."

"You're kidding!" Outside, the woman had stopped pacing and was silent, her head bent, her chin held between thumb and forefinger in a gesture of scholarly contemplation. With a shock I recognized her stance as a favorite classroom posture of my own.

"I wish I were." His thin lips twisted with bitter humor. "Do you suppose she didn't get tenure? Do you suppose that's what happens to you when you don't?"

"Ned." I reached out to touch his hand. "Poor Ned. It's so unfair."

"Yes." He clipped the word off short, as if he was afraid to say any more. Then, "Yes. Yes, it is. Yes—it's so unfair. It's fucking unfair."

To my horror, and probably to his own, his face crumpled and he burst into tears. "Oh, God," he sobbed, "I'm so sorry. I am so sorry." Then he hid his face in his hands and cried, while I alternated between sipping my drink and awkwardly patting his arm.

Two male undergraduates at the next table looked over at us. The one in blond dreadlocks said something to the one with a cap of brown curls on top of an otherwise totally shaven head. Both laughed derisively: Real men don't cry. I couldn't decide whether to snarl at them or to hide under the table. Around us, heads turned in our direction, then turned quickly away.

Finally Ned accepted the wad of tissues I held out to him and wiped his eyes, one at a time. "Okay, I've got that out of my system. I'm sorry. I didn't mean to embarrass you like that."

"It's perfectly understandable. You're under a lot of stress. Anyhow, I'm not embarrassed at all." The latter was a bald-faced lie. I was hot with embarrassment to the tips of my fingers and toes; I hate being part of a public scene. Yet I was genuinely worried about Ned. Piotrowski had asked me if he was *unbalanced*. It was a good word. Ned was a man staring into a perilous psychic abyss; tears and sympathy were not going to be enough to pull him back from the edge. And I wasn't at all certain about his balance.

For academics, the tenure process is a rite of passage; survive it and you're a full-blooded member of the tribe. Don't survive, and you're thrown to the lions. In other words, it's a lousy job market out there, and you may be doomed to teach adjunct courses for the rest of your professional life. Or drive a cab. I don't know *which* is the more dangerous occupation.

Ned began to talk, in his highly emotional condition throwing discretion to the winds. He had come to Cambridge today to meet with his mentor, the professor who had supervised his Ph.D. dissertation at Harvard. She was helping him plan his strategy. She had advised him not to accept the tenure decision, to appeal it to Enfield's Tenure and Renewal Committee. Neither Ned nor I said it, but we both knew that an appeal was much more likely to be successful now, with Randy gone.

I thought about the implications of that while Ned talked on. From what everyone was telling me, Ned's scholarship, though not intellectually trendy, was strong. Without Randy's influential opposition, Ned would have been an easy tenure, a shoo-in. Now, here he was, with a homemaker wife, two small children, and, after next year, no job. How badly did he want to stay at Enfield? To what extremes would he be prepared to go to keep his position at that prestigious school?

Tainted by the miasma seeping from the Enfield rumor swamp, my imagination proliferated irrational, unwanted images—images of a desperate Ned choking the life out of his colleague. He was slender but tall, and—I looked—he had large, powerful-looking hands. But, if so, if he had killed Randy, why kill Bonnie? Why ransack Randy's office? It didn't add up.

But once these images had entered my mind I wasn't comfortable sitting with Ned, even in such a well-lit, public place. I kept looking at his hands with their long, spatulate fingers. Until these murders were solved, even the most casual contact with my Enfield colleagues would be clouded with suspicion.

It was dark when I left the coffee shop, parting from Ned at the door and pausing to pull on my wool-lined leather gloves. Our encounter had left me suspecting that Ned was a man with very few inner resources. To tell the truth, I didn't want him to know which way I was going. He was, if anything, even more miserable than when I'd first run into him. I knew a good Japanese restaurant out in Porter Square, and, selfishly, I didn't want a despondent dinner companion. I'd go back to Charlotte's, unpack, shower, make my phone call to Piotrowski, have a late tempura dinner and an early bedtime. Tomorrow was time enough for my research. I looked down the street to make certain Ned wasn't lurking about, waiting to follow me. Surely that was his tall, weedy figure at least a half-block away by now and moving dispiritedly in the opposite direction. Or was it? I shrugged and turned left to begin the trek back to Huron Avenue.

The wild-haired woman sat slumped, silent now, on the stone bench, her eyes open, staring at me, the wool cap tugged down low over her curls. I found it impossible to pass her by. She watched me truculently as I approached. Equally silent, I reached in my coat pocket for my wallet, took out a twenty-dollar bill, and pressed it in her hand. Her eyes narrowed with suspicion as I nodded at her. Without waiting for the outburst I suspected would follow, I moved away.

She looked familiar. Like Ned, I thought maybe I had been at graduate school with her.

Like Ned, I thought how easy it would be to become her.

Twenty-five

THE GUARD at the desk of the Houghton's bookcase-lined foyer was a lean and literate-looking man of about fifty wearing horn-rim glasses and a brown tweed jacket with elbow patches. He scrutinized my Enfield faculty ID and my driver's license, registered me, and handed me a locker key. I took my coat and bag to the cloakroom with its secluded lockers. By the time I had disposed of everything but a yellow pad and two pencils and started back toward the brass-studded, red-leather-upholstered doors of the reading room, the library's worshipful hush and the elegance of the beautifully proportioned oval foyer had gotten to me. I pressed the white button recessed in the wall by the reading room door with an almost reverent touch. Herein lay access to the past: to papers of Emerson and Hawthorne, poems of Emily Dickinson—actual manuscripts she had written with her own small, freckled hand. As I waited for the click that would unlock the doors from inside and allow me to enter, I experienced the brief shiver of religious awe library ritual always elicits from me.

By the time I had pushed the door open and entered the reading room, however, my feeling of reverence had vanished. I was at Harvard, seat of power and privilege, whose wealthy imperialist library had ruthlessly pillaged the past. I reminded myself of what I had always known—I had no reason to feel like an interloper. Knowledge was far too important a tool to be left to the disposal of the rich.

The reading room was as busy as I had ever seen it, full of academics taking advantage of the few short weeks of semester break to do that last little bit of research necessary to make this book, this article, this scholarly note truly the definitive word on the subject. Because all seats are arranged so that researchers are thoroughly visible to librarians sitting at the massive elevated desk, I had a full view of everyone as soon as I entered the room. To my surprise, I saw, hunched over a manuscript box in the far corner, the stocky form of Margaret Smith. God! Ned had been right—the denizens of Enfield headed for Cambridge with the homing instinct of spawning salmon.

The only free seat was one at the table directly in front of the librarians' desk. I sat down to establish a claim on the space, and the young woman seated next to me twisted slightly away, perhaps so I couldn't see the contents of the leather-bound journal she was reading. Academics are irrationally territorial. Why she would think I had any interest in her work I couldn't imagine. Leaving my notepad on the desk and my russet brown cardigan on the back of the chair, I went through the door into the long hallway that houses the Houghton's card catalog. Forty-five minutes later, when I returned to the table after having given my small mountain of tediously hand-printed call slips to the librarian, my neighbor had turned as far away from me as she could get and still remain at the same table. This, of course, had the effect of causing me to sneak covert glances at her as I awaited the delivery of thirty folders of Henry Ward Beecher letters and memorabilia.

She looked vaguely familiar. Shiny red hair cut stylishly short and spikey, an ordinary face whose best features—shapely lips and huge green eyes—were highlighted by dark red lipstick and taupe eyeshadow, slightly overdone. She wore a loose black nubbly jacket over a black turtleneck. From her right earlobe dangled a huge silver hoop from which swung a dozen tiny coral and turquoise birds. Her left ear sported a half dozen or so small silver studs, hoops, and cuffs. Where had I seen her before? Had she been a student of mine at some point, now pursuing a graduate career? But if so, why the cold shoulder? Was it someone I had inadvertently offended at some distant point in the past?

The librarian, a young man with the delicate features of an archangel, dumped a pile of folders and a gray pasteboard box on the desk in front of me. I turned eagerly to the material as his rubber-soled shoes squeaked away across the polished floor.

The top folder contained two letters Henry Ward Beecher had written to the author and activist Thomas Wentworth Higginson. I pulled it toward me and opened it, groaning as I saw the handwriting. Beecher had a hasty and impatient hand, difficult to read—just what you would expect from an important, busy man with multitudinous claims on his time. Other folders held letters to friends accepting or turning down dinner invitations; letters to strangers, granting or denying some requested boon; letters to his banker, consistently adding to his comfortable bank account. I read through a sermon brief, amazed that the man could build such reputedly charismatic sermons upon such a skeletal outline. Evidently he worked with hackneyed truisms as a base, and made the rest up as he went along. I handled with befuddlement a printed ticket of admission to the 1875 Beecher/Tilton trial:

ADMIT BEARER TO TRIAL
Tilton Vs. Beecher
At the City Court Room

This much-coveted bit of pasteboard was addressed to an acquaintance in Beecher's own hand, leading me to speculate that he may well have gloried in this, the most public dramatic role of an intensely public career.

Although not ultimately illegible, all the documents in Beecher's bold, sloppy, right-slanting hand required careful deciphering if I was to read them with the meticulous attention of a professional researcher. It was tedious and uncertain work, especially since I had absolutely no idea what I was looking for.

As I made conscientious notes with my pencil on my yellow pad, I became increasingly aware of the tap, tap, tap of my table companion as she copied, seemingly verbatim, the contents of her leather-bound book into a really spiffy little PowerBook computer. From all around me came the tap, tap, tapping of other researchers on their high-tech electronic notebooks. With my pencil and pad I was back in the Stone Age, and, as I flexed my cramped fingers, all too well aware of it. I took a little break to figure out on my pad how many days I'd have to work for Piotrowski before I could pay off pressing debts and purchase a PowerBook for myself. Too many days, as it turned out—weeks, actually. I'd have to stick to my pad and pencil for another year or two.

By the time the huge gold hands of the clock over the librarians' desk pointed to noon, I was only too glad to close the folder I was working on and take a break for lunch. So far the files had held no surprises. They contained only the routine correspondence of a well-regarded public figure. The only intriguing item I'd found was in a folder titled "Recipient Unknown." It seemed to be a conventional thank-you note. On a small sheet of thick, creamy paper embossed in the upper left-hand corner with a full-blown rose, Beecher had written an innocuous message: *"Thank you, dear friend, for the most pleasant afternoon walk in the lovely countryside. It will, believe me, live forever in memory. —H. W. Beecher."* The note was dated July 1859 and had no address or salutation.

What piqued my curiosity about this innocent communication was not its contents, but, rather, the marked contrast in the handwriting to Beecher's usual hasty scrawl. The Reverend Henry had taken great pains with this note. His handwriting was clear, graceful and flowing—very careful calligraphy. Style, they say, is content, and the style here spoke to me of the precise attention to the details of self-presentation paid by a person involved in an affair of the heart. Was this one of Beecher's attempts at dalliance?

Suddenly, unbidden, a few lines from an Emily Dickinson poem sprang into my mind: *"There came a Day at Summer's full, / Entirely for me— / I thought that such were for the Saints, / Where Resurrections—be—"* This is one of my favorite Dickinson poems, a poignant prelude to heartbreak.

"A Day at Summer's full . . ." Hmm. When is summer "fuller" than in July?

Dickinson and Beecher? Could it be? At the very thought of this ludicrous coupling, I snorted with derision. I must have snorted aloud, because the young woman sharing my table shot me a rude, searching look, and seemed about to speak. I suppose I was being disruptive in the sanctum sanctorum. Unwilling to accept a reprimand from someone I perceived as a snippy upstart, I smiled an aloof apology, swept the folders up into one pile, took them back to the desk, and asked the angelic-looking librarian to hold them for me until after lunch.

After a visit to the women's room, located down a curving staircase in a corridor of library offices, I left the Houghton, wended my way across the snowy Harvard campus, crossed Massachusetts Avenue, and ordered a burger at Mr. Bartley's. While I waited for my lunch at one of the crowded communal tables, I glanced around at my fellow diners—Cambridge always rewards people-watching. I was struck by the number of men with ponytails. Short thick blond ponytails, long wispy gray ponytails, otherwise bald ponytails, ponytails with earrings, ponytails with bare ears. I wouldn't be surprised to find that there are more male ponytails and earrings in Cambridge than in all other cities in the United States combined. I spent a few happy moments just perusing the scene.

As the waitress slapped a hefty burger and fries on the table in front of me, someone jostled me in passing. I turned to see Margaret Smith push behind me without a word of acknowledgement or apology. She sat at a small table in the far corner. She neither looked at nor spoke to the young woman researcher from the Houghton, who was deeply immersed in a copy of the *New York Times* at the same table. I had taken an irrational dislike to my library tablemate.

With any luck, I thought, maybe she's completed her infernal tapping and will now go home.

But no. Shortly after I returned to my batch of Beecher files, she was sitting next to me again, her body half turned away, tap, tap, tapping at top speed.

The afternoon passed in much the same way as the morning. I learned a great deal about Henry Ward Beecher, some of it actually interesting, but none of it in any way possibly relevant to two cold-blooded murders that had taken place over a hundred years after he had shuffled off this mortal coil. Well, maybe not *cold-blooded* murders. From what Piotrowski had said, there was certainly some passion, however twisted or obscure, involved in this.

Giving myself a little break for stretching, I rose from the table and walked over to one of the floor-to-ceiling windows that overlooked the campus. Late sunlight illuminated the piles of snow that bordered the college paths. Watching a couple walk hand in hand toward the brick-arched gate, I thought again about Beecher and Dickinson.

Ludicrous? Well—perhaps I was allowing my own erotic tastes to color my perceptions. And face it, the only sense I had of H. W. Beecher's attractiveness came from grainy old photographs and a marble bust. It was certainly possible she might have fallen for him, I mused. After all, what did good looks count for, anyhow? Language was the chief passion of Dickinson's life, and Beecher was reputed to have been a charismatic speaker who enthralled men and women alike with his spellbinding orations. At one Amherst College commencement—I seemed to recall it was 1862—he spoke passionately about the Civil War as "the storm in the North, and the earthquake in the South." Whether Dickinson heard him speak or not, she certainly must have seen or heard him quoted somewhere, because she uses the same metaphor; a poem from that very year refers to an "Earthquake in the South——/And Maelstrom, in the Sea——."

In addition, Beecher had a number of close associations with Amherst, where Dickinson lived. He'd gone to Amherst College—before Emily was born, of course. In later years he'd been a trustee of the college. As a great public man, he would have been invited to Edward Dickinson's commencement receptions; Emily's father, treasurer of the college, hosted notables and alumni at an elegant tea at the Dickinson home each July. While her mother and her sister Lavinia entertained the guests, the reclusive Emily was reported to have wafted down the stairs into the spacious front hall, nodding to the right and to the left as she made her silent way through the crowded double parlors, only to disappear as soundlessly as she had come.

Well, okay. As distasteful as it might appear to me, I suppose it was possible that she was attracted to this charismatic man of the world. Love whets odd appetites. But what of it? It might bear looking into some day, but there certainly was no way in which such an ancient liaison could be brought to bear on the solution of two modern-day homicides.

I stretched again, looked up at the clock—three-thirty, only an hour and a half to finish up here—turned from the window, and went back to my table. If I hustled, I could get through these folders today and move on to Yale tomorrow.

At a quarter past four I pulled the penultimate folder toward me. Its title indicated that it was from a "Correspondent Unknown." I opened the folder and then sat back in bafflement. It was empty. I closed it, picked it up, looked under it, put it down, opened it again. Nothing. My indefatigable neighbor ceased tapping for a moment to look over at me. My eyes caught hers, and she turned hastily away. I had seen that face quite recently, I was certain—or if not exactly that face, at least one almost identical. Puzzling. But not as perplexing as the missing document.

I looked one more time, just to make certain I wasn't suffering from some neurotic selective blindness, and then rose to take the folder over to the librarians at the desk. My finding—or lack of it—caused a small flurry of consternation among the library staff, who assured me they would look carefully into this disappearance.

It only took me another five minutes to glance at the final file, which contained a letter from the abolitionist Wendell Phillips asking Beecher to give a speech. Nothing new or shocking there. I leaned back in my chair, stretched my arms high over my head (not caring now whether or not I disturbed my snooty neighbor), then piled up the files to return them to the desk. Quarter of five. Not bad. I'd have a cup of tea, case out the bookstores, call Piotrowski with my nonnews, and have something exotic for dinner, something Enfield didn't offer—Thai cuisine, perhaps.

After all, I might as well live it up. It wasn't often that I got to dine compliments of the Massachusetts State Police.

Twenty-six

THE WOMEN'S ROOM at the Houghton is a kick. Trust Harvard to have
such a grandiose john—done entirely in light brown
marble. Matching marble stalls, marble paneling,
and marble floor tiles. The pedestal sinks and the
black art deco vanity suggest that this bathroom
was furnished in Woodrow Wilson's administration.
We're lucky that in those benighted days they
thought of having a women's room at all.

When I came out of the stall, I found myself sharing the bathroom with the redheaded researcher and
Margaret Smith. The redhead sat on the vanity seat
intent on her image in the mirror, doing something
elaborate to her hair with fingertips and a spray can
of mousse. Margaret was washing her hands at one
of the sinks. She looked up and saw me reflected in
the mirror. I nodded at her reflection as I commandeered the other sink, but she didn't respond. She
just kept washing her hands, lathering them up with
soap, and rubbing them together over and over, as if

she were a surgeon about to undertake a very delicate operation. Once she slid her eyes over to glance at me, but as soon as she realized I'd seen her, she stared down at her hands again. She gave me the creeps. I was glad I wasn't alone in the room with her.

The redhead finished spiking her hair. She pulled out a mascara wand. I rinsed my hands, splashed water on my face, and reached for a paper towel, accidently brushing Margaret's shoulder. "Sorry," I said. She was taking a long time to dry her hands. I threw the damp towel in the waste container, and turned to leave. Margaret stood directly in my way.

"Excuse me." I smiled a polite apology. *Oh, God,* I thought. *Another weird little Margaret Smith scene. I'm too tired for this shit.*

This woman seemed to have some secret grudge against me. Maybe it was because my career appeared to be on the fast track whereas hers seemed to have derailed decades ago. But should that matter to anyone who had any sort of life? What I was dealing with here, I decided, was a pitifully unhappy woman with a bad case of personal envy. I could feel sorry for her, but I wasn't going to put up with much more of her crap. If it weren't for the other woman obliviously absorbed in reshaping her lips in front of the vanity mirror, I would have confronted Margaret then and there. But a public scene was more than I could tolerate at the moment.

"Excuse me." This time I didn't smile. Margaret moved fractionally to one side. I brushed past her, picked up my pad and pencils from the shelf, said "Good night, Margaret" and walked out.

I had promised myself a cup of tea, so I maneuvered around clumps of frozen snow and garbage to cross Massachusetts Avenue. The gray-haired wild woman was gone from in front of Au Bon Pain, but her place had been taken by a saxophonist playing "Am I Blue?" with remarkable verve, given the cold, the sparsity of the audience, and the Bill Clinton mask he was wearing. I threw a handful of coins in his open case.

But tea and then an hour's browsing among the books at Wordsworth did not distract me from my own personal blues. I was supposed to be conducting an investigation, and I had wasted an entire day combing through irrelevant trivia. At six-thirty I was plodding back up Massachusetts Avenue toward Charlotte's house, an aimless integer in a crowd of seemingly purposeful individuals pushing past in their rush to be anywhere else but here.

The gray-haired woman had found a new platform. She was haranguing a crowd of activist pigeons in front of the Coop. I heard her scream something about patriarchal oppression and the military-industrial complex as I edged past on the sidewalk. All her misgivings about this nation would have been confirmed if she had known what I was up to. In the pay of the state police, I was using my elite intellectual training in a covert operation designed to deprive an American citizen of all rights but the right to breathe incarcerated air.

The walk back to Charlotte's seemed interminable. As I left Harvard Square, the crowds thinned out somewhat, but the slick sidewalk was still swarming. I was jostled by fellow pedestrians with more energy than I had—professors, businesspeople, street people, graduate students, hustlers, and the occasional fourteen-year-old prostitute out to make the price of a fix. And what was I out to make the price of? Food, shelter, and clothing, the same as anyone else here. Add a little occasional happiness, minus the syringe if possible, and I would be content.

Slogging through more freezing slush as I turned

onto Huron, I began to brood about Piotrowski. How did *he* manage the tedium of constant investigation? What did they call a police officer in England? P.C. Plod, wasn't it? How did Piotrowski do it? Plodding along, day after day after day, sifting through landfills of irrelevant information with seldom anything to show for it. What kept him going? I was terminally exhausted and discouraged after a single day and beginning to be humbled by this whole experience. Who was I to think I could participate in a criminal investigation? Maybe Tony was right. Maybe I didn't have a clue about what I was doing. My foot slipped on an icy spot. This sidewalk hadn't received municipal attention. It was shoveled only in random places, and I decided belatedly to pay very close attention to my feet. Plod. Plod. Plod.

Good thing Huron didn't get the kind of traffic with which Massachusetts Avenue had to contend. To go along with their lack of shoveling, the sidewalks here were rimmed with four-foot snowplow piles. Occasionally a streetlight was dark. Aside from a couple of stragglers behind me, I was the only pedestrian.

I shifted the heavy briefcase hanging from my shoulder by its leather strap and started thinking about police work again. Piotrowski had accused me of being "off" in my thinking. I didn't think he was accusing me of being crazy. I wondered if he meant that I didn't think like a cop. Hmm. How *would* a cop think about this day? I slipped again and grabbed a signpost for support. One of these times I was going to go down. How much farther to Charlotte's? About two more blocks. If I had to walk this again, I'd call a cab. Or, even more drastic, I'd drive. Well, maybe not. Not in Cambridge.

I tried to compose my thoughts in preparation for calling Piotrowski. Policethink: What would it tell me about the events of this day? I thought long and hard. Nothing. Two annoyances kept getting in the way of any Holmesian deduction—the missing Beecher document and the curious behavior of the redheaded researcher at my library table.

As I turned finally into Charlotte's front walk, I still wasn't satisfied that my thinking was "on," in Piotrowski's terms. If I were really thinking like a cop, I thought with a snort of amusement, I'd probably decide someone was following me. Although the area was generally deserted, there had been fairly steady footsteps behind me. And they'd stopped when I turned off the sidewalk. All at once a wave of panic overtook me. The footsteps! I became convinced that someone really was watching me, had been watching me for some time. Had really been following me. As I reached the steps of the porch, I turned quickly and peered back down the street. The only person nearby was turning up the walk of a house half a block away. Farther down, a drunk sprawled across the hood of a car. In the far distance, a student hefted a heavy bookbag to her shoulder.

I resumed breathing. Just paranoia. A pro would have known better than to panic. And yet, I was happy to get inside.

Piotrowski was still in his office when I called. "Don't you ever go home?" I asked. "It's after seven."

"Not often enough." His voice sounded weary. "What havya got for me?"

I ran through my pathetic list—the number of documents I'd looked at, Beecher's dreadful handwriting, the note I suspected was a camouflaged billet-doux, the empty folder, the annoying tablemate, Margaret Smith's rudeness, the slippery streets, my exhaustion, my plans for dinner. I must have gone on for about fifteen minutes, with occasional questions from the detective. To my surprise he wasn't particularly interested in the redheaded researcher, brushing her off as "just some oddball. Cambridge is full of them."

"But don't you think it's possible she has something to do with this case? I mean, she just kept hanging around. Maybe she's connected with Randy in some way. An ex-lover? A scholarly rival?"

"Well . . ." He sounded doubtful. "We haven't come across anyone like that. But I'll run her through."

I had to be satisfied with that. I didn't think to ask him *what* he would run her through.

What did interest him was the folder with the missing document. He pressed me intensively on what I could tell about it.

"The catalog describes it as a single-page manuscript letter, correspondent unknown, Piotrowski. That's all the librarians could tell me. Ask them yourself."

"Oh, I will. When does that place open? And how likely is it that this document would simply be mislaid or misfiled?"

"Extraordinarily unlikely. They take 'the most stringent measures' to assure against that happening. At least that's what they told me when I asked. I think it might actually be easier to steal it than to mislay it inadvertently."

"Really?" he replied. "Really?"

"Yeah. They just check your notes when you come out of the reading room. They don't do a body search. If you had the right kind of clothing, the document was small enough, and you picked your moment perfectly, you could slip it in a pocket and walk out. It's been known to happen."

"Would Beecher stuff have any monetary value?"

"God, I don't know. I have no idea what the market would be for it. And this was an *unknown* correspondent. . . . I don't think money would be the issue. But, Piotrowski, there could be a dozen reasons for this. It really could be misfiled. Why are you so interested?"

"Things that are missing always interest me, Dr. Pelletier. Things that are not where they're supposed to be. Especially when it's something as well-protected as this letter was. This is an intriguing—er—absence." He paused.

"You think this 'absence' could have some significance?"

"Yeah. It could. On the other hand—"

"On the other hand," I broke in, "it could be totally meaningless."

"Right."

"Hmm." A half-formulated notion was beginning to develop. I'd have to give this some thought.

"What?"

"Oh, nothing. . . ."

"Don't hold back on me, Doctor."

"It's nothing, Lieutenant. I was just wool-gathering."

"Are you sure?" He was testy again.

"Yes!" It was a crazy notion. I wasn't about to risk being told again that my thinking was "off."

I remembered my thoughts about plodding through a landfill. Plod. Plod. Plod. Fleetingly, I thought of the footsteps behind me, but didn't bring them up. He might take my paranoia seriously, and I didn't want to complicate the evening. All I wanted to do was shower, change my clothes, and go out for a well-deserved meal. In addition, I was too tired and hungry to engage Piotrowski in a discussion about how to handle the tedium of criminal investigation. I didn't think this was a propitious moment anyhow. He sounded cranky. I told him good-bye. Before I got involved in a theoretical discussion of investigative procedure, I'd wait and see if I actually did anything to help solve the crime.

Twenty-seven

MUCH TO MY SURPRISE, Ned Hilton and Magda Vegh were leaving the Thai restaurant as I walked toward it later that evening. Ned wore his little-boy jacket and scarf, and Magda was still in her American incarnation of jeans and leather bomber jacket. I slowed my steps so I wouldn't run into them; I was preoccupied with my thoughts and didn't want to have to talk to anyone I knew. Finally I came to a stop in the shadowed doorway of a New Age bookstore and watched as Ned made ineffectual efforts to hail a cab while Magda looked on, attractively fragile and helpless in her oversized jacket. Then it struck me—*leather bomber jacket*. That's what had caught my attention in Rudolph's bar, the last time I'd seen Magda. She'd been wearing Randy's bomber jacket then, too. From my current vantage point, I could tell it was his by the distinctive yellow-and-red pseudomilitary insignia. That's why the jacket was so big on Magda; it was the one I'd last seen discarded on the floor of

Randy's ravaged office. Magda must have snagged it after the police had released the scene. But what right did she have to the coat? Not that I was about to inform anyone; Randy had no further need for fashionable outerwear. But, still, I marveled at the nerve of the woman: stealing a dead man's clothes!

When a taxi finally pulled up, Magda got in, and Ned shambled off down the icy sidewalk. As the cab pulled away, Magda's eyes raked over the crowd of pedestrians. I didn't think she saw me, but I couldn't tell for sure.

And—Ned Hilton with Magda Vegh? An unlikely pair. Again I remembered what Ned had said about most of Enfield heading for Cambridge at semester break. This must have been just another happenstance encounter. They must have bumped into each other on the street, and Magda had latched on to him. She wasn't one to let an available man get away. Or an unavailable one.

The coincidence unnerved me, though. Who else was I going to run into, for God's sake? Avery Mitchell? I moped through my Pad Thai. My research had been unproductive, and Avery had rejected me. I was a failure as an investigator. I was a failure as a woman.

I brooded about Avery until I left the restaurant. He was "intrigued," was he? Well, goddammit, why didn't he do something about it? Get me all worked up and then walk away without so much as a lousy little kiss! Was he a man, or was he a mouse?

As usual in affairs of the heart, my thinking was sophisticated and complex.

The bone-chilling walk home revived me. I began to speculate on the significance of the missing letter that had so interested Piotrowski. I had changed into jeans and sturdy boots and my footing was a little surer on the treacherous sidewalk, so I was free to think about the details of the day's research. I was developing a hypothesis about a possible connection between the disappearance of a letter from a scholarly archive and the murder of a scholar who had frequented that archive. My theory was so farfetched and unbelievable that I kept shaking my head to clear it. It really wasn't like me to indulge in such wild flights of fantasy. But . . .

Deeply absorbed in my speculations as I approached Charlotte's place, I didn't notice until the last minute that the streetlight in front of the house had joined the ranks of the unlit. What really irritated me was that the porch light was also off. Hadn't I remembered to turn it on? Sometimes I was so dim. I fumbled in my bag for the key as I mounted the steps to the dark porch. "What if . . ." I was thinking, "what if . . . ?"

I inserted the key in the lock and turned it. I was just reaching down to twist the knob when someone grabbed me from behind and slammed me full length into the still-closed door. As my left arm was twisted violently behind me, I felt cold metal press against my temple.

Oh, my God, I thought. *Oh, my God!* The force of the impact had expelled my breath with a violent whoosh; I gasped for air as I heard a hoarse whisper in my ear.

"I have a gun, and I will use it. Don't make a sound. Open the door and go inside. Go inside, shut the door, and turn on the light. Do you understand?" The gun was pressed even more firmly against my forehead. I was afraid to nod. I was unable to speak. I opened the door, went inside, closed the door, fumbled for the light switch. My heart was racing like mad; I was colder than I'd ever been in my entire life.

With a final vicious twist of the arm, my captor thrust me through the archway of Charlotte's living room and gave me a fierce push. I cried out in pain and, stumbling into the dark room, smashed into a small table, knocking over a pile of books with a loud crash.

The noise wouldn't matter. There was no one else in the house.

"Turn around," commanded the voice, and I did. In the dim light from the hall archway I wasn't really surprised to see the stolid figure of Margaret Smith. She was staring at me with cryptic intensity. She held a small deadly-looking handgun trained directly at me. For the first time in my life I knew what it meant to be scared to death.

"Margaret. . . ." The syllables rasped painfully out of my constricted throat. My brain was racing to figure out a way to deal with this insane situation, but my heart was racing even faster. Tears of pain streamed down my cheeks. My wrenched left arm hung limp at my side.

"Close the blinds." With the gun, she motioned toward the windows. The long room ran the entire width of the house and, as I walked from window to window pulling down blinds, I looked frantically around in the faint light for something I could use to protect myself. Aside from the heavy old-fashioned furniture, there was little in the room but books, ranked row upon row on shelves, piled crazily in corners, displayed on tables.

Margaret flicked the switch, and the overhead light went on. She motioned me back to the center of the room. I stood staring at her while crazy speculations whirled through my brain. Had my half-baked hypothesis been correct?

"Margaret." I decided to risk speech. "What's going on here?"

Margaret narrowed her eyes. She was dressed as she had been at the library, loose gray jacket swinging open over brown crewneck sweater and tweed pants. Her salt-and-pepper hair was unkempt, and her gray eyes were fixed on my face. I remembered seeing her work out on the Nautilus machine, the unexpectedly well developed muscles of her arms and legs gleaming with a faint film of sweat. With that memory, she became even more menacing—a figure of strange camouflaged capacities intent on playing out some murderous agenda that was only now beginning to come clear to me.

"I know what you're doing here." Only the madness in her eyes inflected her words. "You're trying to destroy her, aren't you? That is your sole purpose in being here, isn't it? To destroy her completely."

I thought I knew to whom she was referring, but I was afraid to risk a guess. "Who?" I croaked.

"Don't play innocent with me. You know who."

I gulped. "You mean—Emily? Emily Dickinson?"

Margaret's eyes lost a fraction of their hardness. I had spoken the magic name. Her gun, however, remained steady. It was pointed directly at my head.

"She appeared to me, you know." She spoke in a tone of intimate disclosure.

"Appeared?"

"Yes. Do you doubt that?"

"Oh, no. No, I don't." It was the gun I didn't doubt. The gun was a palpable fact, and it gave credibility to anything she wanted to say.

"She appeared to me in her bedroom."

"Her bedroom? You mean, at the Dickinson Homestead?"

I'd been there. Amherst wasn't far from Enfield, and one of the first things I'd done after moving to the area was to sign up for a tour of the Dickinson house. I'd found Emily's room poignant, with its artifacts of the poet's life—the white dress, the shawl, the sleigh bed—but I hadn't been overcome as one of my fellow visitors had. A scrawny woman with the worst perm I'd ever seen had actually swayed and started to pass out upon entering the poet's bedroom. She had to be helped to a seat in the hallway and revived with a glass of water. "Ohhhh," she kept saying. "Ohhhhh. Ohhhhhh."

The tour guide, a knowledgeable woman with white hair and no-nonsense country clothes, had glanced at me sideways and rolled her eyes. Like Elvis, Emily Dickinson had her cultists. I'd smiled at the guide. She was handling the situation as if she'd done it before.

"Yes, at Emily's home." Margaret's plain face had taken on a look of mystical rapture. "I saw her there. I *saw* her. Have you been to her room?"

I nodded, encouraged that she was talking to me. Maybe I could form a Dickinson bond with her, and she wouldn't kill me. Feeble hope, but maybe at least I could buy some time.

"Do you remember the mirror in the bedroom?"

I nodded again. An ancient mirror with a dark, crazed surface hung over the dresser.

"Did you look in it? Really look?"

"I—I don't know. I suppose I did. . . ."

"Thrice. . . ." Her voice became dreamy. "Upon three different occasions—I looked into that mirror and I saw . . . a face that was not my own."

A cold shudder ran down my spine.

I nodded again but she wasn't really seeing me.

"And that's how I knew that she had chosen me."

"Chosen you?"

"To be her prophet. As Christ chose John the Baptist. To cry in the wilderness."

"Margaret." I wasn't above hypocrisy if it would save my life. "How wonderful. . . ."

But the sound of my voice snapped her back to the present moment. Her eyes narrowed. Her gaze hardened. "But you don't believe that, do you, Karen? This is what you want, isn't it?" She reached into the pocket of her jacket. "This is what you've been looking for. *This* is what would demolish her."

From her pocket she pulled a sheet of thick, old-fashioned writing paper that had been folded over twice. Margaret held the paper by the edges with the tips of two fingers, as if it were somehow contaminated. If my speculations were correct, this would be the missing document from the "Correspondent Unknown" folder.

The straight narrow line of Margaret's thin lips was replaced by a twist of the mouth suggesting personal hatred. The blue steel gun never wavered. She unfolded the sheet of writing paper and thrust it in my face, but as I moved to take hold of it, she snatched it away. "Just read; don't touch," she hissed.

I looked at the paper. It was a letter, undated, in brownish ink on a sheet of cream-colored, blue-ruled stationery. The handwriting was fine, flowing, right-slanting, with distinctive looping capital letters—oddly familiar. With a sudden lurch of the heart I recognized it as Emily Dickinson's. I *was* right! I looked up at Margaret, my mouth open with amazement.

"Twenty years and more I pored over those poems as if they were sacred texts, trying to comprehend—to *encompass*—Emily's relationship with the Almighty. This was my contribution to the ages—an exegesis of the ultimate mystery as revealed to a sanctified mind. I struggled with each word, as if it alone were the final barrier between me and revelation. Finally, like Jacob wrestling with the angel, I overcame. And I knew that Emily Dickinson was a saint of God. His emissary on earth. And—that she is not dead."

"No?"

"No. Not dead." Margaret's dun-colored eyes gleamed. "She lives in the shadow world. In the dark windows. In the world behind the mirrors. And thus I began my sojourn in the wilderness. . . ."

Her gun hand wavered, as if she were overcome with emotion. I tensed myself for action. But Margaret steadied herself. Her eyes became glittering slits. Her mouth twisted. "And, then, after my long preparation, *he* comes up with this." She shook the letter in my face.

"*Randy* found this?" My voice was no more than a whisper. "He found a Dickinson letter? In the Beecher archives, right?"

"Yessss." She actually hissed. "The destroyer! He was so proud of himself, strutting, like an arrogant banty rooster. Cock of the walk. He told me about it. He thought I would be impressed. But I saw the implications right away—" She broke off.

"Read it," she commanded. I did.

Mr. Beecher, Sir—
  Angels are few. And those—Beyond the Mound.
Satan flew once. And you Master—bear on silken Wing. Who should Know but I—
Lucifer had a Secret. He was scarred too, Master—only, on the Eyes. They opened, he spoke—and he Flew. Daisy's roots clutch Stone.
Angels—too—Thunder from on High.
Dear heart—unless you Speak—this is the last.
                                        Your—
                                        Daisy

My God! This was a letter from Emily Dickinson to her "Master"! Randy had discovered a fourth Master letter, and it had been written to Henry Ward Beecher! Dickinson's Master was Henry Ward

Beecher! This was what Randy had tried to tell me. This was the lethal secret he had blabbed to poor little Bonnie Weimer.

In spite of the circumstances, I yearned to hold the letter in my hand—a material connection with the woman whose poetry was my passion. The longing for contact was so strong it was almost erotic, as if Dickinson's hand could reach out of the dusty past and for a brief ecstatic instant caress mine. I glanced up at Margaret, not knowing what to say or do. What did this letter mean to her? One thing was clear to me now: I had stumbled into the middle of a murderous psychotic delusion.

Margaret placed the letter carefully on an end table by the couch. The gun stayed aimed at me. "I wanted you to see this—before I destroy it."

"You can't destroy it!" I blurted out. "It belonged to her, to Emily. She touched it. Her fingers were right there, where yours are now." For an instant my concern was more with the preservation of the letter than with the preservation of my own life. But only for an instant.

"It's a fraud." Her colorless eyes were fixed on my face. "A fraud and a delusion. Emily loved only in the spirit. She never knew the filth of the flesh. No man touched her. God was her Master. God and God alone."

Her eyes glittered. In them, I could see insane purpose. I knew then that she would go to any lengths to destroy this letter, to obliterate any memory of it from the earth. Including mine. I could feel sweat breaking out on my forehead and upper lip. Sweat was rolling down the middle of my back. I thought about Amanda, and her image gave me strength. I knew I had to do something to save myself. But *what?* My usual weapons of wit and words weren't going to get me out of this alive.

"Poor Karen Pelletier." It was the first time I had ever seen Margaret smile. It was an unnerving sight. "She's about to have a regrettable accident." She was now perusing the room, as if checking out its lethal possibilities. Her eyes roved, but the gun held steady.

"Hah!" With a swift movement, she was at Charlotte's desk, swiping a pile of a half dozen or so books into a heap on the carpet. Dropping into an easy crouch, she kept the gun trained on me while she arranged the books in a loose heap, pages fanned open.

"These old houses," she said. "They're dry as tinder, aren't they? After a century or so, these old wood floors and walls . . . I imagine it wouldn't take much to set one off. Poor Karen Pelletier . . ." Her smile had become a lunatic grimace in a stony mask. "She's going to die in a tragic house fire." My blood turned to ice. Margaret was crumpling papers from the desk and throwing them on her ghastly hearth. I had to do something. Maybe, now, while her attention was diverted . . .

I made a sudden dash for the door. A shot rang out. I froze as a bullet splintered the woodwork near my cheek.

She seemed totally crazed now. Her eyes were fixed, the pupils dilated. "I—don't want to shoot you." I breathed a sigh of deluded relief, but she went on. "I'd rather knock you out before you burn. I don't want to leave a bullet in your body. This is going to be an accident. Enfield College is going to have another tragic loss." She treated me to a humorless grin. With the gun she motioned me back into the center of the room, and I obeyed. With the clear, precise, absurd detail of extreme situations, I noticed that I stood next to the table on which Charlotte kept her three-volume first edition of *Jane Eyre*. Its red cloth covers and faded gold lettering reminded me of happier times in this comfortable, book-lined room. Poor Charlotte. She was going to lose her home. Poor Karen. She was going to lose. . . .

"Don't—move—again." From a jacket pocket, Margaret pulled out a flat red-and-white can with a narrow pointed tip. Appalled, I watched her squirt paint thinner copiously over the pile of books and papers. With an added twist to her ghastly smile, Margaret directed one long, last squirt at my eyes. I gasped and tried to dodge the reeking liquid, but a sharp jerk of Margaret's gun hand brought me up short, and the flammable fluid sloshed over my hair and shoulder. I could feel liquid dripping down my right arm, off my fingers. As I froze, I thought I heard a noise in the dining room, across the hall. A slight scratching sound. Charlotte's cat, I decided. Then I remembered Charlotte didn't have a cat. In my terror I must be imagining things. Margaret tossed the empty can onto the drenched heap of books. I thought about how it would explode into tiny lethal fragments in the intense heat of the fire.

With a peculiar grimace of gratification, Margaret took the Dickinson letter in her left hand and rolled it into a long narrow cylinder. Then she twisted it tightly between her fingers and thumb. "Emily would call this a lamp-lighter," she said in her flat voice, and smiled again. She pulled out a yellow lighter, flicked it on, touched the flame to the end of the twisted paper. It blazed up instantly. Her eyes never left mine as she crouched, gun steady, to light the pile of paper and books.

What it came down to, then, was whether I would rather die by bullet or by flame.

It was no contest.

Swiftly, I reached over to the table at my elbow, grabbed a volume of *Jane Eyre,* and hurled it at Margaret with all my might. The book hit her square in the chest. She emitted a sound somewhere between a grunt and a cough as, startled, she lost her balance.

I took a few swift steps toward the door as Margaret dropped the flaming letter. With a tremendous *whoosh,* the papers in the center of the room ignited.

Regaining equilibrium, Margaret whirled toward me and fired the gun. A searing pain invaded my left shoulder.

As I reeled back from the impact, an amazing vision met my eyes. On the far side of the rising flames, in the elaborately arched doorway of Charlotte's living room, my library tablemate crouched. Her red hair was disordered, her hoop earring swinging, her gun steadied in a sturdy hand. With her left hand, she motioned me sharply down. "Police!" she yelled. "Freeze!"

I fell flat as three shots rang out. In the seconds before Margaret's body toppled heavily on mine, I recognized under the crazy red hair, the wild earrings, and the garish makeup, the plain, reliable features of Piotrowski's Trooper Schultz.

Twenty-eight

PIOTROWSKI was sitting by my bed when I regained consciousness in the ICU of Massachusetts General Hospital. He was wearing his baggy gray suit jacket over his atrocious green-and-red sweater. I blinked and smiled loopily at him. He was a beautiful sight.

The lieutenant's expression was solemn. "Dr. Pelletier," he said, "Dr. Pelletier, I'm so sorry."

"Sorry?" I couldn't think quickly enough. "Sorry? What's wrong? Is something wrong? Amanda—?"

"No! No, everything's all right—now. I'm just sorry for putting you in such jeopardy. If I had only known . . ."

But I couldn't really remember having been in jeopardy. My head throbbed and everything was a little fuzzy, including Piotrowski's anxious face. The last thing I remembered was walking up to Charlotte's porch and inserting the key in the lock. I figured he needed to know about that. "The . . .

streetlight . . . was out . . ." I informed him, owl-ishly.

He smiled gently. "Yes, I know."

"That's enough, Lieutenant." A thin woman in a white coat moved into my field of vision. "We need to have a little rest right now."

I spent a week in Massachusetts General being treated for concussion, a gunshot wound in my left shoulder, and minor burns on my right hand. I never did remember how I got the burns. When I fell, did I try to grab the flaming Dickinson letter? I couldn't have been that stupid. Could I? But, in spite of how battered I was, I was lucky; I was alive. Margaret Smith was dead. Trooper Schultz had shot her twice in the chest. One bullet had penetrated her heart, and she'd died immediately. Margaret's bullet grazed the officer's cheek, but I hadn't known about that. When Margaret fell, her head crashed heavily into mine. Unconscious, I'd missed the fire trucks, police cars, ambulances, the whole cockamamy sound-and-light show of sirens and flashing lights. I figured Amanda would never forgive me: I had stuck it out for three interminable acts, and then missed the thrilling de-nouement. But at least Charlotte's house had been spared, as had her Brontë first edition. Thanks to Trooper Schultz's quick action, the flames had been confined to part of the living room, and the *Jane Eyre* volume had evidently skittered into the hall af-ter it caromed off Margaret's chest.

When I regained consciousness for good, the doc-tors stopped babbling about "talk and die" head in-juries, moved me out of the ICU, and let Piotrowski at me again. This time I remembered most of it. He took me slowly through the entire encounter, bit by bit by bit. It was all news to him. Trooper Schultz hadn't come on the scene until the minute before I hurled *Jane Eyre* at Margaret and the pile of books burst into flame. She hadn't seen Margaret grab me because the porch was so dark, but she had gotten suspicious when she saw me pull down the living room blinds before I turned on the light. That had seemed strange to her: Why would I walk all the way through a dark room and risk crashing into furniture? Schultz had decided to conduct a quiet investigation. It had taken her some time to pick the locks on Charlotte's kitchen door. When she finally got into the house, she heard Margaret's first shot and was outside the living room door in time to prevent my death and incineration. But just barely.

I must have had a flicker of consciousness in the Emergency Room, because I had a vivid memory flash of seeing Trooper Schultz bedraggled and anxious, her right cheek bandaged, her dyed red hair disheveled, her hoop earring gone. I thought now that she must have been terrified she'd flubbed the job. She must have thought her charge was headed straight for the boneyard.

I told Piotrowski about the manuscript letter and about Margaret's deranged obsession with Emily Dickinson. It was coming back to me in flashes, and I wasn't terrifically coherent. But he was very patient. The first time he interviewed me, he had Sergeant Daniels with him to take detailed notes. Then, as I became clearer in my mind, he came back alone two or three times to fill in details. I began to look forward to these conversations; they helped keep the nightmares at bay.

What we came up with was this: Researching Beecher's papers, Randy Astin-Berger had recognized the handwriting on the Dickinson letter. He knew his find was a scholarly coup, clearing up a literary mystery over a century old. Randy must have made a copy and kept it from the scholarly world as he thought about how best to publicize it. At the Christmas party, I conjectured to Piotrowski, he got smashed and started dropping hints. When I was too inattentive to pick up on them he got frustrated— "In more ways than one, I bet," Piotrowski broke in. Then he blushed, obviously afraid he'd offended me.

"Probably," I responded. "He had a low threshold."

Randy got frustrated, I went on, and disclosed his find to Margaret. She had, as she'd told me, seen the implications instantly. If Emily Dickinson had had a love affair with Henry Ward Beecher, and it were proven, then Margaret's passion for Saint Emily was groundless, her endless years of work were all in vain; the Emily Dickinson the world would know would not be *her* Emily, the New England Nun/Holy Virgin/Prophet of God she had constructed in her theological deliberations on Dickinson's poetry. Her life's work would have been wasted. Her life's love would have been all a long, empty dream.

Piotrowski had told me earlier he believed the killings were reactive rather than planned. When Randy told me he had to see someone at the party, it must have been Margaret. And she must have been galvanized into action on the spot. She was extraordinarily muscular, the medical examiner had told Piotrowski. She would have had no problem strangling Randy. His face, swollen and distorted in death, flashed into my memory. Randy never could keep his mouth shut, and, just look, it had killed him.

And what about Bonnie? Randy had evidently given into temptation and shared his find with her sometime earlier in the day. We knew he was an obsessive talker. Any audience suited him; he wasn't particular. And Bonnie had had no reservations about blabbing it. A memory of my final conversation with her in the Commons flashed into my mind:

her almost teasing mention of some unknown letter, Margaret Smith seated at a table in the background reading the *Christian Science Monitor*.

For me, however, Margaret had obviously changed her M.O.: she'd come prepared. I had no idea how long she'd had the gun. I was quite certain, however, that she didn't usually walk around with a can of paint thinner in her pocket. She must have picked that up in Cambridge after running into me at the library. Maybe at lunchtime, so she'd be prepared to follow me home.

My head hurt. I didn't want to think about it any more.

"We sent a team to Smith's house," the lieutenant informed me. "They found a manuscript. It's about Emily Dickinson, but it doesn't make any sense to me. Can we ask you to read it? Not *pro bono,* acourse. And, acourse, when you get better. We need an expert's opinion on its significance to the case."

I groaned. A dull weight settled directly on my brain. I couldn't wait.

The afternoon of my third day in the hospital, I was sitting up in bed, wearing a new nightgown Amanda had bought me, and feeling almost alive. Piotrowski entered, carrying a huge bouquet of daisies and looking somewhat embarrassed about it. Daisies, I thought, what is there about daisies . . . ? But I couldn't recover even a trace of the memory.

As I said, I remembered *most* of what happened. What I couldn't remember, for the life of me, was exactly what the Dickinson letter had said. Given the trauma I had suffered and the knock on the head, it had been a challenge to remember my name; a letter manuscript seen only once under conditions of extreme duress was simply too much of a stretch. Whenever I thought about the letter, I got terribly confused. I asked Piotrowski if there was any way a forensics specialist could find traces of words on the ashes.

"You read too much detective fiction," he replied, shaking his head. "The documents specialist just laughed when we took him in that pile of ashes. 'No way,' he said, 'No fu . . . uh . . . no way.'" I guess my dejection showed, because Piotrowski looked at me quizzically. "This really matters to you, doesn't it? I mean, *really* matters?"

How could I make him understand the enormity of the loss? Emily Dickinson's final Master letter had been utterly incinerated, not a word, or even a letter, could be reconstructed except what I could remember—which, at the moment, was almost nothing. Margaret had achieved her objective: The letter was gone forever.

To Piotrowski this was not a setback. My testimony, with supporting evidence, was enough to close his case. But to me it was a tragedy. Other scholars most likely would believe my account of this letter, but the material trace of the forgotten passion—and the language of it—had vanished forever.

"To you, Piotrowski, that letter was the cause of two deaths." He nodded. "Almost of three," I added as an afterthought. His responding grunt was eloquent. "But to me, at least for the brief time in which I actually *saw* it, that letter was a way of defeating death. Of getting past the silence that death enforces." I was now talking more to myself than to him, but he seemed to be listening attentively. "That letter spoke to me of love and betrayal. Of a passion that was so alive at the moment Dickinson's hand traced those words upon the page, that it was still living almost a century and a half after the words were read, folded away, and forgotten. That letter brought her to life again, if only because through it

she spoke to my imagination and my consciousness—to my *heart,* if I can be corny about it."

"Yeah." Piotrowski's reply was thoughtful. I
started, because I had forgotten he was there, that I
was actually talking to someone. "Yeah, I see," he
said. "I suppose that's how it is."

"I'm sorry." My head ached. "I'm getting carried
away here. You're not interested in all this—aesthetic
stuff." I was looking at the way the sunlight through
the window illuminated the daisies in their yellow
vase.

"Oh, but I am. Who else do I know that could talk
like this? You make me think there might be something in all this poetry sh—er, stuff. That it might
really let the past talk to you. . . ."

"She knew that about language." I was amazed I
was having this conversation with him, and I also
wasn't really certain I was making any sense. "She
knew that words chosen with care and arranged in
just such a . . . a . . . felicitous way could bring
old passions back to life. Could resurrect them, so to
speak."

He was silent for a moment. Then he said, "I suppose it's something like what I feel whenever I hear
'Fats' Domino singing 'Blueberry Hill.' "

"Yeah," I said, "something like that." It hurt to
grin, but I couldn't help it. "Yeah, really. Quite a bit
like that, actually. Quite a bit."

Piotrowski saw my smile and immediately backed
onto safer ground. "What I don't get is, if this note
was so important and it was sitting there in that library for a hundred years, how come nobody found
it before now?"

"I've been thinking about that. It does seem
strange, but maybe it's because Dickinson's Master
letters are really rather specialized knowledge.
They're known mostly to literary scholars. And al-

though he did write a novel, Henry Ward Beecher is not exactly considered a literary figure. I imagine that most of the people who have looked through Beecher's archives have been historians or theologians. A folder marked 'Correspondent Unknown' with a slightly hysterical letter in a difficult handwriting would have been of no interest to them. It was only by happenstance that Randy went into those files. I imagine he was looking for material relating to homophobia or latent homoeroticism, and of course he recognized Dickinson's distinctive prose style and handwriting."

"Too bad for him."

"Yeah," I responded. "Too bad for him." And almost for me, I thought. But I knew Piotrowski felt guilty enough already, so I kept my mouth shut.

The sunlight continued to shine on the daisies. As the afternoon sun dipped toward the horizon its rays began to blind me. I reached up automatically with my right hand to shield my eyes and winced with pain as I jarred the burn wounds. Piotrowski noticed, clucked sympathetically, and got up to adjust the window blinds.

"Do you think it's possible that the words of Dickinson's letter are seared into my flesh?" I would never have attempted such whimsicality with him if he hadn't confessed his response to "Blueberry Hill."

With a perfectly straight face, he replied, "I suppose that would be too much to hope for, Doctor, but I'll have our documents specialist take a look."

He was still standing by the window, and I looked over at him in astonishment. This time it was his turn to grin, the hundred-megawatt grin I remembered seeing only once before. I smiled back at him, slowly, but with increasing appreciation. Really, this was a most surprising man. And he had one hell of a knock-out smile.

Twenty-nine

PIOTROWSKI insisted on driving me home from the hospital in his Jeep. No, he said. That was all right. He knew he didn't have to, but he wanted to. It was Saturday; he had nothing else planned. At my insistence, Amanda and Sophia were crashing at the Samoorians' until I got home, and my daughter had already driven my car to Enfield. This way she wouldn't have to come back to fetch me.

"Can I get you something to eat? Ya need a pillow for your head? A blanket? A cup of tea? Something to read for later?"

"Just make sure I don't have to pay the damn hospital bill and get me the hell out of here."

As we drove west on the Massachusetts Turnpike into the late afternoon sun, we didn't seem to have much to talk about. The turnpike was the long way home to Enfield, but at least it wasn't as winding as Route 2, and the road was in good shape. For that, my aching head was grateful. Each bump of the car threatened to sever the top of my skull from the rest of my body. I was still drugged and intermittently confused, and as for Piotrowski, he seemed to be brooding deeply over some private thoughts.

I looked over at him, at his square, practical profile outlined against the passing scene of speeding cars and filthy snowbanks. He looked good. His brown hair had been recently cropped. He was wearing a gray turtleneck and black pants that actually fit him. He had lost more weight, but his shoulders still bulked out the new blue jacket nicely. He looked *very* good, as a matter of fact. But he was quiet and distracted. I thought maybe I should try to get him to talk.

"How's Trooper Schultz?"

His response was slow in coming, as if he were thinking of something else and was reluctant to change gears.

"She's taking it hard. It was her first time undercover, and she almost lost you. She's beating on herself for that. *And* it was her first shooting." He shrugged. "But Felicity's tough. She'll be okay."

Felicity? I remembered her crouched in the doorway, gun aimed straight at Margaret Smith's heart. Felicity, indeed.

"Would it be okay if I called and thanked her?"

"She'd probably appreciate that." He laughed, brightening up briefly. "But I got to tell you she didn't like you very much."

"Oh, no?"

"No. She thought you were arrogant and rude. 'Arrogant and rude,' those were the words she used."

I remembered with a blush how brusque I had been with her in the library. "Tell her I'm sorry. If I'd only known . . ." Then I got pissed. "Why the hell didn't you tell me? You never told me stuff! You let me make a fool of myself again, just like when I called you that night—"

"Well, we wanted you to act natural, so we didn't want you to know we had protection on you. . . ." He let his words trail off and again seemed preoccupied with his thoughts. But I wasn't about to let it go.

"You *wanted* me to act arrogant and rude?"

"If necessary." Then he looked over at me, his brown eyes briefly animated. "You know, I've felt that way about you, myself, actually."

I was deeply hurt. "I thought you liked me!"

He gave me a fleeting brilliant smile. "Oh, I do. But that doesn't mean you're not obnoxious sometimes."

"Well, the feeling's mutual. And while we're on it—"

But he interrupted me, grim again. "Look. There's something else, something I gotta tell you." The car whizzed through a deep rock cut. Huge icicles hung perilously close to the road. We must have been doing close to eighty miles an hour. Piotrowski looked so serious that the fight instantly went out of me.

"What?"

"Last night there was an intruder in your house."

"What!" Pain stabbed through my head, and I suddenly felt nauseous.

I must have gone pale, too, because Piotrowski said solicitously, "You gonna be okay with this?"

"Yeah." I swallowed hard and hoped I wouldn't disgrace myself.

"It was a bad scene. He shot one of our officers. But we got the bastard." Piotrowski's expression was grim. "We got him, and, goddammit, the courts better not let him slip through. He damn near killed Brita Johansson."

"God. . . ." I was going to be sick.

Piotrowski's expression grew anxious. "You're not gonna pass out on me, are ya?"

"Just give me a minute." I took four slow, deep breaths. "Okay. Go on. Is Brita Johansson the tall blonde? The one who came to my house that time?"

"Yeah. And last night she took a bullet in the gut." His hands gripped the steering wheel so tightly I feared he'd lose control of the car.

Dear God. She seemed just a kid, not much older than my students. Or Amanda. "Will she be okay?"

"She was in surgery six hours. But they say she'll recover. I saw her just before I came over. . . ." His voice trailed off.

"Oh, God, Piotrowski. I'm so sorry. I'm so sorry. I'm so sorry." I remembered the blond officer's impudent grin the night of my call to Piotrowski, and I was trying hard not to cry. Then I realized that Piotrowski was still holding back on me.

"Who was it, for God's sake? Who was at my house? What did he want?"

Piotrowski's lips were tight. "Stan Warzek."

"Warzek? What the hell was he doing in my home? How did the trooper find him?"

"You remember that night you called me?"

"I'm not likely to forget."

"It's a good thing you called." He glanced over at me, reached out, and squeezed my hand. If I hadn't been so horrified with what he was telling me, I would have jumped out of my skin with astonishment.

"You told me about Warzek harassing you, and I made the connection with the car, you know, the one going by your house at odd hours. And those anonymous phone calls . . ."

"Oh!" I had forgotten.

"And just in case you were right about Warzek being the killer, I put surveillance on him."

"You did?"

"Yeah. His was the car that followed you out of Enfield. The beat-up brown one. We were following him."

"And you didn't tell me—"

"You were well out of his way by then. We kept the tail on him until we knew he wasn't the killer. That was a week ago. But yesterday Johansson was on patrol, and she saw his old Plymouth pulled over in the woods near your house—"

"Oh, God. . . ."

"She handled it right. She radioed for backup, so there was three of them went in. But it was her he went after."

He concentrated intently on the highway. The stretch of road ahead was straight, flat, and dry.

"The guys said it was weird. It was like he didn't even see them. Like she was the only one in the room. He kept staring at her, pointing the gun. He called her a lezzie bitch and a bull dyke. And that wasn't the worst of it— You're a lady; I'm not gonna repeat the rest of it."

Any other time I would have told the lieutenant he couldn't shock me. That I'd already heard all the words there were to hear. But at this moment I respected his need to try to protect me, if only in this extremely old-fashioned way.

And, as I thought about what he was telling me, guilt overwhelmed me. "It was me he wanted, you know. He hated me. He really hated me. And when he couldn't get at me, he went after her. Officer Johansson took the bullet for me." Then I did cry. I tried to do it quietly and with some dignity, but I failed. Piotrowski handed me a fistful of his outsized tissues. I wondered if he kept them specially for sobbing women. In his job he must see a fair number of them.

I cried and cried. This nightmare was never going to end. Even my own home wasn't safe. Panic seized me. I had to get out of that place. I had to go live somewhere where there were people around. I had to . . . Then it struck me. "So, if I hadn't called you that night, I might have found him waiting for me when I got home." *Or Amanda,* I thought. *Oh, God. He would have gotten Amanda.*

"Right." He bit the word off sharply. "But you did call. Smart thing to do. You noticed the right things, things I didn't have a chance to see. You just put them together a little crooked."

"Yeah. I guess." I sniffed.

"Looks like he's obsessed with you. He says . . . you're a lesbian."

"Oh, yeah?"

"Yeah." Then silence. Was he waiting for me to deny it? Well, he could just wait. He was a detective, wasn't he? He should be able to figure it out.

When I didn't speak, he went on. "Not that it would matter. But what he thinks is that you're after his daughter. He keeps saying he was just trying to protect his kid." He shook his head. "The guy's crazy. A real squirrel."

"Squirrel?"

"Yeah. A nutter. A sociopath, I think. One a those guys hates women, ya know? I see a lot of that. Gotta be the big man all the time. Gotta be in charge." He kept shaking his head, as if this were inconceivable to him. "And you being so damn decent to that girl . . ."

His eyes softened, then he continued. "So . . . Anyhow, I'm not taking you home."

"What?"

"Your daughter's gonna meet you at the Samoorians'. They're gonna keep you both for a few days, until we release the crime scene, and you can get your place cleaned up."

I didn't ask him what needed to be cleaned up. I didn't want to know.

"And Miss Warzek's gone home to her mother."

"Shit." On a long uphill grade, we passed a laboring tractor-trailer. The driver had adorned its mud flaps with shiny silhouettes of naked women. "Shit. *Shit*. I thought maybe we could get her out of that wacked-out place."

"Well, we've got Warzek on enough charges to keep him away for awhile, so she should be all right. Assault with a deadly weapon, assaulting a police officer, burglary, aggravated harassment, stalking . . . If the courts do their job, no one should have to see him for a long, long time." He hesitated. "We held off on the charge of possession of an unregistered handgun. At least at first." His eyes slid sideways toward me.

"Why?" I was baffled.

"He says the gun is yours."

I went cold with horror. The gun Tony had given me! Warzek had been going to kill me with my own gun. He had shot Brita Johansson with *my* gun!

But that wasn't what was on Piotrowski's mind.

"So I talked to Captain Gorman—"

"Why on earth . . . ?"

"Because, Dr. Pelletier, when I come across an unregistered gun with serial numbers filed off and no identifying characteristics that belongs to a woman that has had a close relationship with a member of the law enforcement profession, I begin to wonder— well—where it comes from. You know. Guys sometimes have throw-downs—"

"It's mine," I said immediately. "Tony doesn't even know I have it."

"You're a rotten liar, Doctor. Captain Gorman

admits to the gun. In my conversation with him there was a—a lot of discussion—some, you know, general—er, speculation—about how disappearable this gun might be. But it doesn't look real disappearable now that there's a shooting charge. But"—he paused and looked over at me for emphasis—"we might be able to forget that he found it at your place. . . ."

"You'd do that, Piotrowski?" I filed away the word *disappearable* for future contemplation.

"What would I have to do? The bastard's lying through his teeth. You never saw the gun. What would a nice lady like you be doing with a handgun? And Captain Gorman woulda known if you had a weapon, but he never heard anything about it. Is that clear?"

"Yeah. But you can't just do that, can you? What about fingerprints? Mine must be all over it. Tony's too. He was the last one who cleaned it."

"Well—there was some kind of stupid foul-up last night. Maybe because it was late and the guys were so tired. Anyhow, somehow the weapon got smudged up—wiped almost clean. Damned shame. No one knows how it happened."

"Piotrowski, don't get yourself in trouble."

"I know what I'm doing. And *you* know, don't you, that we never had this—er—little discussion."

"Yes. I understand. Thanks." Tears spilled out of my eyes again, embarrassing me. In spite of the pain in my shoulder, I leaned over and kissed his cheek. Now he looked embarrassed, too. The road must have been demanding all his attention; he didn't take his eyes off it. He switched on his turn signal for the ramp to I–91.

"You've had enough," he said gruffly. "Besides . . . I owe you."

"Yes, you do. Damn right! And then—there's the brotherhood of the badge, isn't there?"

"Well . . ." There really was nothing more to say.

My head ached and I was getting confused again. I knew I was going to have to think seriously about the implications of all this. Warzek hated me. He wouldn't forget it. He knew where I lived. He'd be out of prison sooner than he should be. Both Piotrowski and I knew that. Maybe when Sophia moved into the dorm . . . Maybe if I moved into college housing . . . Maybe . . . Oh, God. Maybe I'd be safe someday.

Epilogue

I WAS ON temporary disability leave. The college got someone to teach my courses for a month or so until my head stopped aching and the confusion abated. Amanda was persuaded to go back to school only after I accepted Greg's offer to stay with Irena and him for as long as I needed to. Since I was forbidden to drive for at least six weeks, I had little choice. Besides, I didn't want to go back home. I'd decided to look for a house in Enfield. I wanted to live where there were people around. Where I had some friends.

Speaking of friends, Earlene Johnson and Jill Greenfield must have made a pact to keep me occupied. When she got back from Cleveland, Earlene took me shopping and out to dinner, and encouraged me to talk about the nightmare encounter with Margaret and the specter of an intruder in my home. Jill took me shopping and out to dinner and encouraged me to listen to her agonize over her tangled feelings for Ned Hilton. Both kept me up to date on college gossip. Ned had decided to bring his tenure decision before the Tenure and Renewal Committee. It would be a prolonged and complicated procedure, but Earlene thought TRAC would look favorably on Ned's appeal. Miles was steadfastly blocking Avery's proposed college-wide curriculum revision initiative. I remembered Avery leaving Randy's office just before Christmas with the curriculum revision folders; then I flashed on an image of Randy's distinctive handwriting as I'd seen it on the yellow, lined pages on Miles's desk. Avery hadn't been the only one interested in Randy's curriculum jottings; Miles had been attempting to check out the opposition. Magda's attempts at securing herself a future at Enfield had fallen through, and she was heading back to Budapest in September. Presumably Randy's jacket would go with her; "Chust a little keepsake," she told Jill when my intrepid colleague asked about the jacket.

Most of my coworkers seemed to feel pretty awkward around me. What do you say to someone who has been shot, knocked on the head, and almost burned to death? My colleagues tended to send a lot of flowers. When the dozen long-stemmed white roses arrived with the note on the stationery of the Enfield College president's office, even Amanda was impressed.

"Classy," she said. "Who is this guy?"

I gave the roses a sour look. "My boss," I replied.

I saw Piotrowski a few times. He came by with Margaret's book manuscript, which insisted, with fevered incoherence, that Emily Dickinson was the Bride of Christ. He came by with information about Stan Warzek's trial dates and about Trooper Johansson's progress. He came by with a check from the BCI. It was stupendously large. He said I'd earned every penny of it, and more. He said that with some feeling. I had to agree.

I still have bad dreams. Dreams that wake me in the middle of the night with my heart pounding and my body sticky with sweat. But I think at least I'm safe from Warzek now. Against my ardent counsel, Sophia dropped out of school to live at home and take care of her mother. That should satisfy him. She got a full-time job working in the Bread and Roses Bakery and Café and registered for only one course at Enfield.

"Sweetie." I spoke with as much vehemence as I could muster with my throbbing head. "Sweetie, you've only got one semester to go. You've got to finish. Don't get trapped now."

"Karen." She seemed disconcertingly more resolute now that she was the head of a family. "There's no money." She paused, and then went on. "Maybe you know how that is."

"Yes." I nodded only for a microsecond. Nodding was always a mistake. "Yes, I do know how that is."

"And *you* made it."

"No one should have it so hard, sweetie. Think of your own life. Your mother's a grown-up woman. Surely she can take care of herself."

But she wasn't listening.

And, oh, yes. Once I'd been out of the hospital for a few weeks and was becoming bored and very restless, I decided to walk over to campus and get some notes from my office. I might as well use the time to begin work on my new book. The English Department secretaries hovered around me with motherly concern. "You can't really write now, can you?" Shirley cautioned. "Won't that be too hard on you? Sitting in front of the computer like that? You've got to be careful."

"You know," advised Elaine, "you should really

use the laptop. You could take it to bed with you and lay it right out on your stomach. That would make things so much easier."

"I don't have a laptop. And it doesn't look like I'm going to be able to afford one soon." Piotrowski's money had been handy, but it had vanished into the black hole of my personal debt. There was nothing left over for self-indulgences.

"I meant the department laptop." Elaine took a key out of her desk drawer.

"I didn't know the department had a laptop."

"Oh, yeah. People use it all the time for research." She walked over to a closet, unlocked it, and took out a flat, gray laptop computer, about the size of a portable typewriter. "Poor Randy was the last to use it."

Randy. I swallowed hard, took the proffered computer, and carried it to my office. I closed the door. I placed the computer on my desk, plugged it in, opened it and pushed the *on* button. When it had booted up, I keyed in the files listing. All sorts of incomprehensible file names appeared. I scrolled through them until I came to one that said: "ED.ltr." Holding my breath, I pushed the "retrieve" key. In front of my eyes in little impulses of light I read:

Mr. Beecher, Sir—
    Angels are few. . . .

Permissions

Excerpts from poems #45, #281, #311, #322 and #502 from *The Poems of Emily Dickinson,* Thomas H. Johnson, ed. Reprinted by permission of the publishers and the Trustees of Amherst College from *The Poems of Emily Dickinson,* Thomas H. Johnson, ed., Cambridge, Mass.: The Belknap Press of Harvard University Press, Copyright © 1951, 1955, 1979, 1983 by the President and Fellows of Harvard College.

Excerpts from letter #248 and letter #283 from *The Letters of Emily Dickinson.* Reprinted by permission of the publishers from *The Letters of Emily Dickinson,* edited by Thomas H. Johnson, Cambridge, Mass.: The Belknap Press of Harvard University Press, Copyright © 1958, 1986 by the President and Fellows of Harvard College.

Grateful acknowledgment is made to Warner Bros. Publications for permission to reprint song lyrics from *torn* by Glen Phillip, Todd Nichols, Randy

Guss and Dean Dinning © 1990 WB Music Corp. (ASCAP), Wet Sprocket Songs (ASCAP). All Rights administered by WB Music Corp. All rights reserved. Used by Permission. Warner Bros. Publications U.S. Inc., Miami, FL 22014.

About the Author

JOANNE DOBSON is Associate Professor of English at Fordham University. She is a former editor of *Legacy: A Journal of American Women Writers* and the author of *Dickinson and the Strategies of Reticence: The Woman Writer in Nineteenth-Century America*. She lives in the New York City area.

If you enjoyed Joanne Dobson's debut mystery, QUIETER THAN SLEEP, you won't want to miss the next tantalizing novel in this series of literary mysteries, THE NORTHBURY PAPERS.

Look for THE NORTHBURY PAPERS in hardcover from Doubleday at your favorite bookseller's in October 1998.

Turn the page for an exciting preview.

THE NORTHBURY PAPERS

by Joanne Dobson

The bookplate was ornate in the nineteenth-century manner, a rich cream-colored rectangle with a wide border of morning glories and tangled vines. In Gothic lettering it read EX LIBRIS MRS. SERENA NORTHBURY. I closed the book and turned it over to look at the title. Mrs. Northbury's bookplate was affixed to the inside front cover of a well-preserved, half-morocco-bound copy of Charlotte Brontë's *Jane Eyre*.

"Wow," I said to Jill, "where'd you get this?"

Jill Greenberg slid her tray across the Faculty Dining Commons table, pushed the unruly red hair back from her forehead, and sat down next to me. "You know that antiquarian bookstore in Pittsfield, the one on North Street?"

I nodded, fanning lightly through the pages in search of any possible Northbury artifacts; you never know what you'll find preserved between the pages of an old book.

"Well, I was browsing there with . . . well, I was browsing, and the cover caught my eye. Then I saw Serena Northbury's bookplate and knew you'd be interested. It's beautiful, isn't it?"

"Yeah, they really knew how to make books in those days." The title was stamped in gold on the leather-bound spine of this one, and the dark blue covers were speckled in green. "A lot of the time it didn't much matter what was inside, but the book itself had to be a work of art." Finding no treasures between the ragged-edged pages, I handed the volume to Jill.

"Keep it, Karen," she said, pushing it back toward me with both hands. She picked up her ham and Swiss on rye and nibbled. "You're probably the only person left in the entire universe who cares about Northbury."

"Jill, I can't take this." I wanted the book. It had been owned—been touched, been *read*—by a nineteenth-century American novelist with whom I was becoming increasingly fascinated. But I couldn't afford to indulge myself in luxuries. On the scale of professional salaries, English professors rank just slightly above church mice, and the average church mouse isn't paying tuition for a daughter studying pre-med at Georgetown. "This must have cost a fortune."

"Nah." Money was never an object with Jill. It had never had to be; she was the daughter of a Park Avenue psychiatrist. A psychopharmacologist, yet. The streets of the Upper East Side are paved almost entirely in Prozac, and Papa had a great deal of money in his pocket. At the age of twenty-five, Jill had no education debts and no one but herself to lavish her salary on.

"It wasn't that much. The book dealer said the book wasn't a first edition or a particularly valuable one, so basically he was just charging for the binding."

"Well," I said. "If you're sure . . ." I turned the handsome volume around and ran my forefinger over the gilt lettering of the title. "I'm a little surprised to find that Northbury read *Jane Eyre*. Her own novels are nothing like it. They're really quite—well—sentimental. But they're so *interesting*. . . ." I drizzled oil and vinegar over my chef's salad and tucked into it.

" 'Interesting,' my foot. Why don't you just admit you like trash."

"It's not trash." I felt defensive; the grip Serena Northbury had on my imagination wasn't easily explained by any of the usual literary or feminist rationales. Northbury wasn't a great prose stylist, and she certainly wasn't a flamboyant feminist rebel. Her forty bestselling novels were conventional tales of young girls who face hardship and moral danger, but through unassailable virtue and mind-boggling diligence win out in the end.

I could relate to that; it sounded like my own life. Well . . . maybe not *unassailable* virtue.

"I know she's no Brontë," I admitted, "but there's something quirky in her stories. I don't know how to describe it, but I think I'm addicted."

Jill laughed and took a second bite of her sandwich. "A Ph.D. in lit, huh? A professor at Enfield, one of New England's most respected colleges? Karen Pelletier, you ought to be ashamed of yourself!"

"Come on, Jill. You of all people should know popular literature is a perfectly legitimate field of study." Jill is a sociologist, and literary studies are becoming more like a branch of the social sciences every day. "I'm simply reconstructing cultural conditions of literary reception." Yeah. Right. I had read every one of Serena Northbury's books I could get my hands on. Her popular novels enthralled me in the same way they must have captivated her multitudes of nineteenth-century readers.

"Lighten up, Karen. Face it; you're reading garbage!" Jill was joking; with a tattoo just above her left ankle and a gold ring where she didn't talk about it, Jill was a pop-culture nut.

I lightened up. "Yeah, Jill, you're right. I'm a lowbrow." I stroked the well-preserved copy of *Jane Eyre* as if it were still warm from Mrs. Northbury's hands, and set it down next to my plate. "Thanks for this. I owe you."

Jill made a dismissive motion with a hand that wore a half dozen silver rings and took another nibble of the sandwich. I picked up my mug of black coffee—I needed a jump start before I went into the classroom—and glanced at Jill over the rim.

My young colleague wasn't looking her best. I was used to the untamable red hair and the funky clothes—today a short, sleeveless cotton shift in a turquoise-and-lime flying-toasters print worn with black Converse basketball sneakers and one dangling garnet earring—but the mouselike appetite and the listless expression were something new. Jill Greenberg usually had the appetite—and the brute energy—of an adolescent hockey player.

"You okay, Jill?" I buttered my crusty whole-wheat roll and took a bite.

"I'm fine." Her tone was abrupt. "I'm just a little tired is all." She put the nibbled sandwich half back on her plate, aligned it with its untouched mate, and pushed the plate away. "And the food here gets worse every day."

The food in the Enfield College faculty dining room is okay. It's *more* than okay. It's downright *good*. And most days Jill proved that by putting away a full dinner entrée at noon and then topping it off with a sundae from the self-serve ice-cream bar. For a college professor—even for the child prodigy she was—Jill usually ate, well, prodigiously. I narrowed my eyes at her. Something was definitely wrong. Could Jill be having boyfriend trouble? As far as I knew, she hadn't been seeing anyone lately. Come to think of it, though, with Jill, that in itself was worth notice.

"Jill?" I ventured.

But she was gazing past me. "Karen, don't look now, but something weird is going on over at the Round Table."

I immediately swiveled around and stared.

The large round table in the far corner of the Faculty Commons is reserved for group luncheon meetings. On Thursdays, for instance, it's the women's studies table; once or twice a month black studies has dibs on it. Today it was crowded with college administrators and department heads. From where I sat I couldn't see everyone, but it would have been impossible to miss Miles Jewell, English Department chair. Miles was holding forth in a voice that had begun to rise beyond a decorous decibel level. He was ignoring President Avery

Mitchell's attempts to quiet him. His round face was even more flushed than usual, and a cowlick of thick white hair had flopped down boyishly over the ragged white eyebrows. Halfway across the large dining room I could hear the outraged tones of Miles's protest—something about insupportable assault on traditional standards.

"Karen, don't gape."

Jill was right; I was gawking with prurient curiosity as my department head made a public spectacle of himself. I turned back to my tablemate. "That's a pretty high-powered bunch there, and they don't look like happy campers."

"Sure don't. I wonder what's going on. Look—I mean, don't *you* look, for God's sake; you're too obvious. I'll *tell* you what's happening. Now Avery's got the floor. The voice of sweet reason, as usual. God, he's a beautiful man. Those hands—like a concert pianist's. Oh, baby—he can play *me* anytime. Now Miles is sulking. You know how pink his face usually is? Well, now it looks like a humongous *strawberry*. Geez, I hope he doesn't have a coronary. Sally Chenille is jabbering on now, probably 'interrogating the erotic subtext' of something or other." Jill's voice suddenly twisted. "I really detest that woman!"

I glanced at her, surprised; as a rule, Jill wasn't given to strong antagonisms.

But Jill didn't notice my reaction. "You should see Sally's hair—no, Karen, don't turn around. I'll *tell* you. Today, Professor Chenille's hair is a lovely Day-Glo orange, a very, *very* nice visual contrast to Miles's strawberry—no—*raspberry* complexion. Okay, now your pal Greg Samoorian is talking— that deep authoritative voice that only bearded men seem to have. I can't hear exactly what he's saying, but it looks like he's on Avery's side. At least Avery's nodding and . . ."

"Okay, okay, I don't need a blow-by-blow. If Greg's involved, I know what it's about. He told me Avery was getting together an exploratory committee to investigate collegewide curriculum reform. As the new chair of Anthropology, Greg's part of that. This is probably the planning group."

Jill whistled softly between her teeth. "Whew, no wonder Miles is so upset. The college might actually stop requiring his course in the Literature of the Dark Ages."

"Yeah." I laughed, but it wasn't funny. In the current culture wars the English Department faculty was factionalized between the old-guard professors who taught Literature (with a capital *L*) as high art, and the avant-garde who taught almost anything that had ever appeared in print—and had completely discredited the very idea of art. And now it looked as if the contest for the hearts and minds of Enfield students was about to draw blood. Miles was representative of the older contingent, completely conventional in his approach to literature: Chaucer, Shakespeare, and Milton were his gods. Henry James deserved serious consideration—maybe. Jane Austen, well, okay, she wrote nice little stories. But beyond that, no woman had produced anything worth consideration. And *minority* literature? A contradiction in terms.

Since I'm in the opposing camp—I'd been hired to teach American women's literature—I was at frequent odds with my department chair. As an untenured professor, I could be made pretty uncomfortable at times. Miles, and the other old boys, seemed to think that the department got more than it bargained for when they hired me. My work on Emily Dickinson was acceptable, of course; after all, the woman had somehow wormed her way into the canon of American literature, that body of texts professors had taught since time immemorial. But now, two years into my position at Enfield College, I—young upstart that I was—was exposing my students to all sorts of *noncanonical* stuff: slave narratives, sentimental novels, working-class literature—the books people actually *read* in the nineteenth century. *Garbage.* And now, God help me, I was also thinking about writing a biography of an obscure woman novelist named Serena Northbury. I hadn't told the department yet, but Miles would freak out when—and if—I mentioned it in my annual faculty activity report.

I sighed and nudged my empty plate away. Time to get back to work. There were papers to grade, classes to teach. And I needed to make time to write a good long letter to my daughter. Even though Amanda had been away at college for two years, I still missed her. We talked on the phone all the time, but letters were better: you got to slit the envelope, pull the missive out, smooth it open—and read it over and over again.

Jill picked up her sandwich, examined it with a curl of her lip, and dropped it back on the plate. "I guess I'm not hungry. Are you finished?"

I slid the canvas strap of my book bag over my shoulder and picked up the copy of *Jane Eyre*. "Yeah," I said. "But I actually ate something. Are you *sure* you're okay?" Jill had the milk-white skin of the authentic redhead, but today she was paler than usual, and her mouth had an uncharacteristic pinched look. She drained her water glass, then rose from the chair.

"I'm fine. It's just that— Karen, watch out!"

But it was too late. As I moved from the table, intent on Jill's response, Miles Jewell stormed away from the curriculum meeting and barreled into me. He hit me broadside, and, in a blind fury, kept on going. I staggered, fell back, and caught my balance by grabbing hold of the table. My book bag slipped from my shoulder, my arm jerked painfully, and the old book in my hand plummeted to the dining room floor.

Miles continued his retreat. As he exited through the Commons' wide French doors, I stared after him in astonishment. Miles may be conservative, even retrograde, but he was *never* rude. What could possibly have been said at the Round Table to cause this gentleman of the old school to forget his manners so shockingly?

"Karen." Avery Mitchell, Enfield's president, was at my side, his hand on my elbow. His tone was solicitous. "Are you all right?"

I wasn't sure. I didn't know whether Miles had knocked the breath out of me, or if my current inability to breathe was due to the close presence of Avery Mitchell. Our distinguished president tends to have that effect on me. Tall, lean, and elegant, Avery is the consummate American aristocrat, the type of man my working-class origins had taught me to passionately distrust as effete and dangerous. A member of the power elite. A parasite on society. I get palpitations every time he comes within six feet of me, but I don't think it has anything to do with my politics.

"I want to apologize for Miles," Avery continued. "He's extremely upset."

"I could tell." I had worn my long hair loose today, for a change, and now, pushing strands away from my face, I struggled to control my ragged breathing. That was particularly difficult, because Avery still had hold of my arm.

"Yes, well . . . You know he would never behave like that if, ah, well . . . under normal circumstances. Please don't take offense." Letting his hand fall, Avery reached for the copy of *Jane Eyre,* sprawled open on the cream-and-rose-patterned carpet. "You dropped this." As he handed me the volume, something fell from between the pages. He stooped again, retrieved a photograph, took a cursory look at it, and held it out to me. I took the picture by its corner.

"I've got to get back." Avery waved his hand in the general direction of the Round Table, smiled at me ruefully, then strolled over to reconvene the disrupted meeting.

"Always the old smoothie, isn't he?" Jill was at my elbow. "God, that man has all the moves." I took the book bag she held out to me, my eyes intent on the sepia photograph in my hand. I had no intention of being sucked into any gossip about our exalted president.

"What's that?" Jill asked, motioning toward the old photograph. A picture of a baby, it must have been pushed deep into the center of the book, or I would have come across it earlier, when I'd riffled through the pages. The infant was about six months old, propped against a plump pillow with intricate lace edging, and dressed in smothering layers of white mid-Victorian ruffles.

"Poor thing," I said. "She looks uncomfortable." I assumed the child was a girl—a waterspout curl on the top of her head was tied with a white bow, and on a chain around her neck she wore a heart-shaped locket in what looked like gold filigree.

"Who do you think it is?" Jill asked. "One of Mrs. Northbury's kids?"

I turned the stiff photo over. On the back was written "Carrie, August, 1861."

"No," I said. "Serena Northbury had her children in the 1840s, when she was in her early twenties. They were named Lavinia, Josephine, and Hortense. There was no Carrie."

"A grandchild?"

"Too early. Her daughters weren't married yet. Must be the child of a friend. Or maybe she just liked the picture, used it as a bookmark."

Jill took the photo from me. "This looks like a studio shot."

"Yeah," I said. "The table with the paisley cloth, the ornate book, the vase of flowers: they're all photographic conventions. Cameras weren't easily portable then. This isn't a casual snapshot. Somebody really wanted a picture of this baby."

"I don't blame them; she's a beautiful child," Jill said. "Those dark eyes, the curls."

I retrieved the photo and looked at it more closely. "Huh," I said. "*That's* interesting."

"What?" Jill seemed enthralled with this long-vanished baby.

"Look." I took the picture over to the window, where the light was better. "Yes," I said. "Jill, I think this is a black child. What do you think?"

She gazed intently at the sepia print. "It's hard to tell, the image is so dim. She's light-skinned, but her features do have an African-American look. I wouldn't be surprised; there were a great many bi-racial children coming off those plantations."

"Yeah. Right." I shook my head sadly. The rape of slave women by their masters was well documented by nineteenth-century slave narratives. "I wonder what Serena Northbury was doing with a photograph of an African-American baby?"

"Was she an abolitionist?"

"Well, yes—she seems to have been. But she was never outspoken in the way that women like Harriet Beecher Stowe and Lydia Maria Child were. She was—genteel, you might say."

"Sounds deadly. I'm surprised you're interested in her."

"Yeah, well . . . There's something there. . . ."

I shrugged, tucked the photograph back into the pages of *Jane Eyre*, where it had reposed for at least a century, and slipped the book into my big canvas bag for safekeeping.

Crossing the quad on my way back to my office, I sipped carefully at a second cup of coffee and recalled the farcical scene with Miles Jewell. Then I thought about the chaos certain to descend on the English Department when we began to reassess our course offerings and curriculum requirements. If Miles and I hadn't been at loggerheads before, we certainly would be now.

It wasn't until I slipped my key into the lock of my office door that I realized Jill had never told me what was bothering her.